CROWNE OF LIES

CD REISS

CROWNE OF LIES

By CD Reiss

This is a work of purest fiction.

Any similarities to persons living or dead is not only a coincidence, it says volumes about who you associate with. That's why I like you so much.

PART I

1

LOGAN

Marriage. A deep and abiding partnership where two people take on separate roles to build a more complete life together. My parents, Ted and Doreen Crowne, were perfect partners and perfectly in love. They'd managed a thriving business and six children in a harmonious house.

I wanted what they had, and no less.

She was out there somewhere, and she'd appear when she was ready. I wasn't looking. Wasn't dating. Wasn't doing much more than working, and that was my choice. My first goal was running Crowne Industries, and when that was in the bag, the marriage would take care of itself.

But my father was a worrier, and if he wasn't content with my life, I couldn't be.

We were in our parents' Santa Barbara place when my father called my older brother, Byron, and me up to his office.

Before I sat in the chair across from Dad's desk, I'd been complacent. I could beat myself up with that for a long time, and I would. Byron had given up his shot at running the company, so Dad had groomed me, trained me, told me everything. I attacked everything he threw at me. No job was too small. No task too

3

menial. In five years, I knew every nook and corner of a company with offices on four continents and a research station in Antarctica.

So I figured he wanted to meet us about Byron's impending fatherhood or the wedding that was being planned for after the baby was born.

"What's this about?" Byron asked before Dad came in, surprising me. I thought he'd at least have a hint.

"Fucked if I know."

Dad came in and shut the sliding wooden door. He didn't do that unless he didn't want to bother Mom with the business he discussed with me.

"Gentlemen." Dad sat behind his desk, which was also weird with Byron here. "So, your mother is getting worse."

Mom had Parkinson's. Neither love nor money could control it. It didn't care about the power behind the Crowne name, and the thought squeezed my lungs like balloons in a fist.

"This was completely expected," Dad continued, totally fucking together and calm. "It's a degenerative disease. You boys don't have to look like I slapped you."

"Shouldn't the rest of us be here?" I asked.

"All of us have an interest," Byron added.

"This is business," Dad said. "Which means it's you two."

"Then why's this guy here?" I asked, half joking to protect the threatened half.

"Logan's shutting up now so you can finish," Byron said.

"Thank you." Hands folded in front of him, our father directed his attention to me. "She's getting the best care available. We're moving a staff in. But..." He tapped his fingertips against one another. "She needs me. More of me, more of the time. And I need her."

More of Dad's attention on Mom meant more responsibility for me.

Was he handing me the keys to the kingdom?

Had to be. That didn't answer why Byron was there, but I was sure that was the upshot of this conversation.

"So, first things first," Dad continued. "We're moving out of Crownestead and back down to Los Angeles."

"Why?" I asked, indicating my mother and Byron's hugely pregnant fiancée, Olivia, sitting at a table on the other side of the glass. Nellie, our housekeeper and cook, poured them both more ginger lemonade. It was sunny, peaceful, and quiet. Why move back to LA when life in Santa Barbara was perfect? "Mom loves it here."

"She wants to be near her children, and whatever she wants, she gets. She has a property in mind. She saw the house. It's easily wheelchair accessible—when it comes to that. I suggest both of you"—he looked at each of us before finishing—"not try to talk her out of it."

"Fine," I said.

"Where is it?" Byron asked. He'd been building houses since he left Crowne industries and probably had something to say about the neighborhood.

"Bel-Air," Dad said.

That explained why Byron was in the room. He'd just finished building a monstrosity of a house in Bel-Air. Olivia had talked him into making it smaller, but it was still massive enough to get interest from sheikhs and movie stars.

"Great," Byron said, hand up as if his opinion would be a relief to our father. "The neighborhood council loves me now. I need to see it sooner rather than later."

"Jesus," I said under my breath. Did falling in love make him thick? He'd just erected a monument to his ego in Bel-Air and Dad, in his infinite generosity, was going to buy it.

"You built it, son."

I felt no satisfaction in being right.

"Ah, Dad…" Byron flattened his hands to punctuate the start of a long explanation on why this was a bad idea.

5

"It's perfect."

"I didn't have you in mind when I started it."

"You didn't when you finished it either. Don't worry, we'll pay market unless we're outbid. Then we'll match it."

What a damn gift that was. A few hundred mill at market, on top of the free money my brother had gotten to build it as his One Big Thing. The OBT was the no-questions-asked, once-in-a-lifetime gift each of us was entitled to, and now Dad was basically tripling it.

"No bidding, Dad," Byron said. "If Mom wants it, it's hers."

Dad shook his head—about to demand Byron take the money he hadn't even used on the house—and I just couldn't sit there.

"Are you serious?" I asked. "His One Big Thing goes to some environmental fund, and now you're paying market for the house it was supposed to build?"

The One Big Thing, the OBT, was the one request we made of our father that he wouldn't refuse.

"What's the difference?" Dad asked.

"We're not negotiating? Just, 'Here... take it'? It should go to Crowne for cost."

"Mind your business, twerp," Byron said.

Screw him for saying it. He was fine giving it to them. He just didn't want me to be part of the decision even though Dad had brought me into that room for a fucking reason.

"Exactly," I said with my finger rigidly pointed in my brother's direction. "It's business. This business. Which is my business. Dad—"

"And there's something else," Dad said. "If you two can get your thumbs out of each other's eyes for a minute, I'll tell you."

"Logan." Dad looked at me, and I felt the torque of a rapidly changing subject. "Your mother and I talked about this... God, if I could count the hours we talked. We've watched you work yourself ragged to prove you can manage an international company the size of Crowne. But every time I ask you what you want out of your life—just a month ago was the last time—you say you want what your mother and I have."

"I do. You guys are perfect. So?"

"How are you going to get it like this? Twenty-two-hour days. Constant travel. The last time you socialized, it was to practice Cantonese."

I wasn't getting his meaning. He'd worked just as hard when he took over from his father. How was I supposed to get the same reward with less effort?

"You managed," I said, pointing to the back again, where Mom and Olivia were still drinking lemonade.

"We were stupid. We got married at eighteen, before Uncle Jerry died. Before I knew it would be mine. You're running into a lonely life like a starving man chasing a sandwich."

"You're telling me to date? Dad. Come on."

I was about to explain that I saw women, but it was a secondary pursuit because I loved what I was doing. But I paused too long trying to formulate a convincing way to explain why loving my work that much was a good thing.

"I'm telling you," Dad said, "to get married."

"What?" My hands shot to the armrests as I slid to the edge of the chair.

"Dad?" Byron asked incredulously. "Are you serious?"

Dad spread his hands on the desk, laying into me with his gaze. "Your mother and I don't care how much money you make in a lifetime. Or how much you grow the business. She said, and I quote, 'I will die weeping if the room dims before my babies find their happiness.' Which isn't her best bit of verse—"

"Just get married?" I interrupted. "Should I pick a girl off the street? Hire someone? What even is this?"

"Dad." Byron leaned forward with me, holding his arm between Dad and me as if that would stop me from launching. "Is this even legal? What did Joe say?"

"The board follows my lead." Dad sat back in his chair. "And management is contingent on my approval. I don't have to put my children in charge, you know."

He was threatening me.

He'd take away everything because I was working too hard to earn it.

"What if I'm like this asshole?" I pointed at Byron, who'd only met the woman he was going to marry at thirty-seven. "I'll be dead before I'm married."

"He has a point," Byron said. Was he actually on my side? Or was he playing a game for the sake of a win?

"The fact that Byron's happy has changed the whole equation for us. So, you can blame him for what I'm about to offer, but it's not negotiable."

"I don't want to hear it." I said, listening anyway.

"Effective immediately," Dad said, "I'm resigning as CEO of Crowne Industries so I can spend more time with my wife. I'll maintain a controlling interest in voting shares, but I'll otherwise take on an advisory role from my new home in Bel-Air."

"Who's *running* it, Dad?" I demanded.

"Byron."

"What?" I must have heard him wrong. I didn't want to have fun. I wanted to fulfill my fucking dreams.

"Whoa, whoa!" Byron held up his hands like a traffic cop trying to understand why Dad was driving on the wrong side of the road.

"Why?" I asked, seeing that my brother wasn't behind this. There was no way he was faking surprise at this turn of events.

"Byron," Dad said, unruffled. "You were raised to do this. You're more experienced, and with what's coming..." He jerked his chin toward Mom and Olivia at the table outside. "You've become a serious, capable, and thoughtful man."

"I don't want it."

Thank God. Thank fucking God.

"That's the point," Dad said. "You're the only one who can do it well *and* easily give it up when Logan gets settled."

"Married," I said. "You mean married."

"Joe says you haven't bought another property." Dad spoke to Byron as if I wasn't even there. "Correct?"

"Correct."

When had my work lost its value?

When had I lost control of my own fucking life?

"Will you do it?" Dad asked Byron.

"If I don't?"

"Yes or no."

"Yes," my brother said. "I got it."

Fuck him. I was going to shred his ass and write an apology to Olivia when I was done.

"So," Dad said to me. "Go out. Have fun. Meet people. Learn what you can from Byron."

"How long?" I barely had enough air for two words.

"If you're not married by your fortieth birthday, we'll revisit." Dad put his hands on the desk and stood. "Meeting adjourned."

"What? So I don't come to the office anymore? You're firing me for working too hard?"

"I'm asking you to wait," Dad said as he slid the door open. "Become the man you're supposed to be."

I knew exactly who I was.

I was Logan Crowne, and Logan Crowne was Crowne Industries.

I just had to prove it.

2

LOGAN

SIX MONTHS LATER

THE LOFT CLUB bar was on the sixth floor of a recently renovated Downtown warehouse. The designers had kept the graffiti from the years the brick structure had been abandoned, cut into the walls to add windows, and covered the bright colors with framed original art.

Mandy Bettencourt sat across from me at a corner table, diamonds in her ears. Light brown, curly hair pinned up in a precise mess to show off the highlights. Yellow sweater with pearls. Red lipstick.

"I've treated him like a full partner, and what does he do? Runs behind my back, changes the route of a major pipeline to run through a scenic valley. The engineers are scrambling and don't get me started on the permitting."

"Mm-hm." She smiled, glancing around the room for someone who didn't talk about work.

"I have to get him out of my hair."

"How old is their baby? Five months? Six? I bet he's so cute."

"I have to get married."

She was the only one who knew about my father's ultimatum, and when I mentioned it, she always shook her head at what an intractable problem it was... until I took a little velvet box from my pocket and put it in front of her.

She tapped the edge of her wine glass with a manicured finger, staring at the wildly expensive square-cut diamond. "Who is she?"

"Someone who could use cash."

"You want me to marry you," she stated the truth with a mix of disbelief.

"I trust you." I'd known her since we were kids. We'd gone to the same upper school, where we'd developed a close friendship that had only gotten stronger over the years.

"Right. And so this means we should get married?"

"Temporary. Just to get rid of Byron. No sex obviously."

"Obviously." She made a face and sipped her white wine. "Renaldo would throw an absolute fit."

Renaldo was a deadbeat actor with a handsome face who didn't have the talent to get cast in a couple of movies, but he didn't have to because he'd married America's Sweetheart, Tatiana Winsome, well before she starred in *Homewrecker* and Hollywood fell in love with her. All he did now was spend her money and give himself a boner when the captions under the tabloid pictures said *"actor* Renaldo DeWitt."

"And that's why it works." I leaned over the table for the big pitch. "His wife suspects something, right? You told me yourself."

"She's so awful."

I'd already argued that her boyfriend's wife had every right to be awful, considering her husband was a philanderer, but she wouldn't budge.

"If you marry me, she's off your case. You keep being discreet with him in private. Show up with me in public. We divorce in three years, and in the meantime, I pay off your family's debts. He doesn't have enough to get your mother's estate in Montenegro out of hock. Not enough for the boats. The debts. The bad habits. Any of it. I do."

As successful as her clothing line was, she didn't have enough either. There weren't many people on the face of the earth with enough generational wealth to dig out the Bettencourts.

"I won't hurt him like that." She snapped the box closed. "Not for money."

That was the Bettencourt problem. Nothing was ever for money.

"Logan," she said, pushing the box to me, "we're friends, right?"

"Yes."

"So you won't be mad if I tell you the truth?"

I pocketed the ring and sat back with my drink. This wasn't going to go the way I wanted. "Go right the fuck ahead."

"Maybe this is a good thing. You don't sleep. You don't go out unless it's for business. Why not just do what Ted wants? Maybe... I don't know? Date?"

"Marry me, and I swear I'll date."

She laughed, and I had to smile at the paradox of the suggestion.

"You really want to go through with this? Marry someone for convenience?"

"It's fucking inconvenient, but yes. And I want to take the wind right out of Byron's damn sails. Send him back to the real estate business where he belongs. Let him"—I waved to indicate the repurposed space—"renovate more warehouses."

She pursed her lips as if she was considering it, and I sat straighter to receive a little good news for a change. She took her time, pausing to drink wine, shake her head a little, take a breath.

"You know," she said, "I think I can help you."

"So you will?"

"There's someone I'm thinking of."

CROWNE OF LIES

"No way. I don't want just anyone off the street. It has to be plausible."

"You know her from Wildwood School."

"It can't be some hippie, Mandy. She has to have social credentials and she has to need something. So if it's some desperate woman who wants children or just wants a ring on her finger, forget it. The divorce has to be clean. You're the only one."

"No." Mandy cut the air with her hands. "The more you talk, the more I know it's true. She has everything you want. Single. A solid name. A definite need. And she'll never fall for you, trust me. You're too boring for her. She's perfect."

Mandy was selling me when I was supposed to be selling her.

"Who is she?" I asked, hoping to regain control of the situation. I could dismiss this person if I knew who she was.

"I'm going to ask her first. Feel her out."

"When?"

"I'm seeing her tomorrow morning. If it looks good, I'll tell you who she is so you can do some background, then you can meet, negotiate, kiss the bride. Boom. You'll make a huge mistake so fast you won't even know what hit you."

"Tomorrow." Because I'd have to run background, the time frame—even if she was perfect—was still tight. "Crowne Jewels is Saturday. I want to announce there."

Crowne Jewels was Mom and Dad's celebration for finally moving to the Bel-Air house, which Lyric had christened Crownehome. Some days, I wished for a name less prone to easy wordplay.

"I'll work it into a conversation and call you as soon as I know. Hopefully, by then you'll talk yourself out of this stupid idea."

Fat chance of that.

"When you talk to her, don't say my name."

"I'll just say you're a young, stunningly gorgeous rich man. The name Crowne will not pass my lips."

"Fine." I raised my glass and we clicked in agreement.

13

3

ELLA

THE MARINE LAYER hung over the city, cutting the bright power of the sun.

The forecast had promised clear skies by seven o'clock, but the forecast had clearly lied.

"They're gonna start on time. Promise you that." Amilcar took the binoculars from his brown eyes and squinted at the sky. The sides of his head were shaved, and a cluster of short dreadlocks stuck up from the top.

My watch said it was three minutes to seven thirty in the morning, the legal start time for any construction in Los Angeles. We were on a rooftop with dozens of other gawkers. A lot of people had showed up to see the destruction of this particular little house in Westlake that sat between apartment buildings. The crowd lined the sawhorses protecting the property, all called by a Twitter account owned by the Guerilla Arts Collective. By design, no one knew who was in the GAC, because what they created involved a host of illegal activities. Trespassing. Vandalism. Maybe a little theft if you wanted to get technical.

"NPR just retweeted," Tasha said. She was sixteen, in tight braids with beads on the ends, and her brother Amilcar's legal ward. He didn't let her contribute to the piece when, late at night, we broke in and worked on it. She did the social media in secret, keeping her hands clean so she could go to college.

"It's not going to work without the sun." I held out my hand for the binoculars and Amilcar handed them over.

"It's gonna work, Fance," he said, using his nickname for me as if he was making a threat. It was short for Fancy, my terrible tag name from back in our graffiti days.

"But it won't be perfect." I scanned the crowd through the binoculars. The construction workers were getting into their big yellow machines. Mandy was in the crowd with her sister and a few people I didn't recognize. Socialites, probably. In a separate group, a white-haired woman of Hispanic descent held a notebook, her eyes on the house. "Selma Quintero's here."

"Damn," Amilcar said when he saw the Pulitzer Prize-winning art critic. "Tasha's good."

"Damn right," she said, poking her phone.

"Damn, damn." I looked at the sky. The marine layer had thinned a little.

The bulldozer rumbled to life, belching smoke.

"It's on," I said.

Our first really big piece. Not well-placed graffiti and street art, but a statement. Something beautiful in the rubble. A city turning hidden treasure into garbage.

At exactly seven thirty, the bulldozer moved. Suddenly, as if the atmosphere had conspired with the forecasters to stress me out, the haze cleared and the sun shone brightly on the little boarded-up house. The crowd went silent, waiting for something. Delight or boredom. The unexpected thrill of art or the inevitable disappointment of raised expectations.

I grabbed Amilcar's sleeve as if I was about to fall. He didn't move.

The bulldozer pushed into the building and it crumbled, exposing the interior walls, which were covered corner to corner in multicolored rhinestones that sparked in the sunlight. The floors, the ceilings—everything came down and exposed the glittering insides.

The crowd gasped.

In three minutes, it was over.

Geode House was a success.

———

PROJECTS LIKE *GEODE House* were rewarding, but they didn't put bread on the table. In fact, they cost enough to impoverish even Basile Papillion's daughter.

Which isn't to say I started the GAC with much money to my name.

My mother had built my father's fashion empire and managed it until the day she died. Basile designed every gown and accessory until the day he joined her, but not before marrying a stepmother who hated me.

Use your gifts. My name is your responsibility now.

Those were his last words to me, uttered in halting breaths while cancer ate the last of his life. The last thing he heard in this world was my voice telling him he didn't have to worry. I'd use my gifts for the Papillion name.

So I stayed at the company I knew like the back of my hand.

When his widow, Bianca, demoted me, I stayed.

When she brought on the moody but well-known Jean-Claude Josef as design director to rescue the couture business, I stayed because I was the only one who knew how to turn his nonsense drawings into garments that would not only work in the real world, but actually honor the Papillion name.

When I was relegated to the fit room, pinning up garments I couldn't afford for people who weren't worth my time, I stayed.

When Bianca added a cheap branded T-shirt line for discount stores, I fucking stayed.

Also, I needed the job, and sometimes I met nice people, like Olivia Monroe, who stood on the raised platform in front of a bank of mirrors while I perfected the hemline of her blue gown.

"You're all set," I said, standing. "Just don't lose another half a size while you sleep."

She'd had Byron Crowne's baby six months before, and I'd had to take her dress in three times as she lost her pregnancy weight. The waist kept sagging and the hem kept dropping, but this was the last alteration, and she looked pretty damn good if I said so myself.

"It's perfect," she said. "Thank you so much for getting another fitting in."

"No problem."

She looked at me in the mirror as I made sure the neckline hadn't dropped. "They're working you pretty hard."

"Crowne Jewels is the biggest event of the year." The party at the new Crowne place in Bel-Air had supposedly started as a small affair, but had exploded into the event of the year. "Everyone wants to look good for the paparazzi. When you move your arm, does it feel tight across the back?"

"You look tired." She lifted her arm to the side, then the front. "The back feels good. Fits like a Papillion."

I didn't address her comment about how I looked. She didn't need to know I'd spent half the night in a crystal-encrusted abandoned building.

"That's my name," I said. "Wear it out."

Olivia smiled when I quoted my father. Basile Papillion didn't have a sense of humor as much as a charming way with puns.

"Are you sure you don't want to come to the party?" Olivia said as I unzipped her dress. "I can get you an invitation, you know."

"Nah, I don't have anything to wear," I half-joked. I didn't have anything to wear, but I didn't feel the urge to go either. Small talk gave me hives.

"You're surrounded by gowns," Olivia said from behind the dressing room curtain.

"They're all spoken for."

"Ella!" Bianca cried from the other side of the outer door, adding a quick knock. "Ute Wente's waiting."

I opened the door. My stepmother waited on the other side with her arms crossed as if my problem was laziness and she'd caught me slacking again.

Laziness wasn't my problem. She was.

"Just finishing up with the Monroe gown."

"Done!" Olivia said, coming out from behind the curtain, fully dressed.

"Oh," Bianca said, stopping in her tracks. "Mrs. Crowne! It's so nice to see you."

"Monroe," she corrected with a smile. "My mother's name."

My stepmother's skull-short black hair hugged her head like a swimming cap, but she'd managed to tuck a Swarovski crystal comb behind her ear. Her skin was soft leather, consistently winter-tanned as if she'd just jetted back from a vacation in St. Croix.

"Of course," Bianca singsonged with a kind smile, banishing the horror of anyone not taking the Crowne name as she turned her glare to me. "We have Theresa and Fiona Drazen both waiting forty minutes for your attention. And Ute, of course." She turned back to Olivia, still smiling. "I hate to rush you, but we're in such a crunch over your celebration." She pressed her palm to her chest and bowed ever so slightly as if she was praying in her direction. "Will you have lunch with me though? We have a spread all set out."

"I have to get to work," Olivia replied, buttoning her jacket. "I'll show myself out."

"I won't hear of it!" She turned her back on me to lead Olivia away. "This floor can be such a maze, and you don't want to get lost in the sample room. It's like those dirty, loud back streets in

Fez where me and June got lost this one time? It was absolutely..."

"Hellish," I grumbled, finishing her sentence to myself as I rolled my eyes.

———

ON HIGHLAND AVE, a billboard sat on the roof of a single-story industrial building wedged between two galleries. A mural with the words BREAK SHIT took the entire front wall. The permits to demolish the building had expired when the owner couldn't buy the adjoining spaces. He rented it to me for a fraction of the market rate as long as I didn't ask him for repairs or refuse to vacate once he could tear it down.

Commercial zoning meant I couldn't officially inhabit it, but it had everything I needed. Two thousand square feet divided in the middle. A bathroom. A hot plate and refrigerator on the side I lived in, and a workspace for the dozen or so artists in the GAC.

Mandy climbed the telescoping ladder I'd hooked to the back of the building. There, in the shade of the billboard, on a patch of Astroturf, I had a little table and chairs set up. Every first of the month—most months—I heard men clonking around the roof to change the ad. They left my seating area alone.

"Thank you for the retweet," I said to Mandy, putting a bag of takeout on the table. "The GAC accounts were on fire."

"Any excuse to look like an edgy influencer," she replied, taking out a plastic clamshell of salad.

"It was amazing," I said, reclining on the chair until I faced the night sky. Though we were on the back side of the billboard, its lights drowned out the stars. "The sun. The stones. The construction guy getting out of the bulldozer to check it out. The whole thing."

"It was. Were you late for work?"

"Yeah, and I got in trouble. Blah blah."

19

"If you worked for me, you could come in any time you wanted."

I waved away the offer and cracked open my chicken sandwich container. Mandy had offered me a hundred jobs and she'd offer another hundred, but her clothes would never say Papillion on the label.

This name is your responsibility now.

"Gotta keep my eye on the evil stepmother."

"For how long?"

"I'm not wishing for anything, but she's gotta die someday. Then it's mine."

"And you still want it? After this morning?"

I tilted my head to get a bite of my sandwich. I was starving. I was always starving. The bomb of a chicken salad hero was no match for my appetite.

"Twitter fame don't pay the bills." I wiped my mouth. "Art with nothing to sell doesn't either."

"What if..." She shoved salad in her mouth. "Just for kicks, let's say you had a piece that made... I don't know, let's say..." She crinkled her face as if calculating. "Ten million. Would you start buying up shares?"

I was right. She'd been calculating. She knew her competition's share price to the penny. "Like a hostile takeover?"

"They call it activist investing now."

"Of my own company? Basically... buy my birthright?"

"You could murder Bianca, I guess." She wrinkled her nose and shook her head as if the idea wasn't just morally bankrupt, but icky.

Ten mill? Fifteen? If I had it, would I scoop up shares and kick the bitch out of the corner office? Return the Papillion name to its former glory?

In three more bites, I had most of the sandwich down and the idea mostly digested.

Juggling the GAC and a full-time job was hard enough. If I ran Papillion, the collective wouldn't fit into my life.

"Maybe," I said, deciding to play the game. "First thing I'd do is fire Jean-Claude, then I'd kill those ugly fucking T-shirts."

"Interesting." She nodded into her salad, and when she looked at me with a gleam in her eye, I realized we weren't playing.

"Mandy," I said with a thick layer of suspicion, "you already have your own fashion house, and I know you don't have that kind of cash lying around."

"Well." She chewed, swallowed, and pointed her fork at me. "Here's the thing…"

———

AFTER WORK THE NEXT DAY, I met Amilcar in his Downtown loft. Still in his creative business casual suit. He ran the tech department for a marketing firm, doing microtargeting and other less savory stuff I didn't understand, which was why he was my go-to as soon as Mandy called and told me who my potential husband was.

Logan Crowne.

I hadn't seen him since ninth grade, but least he wasn't a complete stranger.

"The first guy I hacked for you was doing shit to you I can't even talk about," Amilcar said, tapping the keyboard in front of four huge screens. "So if this is a similar situation, I want to know now so I'll be ready to kill him."

"It's not even close."

"And you're not telling me why I'm looking up the dark web's asshole for Logan Crowne? Because he's rich as fuck. The GAC should be drone-bombing his house."

That was a possible next project. Dropping art from the sky. The idea wasn't quite fully formed. It had to be more than litter.

"Not yet."

"Huh, well…" Pictures of Logan flashed on the center screen. "That is one handsome motherfucker."

"He is."

He'd always been handsome, but the years had strengthened his jaw, hardening his gaze, and turned a nice-looking adolescent into a stunning man.

"He makes me wanna fuck." Amilcar leaned his chair all the way back to take in the visuals. "True story."

"Since when do you admit you want to fuck a guy?"

"No, no." *Tap tap* on the keyboard. "Not a guy. I want to a fuck a woman. A beautiful woman."

"He doesn't look like—"

"Fance. Stop. You're killing me."

"What?"

"Look at him! Damn. All right. Here it is. Business. He likes his privacy."

A scarcity of images and mentions on my Google search had told me that. "Okay."

"He's a hundred percent single for a while now. Was on *LA Seeker*'s list of Los Angeles's Most Eligible Bachelors until two days before it went to print. Then he was pulled."

"How do you know that?"

"Right here." He tapped a side screen with rows of code he knew I couldn't read. "He doesn't like attention. His profile's in this folder and the added date is two days before. Here's a *Vanity Fair* article on rich dudes at Harvard. Early draft, he's there. What they printed? Poof."

"How are his finances?"

Amilcar turned to me with an incredulous look.

"Can you see that or no?" I asked.

"He's a *Crowne*."

"You never met a broke rich person?"

"Actually, no. I only know broke broke people and broke people trying to act rich because they think the universe is gonna be fooled into believing it."

"If, let's say, he wanted to buy something for... I don't know... ten million dollars? Does he have the cash to do it?"

"That is stupid money."

"I know, can you—?"

"What's going on with you and this guy, Fance?"

I shook my head. "Something. It's harmless."

"You pulling off a heist or something?"

"No. Amilcar. Trust me. Okay?"

He shook his head and looked at his watch before turning back to his typing. "I gotta pick up Tasha from school in half an hour, so if I can't pull it up in fifteen, I'll get back to you."

"So late?"

Websites with flames, guys in hoods, green letters on black backgrounds came up and disappeared.

"Rehearsals. The spring production's *Cats*. She's Grizelda. Been hearing *Memories* for weeks already." He paused to scroll. "You coming?"

"Of course. Get me a ticket."

"Boom." Amilcar held out his hand at another website I couldn't make heads or tails of. "God bless the dark web."

"Does he have it?"

"In his fucking couch cushions, lady."

I clapped once. "Awesome."

"You're not marrying him or anything are you?"

Amilcar's instincts were finely tuned. I should have known he'd get it on the first guess.

"Who knows what the future holds?"

He shook his head, part impressed part dissatisfied. "So you're dating."

"It's a long story," I said. "But it's a short story too, so I wanted to make sure he has what he says he has. Not that it matters. I just... well, why I wanted to know about the money is the long story part. And I can't tell you, so don't ask. You just have to trust me."

"Trust but verify. Your judgment sucks. I want to meet him."

"If we get married, you will."

"Before that. I want to give him a look over. Sniff his ass out. Make sure he's not some kinda rapist, or like, I don't know. Whatever."

"Okay. You give me your first impression. I'd like that."

"Hope it's worth it," Amilcar said. "Whatever it is you need stupid money for."

I threw my arms around his shoulders and kissed his cheek, but I didn't tell him I was selling my hand in marriage for stupid money.

4

LOGAN

"I THINK WE SHOULD WIN," Byron said. "That's what I think."

The conference room we'd occupied for the past four hours still smelled of dinner, and the halls outside it were quiet. The head of supply and the VP of operations were catching my brother up on shit he would have known if he'd been around.

"There's no point to winning the contract if we overpay for it," I said.

"We can make money back," Byron said as if there was nothing more obvious. "Losing damages our reputation. Forever. You want to risk that for a few pennies on the dollar?"

This fucking guy. He couldn't read an EPS report or between the lines of an MD&A, but here he was tossing numbers around as if he were on a Mardi Gras float.

My phone rang. Mandy.

"I think we should pick this up in the morning," I said, standing.

The operations VP closed his folder.

I slid into the hall, whispering, "Well?"

"You owe me," Mandy said.

"She in?"

"Open to the idea. It's going to cost you."

"How much?" I closed the door to my office.

"A strategic buyout of her father's company."

"I need you to be more specific. This WalMart or the corner store?"

"If I tell you who she is, you're on for a meeting. Okay?"

The interior walls of my office were glass, and I watched Byron walk down the hall with the VP, talking like a man making a point. Probably selling him on spending a few more pennies on the dollar.

"Agreed," I said.

"The company is Basile Papillion."

"Ella," I said without hesitation.

"I knew you'd remember. See? It was meant to be."

———

ELLA PAPILLION.

What did I remember?

Cute. Very cute, actually. Smart. Dead mother. The age difference was a joke now, but at the time, she'd seemed too young to touch.

I remembered her alongside Millie, my senior year girlfriend and director of the school theater production. Her costumer had been a sophomore, still been young enough to be called a prodigy, pins in her mouth, hunched over a sewing machine or sketching so quickly my girlfriend hardly had to finish a sentence.

Cooper Santon was supposed to be investigating the rest, but I couldn't wait. I had Mandy arrange a meeting for the next evening. Ella insisted on her place. I was already halfway across Beverly before Cooper called. I pulled over to take it.

"You have five minutes," I said when I picked up.

"You didn't give me a lot of time."

"Fast, cheap, and good, Coop. You get two out of three in life and I didn't bother with cheap. So tell me what I paid for."

"Okay. Ella Papillion. She still works at her father's company. Lives on—"

"Highland Ave. I know."

"It's not zoned for a residential lease."

"Anything else?"

"Like I said, I didn't have a lot of time."

"Yes, you said that."

"There aren't any liens against her." He rattled off the relevant facts. "No drug arrests. No mental health issues I can see. And— you said this was important, so I made sure before I called—the internet's clean. No bad publicity with her name on it."

"No drug arrests."

"Right."

"The specificity is weighing on me, Coop."

"That's what you asked about. Specifically."

"Has she broken any laws that matter?"

"She was into graffiti as a kid. Got picked up for vandalism and trespass in 2007. Pled and took the fine. Then again in 2008. Community service picking up garbage on the side of the 101."

That was after I knew her. She'd left Wildwood School a few months before I graduated, leaving Millie without spring production costumes. Must have had a few downhill years after her father got remarried.

All of that was a long time ago. I had a few hours to decide if I could live with it.

"Thanks," I said. "Do you have an opinion? A gut reaction?"

"Depends what you want with her. Would I date her? Yeah."

"Would you marry her?"

"If I loved her. Wouldn't give her my bank account numbers right off."

"Thanks, Coop."

We hung up and I pulled back onto Beverly with a few

27

minutes to ask myself how desperate I really was. How important was getting married? How much time did I have before Byron wedged himself in so deep I couldn't get rid of him? Every day for six months, he'd gotten more comfortable. He kept his woman happy, played around on the floor with his son, and ran a multinational business with me. Every day, he proved he could handle Crowne and a personal life without breaking a sweat, and every day I wasn't married, I proved I couldn't.

My father held the keys. He was in charge of succession and wanted a Crowne to run the business. It had always been Byron, until his first fiancée committed suicide and he left to flip real estate. Then my father turned to me, and I jumped in with an exhilaration I'd never felt before, working at his side for six years until he decided I wasn't happy enough.

Byron was winning. He thought everything was about winning, but it wasn't. It was about getting in the ring and staying on your feet for every round. Beaten bloody, aching from the battle, ears ringing so loudly you could barely hear the last bell— that was the point.

Born two and a half years apart, we'd spent one season in the same Little League division, but on different teams. He hated baseball, and I figured he stayed in another year just to play against me. He pitched. I hit. And when our teams met in the playoffs, the fucker beaned me cold. Swore he didn't do it on purpose. Maybe he hadn't. But I'd be damned if I was going to let a pinch runner take that base. Damned if I wasn't going to steal a second and drag my ass up to the plate in the next inning.

I was a hitter. I knew where to put the ball. And when he sent an off-speed pitch I saw coming a mile away, I sent it right to his fat fucking head. He dodged but couldn't catch it, and I got to second.

It was the last time he let a man on base, but I stole third and made it home on a sac fly. It was the last run we needed to win, so fuck him. When we got home, he apologized and I slept like a concussed baby for fourteen hours.

For him, anything less than total domination was a loss.

I was more surgical. I wanted what I wanted. He could have the rest.

And I wanted Crowne. I didn't want to lie to get it, but I had to, and I had to lie now or let Byron take everything.

The address on Highland was in a semi-industrial zone on a block of converted warehouses built when the neighborhood was one big storage unit for Hollywood studios. Most had been turned into restaurants and furniture stores. Ella Papillion's sat between two galleries and had a billboard on the roof. The barred steel door and small window in front had been integrated into a graffiti-style mural that said BREAK SHIT.

Not a great sign.

My family would have to be convinced I'd marry into a message like that.

I turned around the corner and found the back alley. Two cars were parked behind her building. An El Camino that had been dark blue when it came off the factory floor, but was now a cool gray, and a new black Toyota Camry.

I pulled my BMW into the last available space and got out, then went up the concrete steps to the metal door, which was ajar. I pushed it open. "Hello?"

The space stretched to the front of the building. Clean white wall on one side. Fucking mess of small, stacked canvases on the other, along with shelves of paint, brushes, a slop sink, a drafting table, and a mismatched couch and chairs that looked as if they'd been dragged in from the street.

The white wall had a single, seven-foot-high, five-foot-wide blank canvas on it. The fluorescent light made it seem to glow.

A door in the back of the white side opened, and Ella stepped through. "Hey, Logan."

Not the same girl. First off, she was pierced. Nose. Ears all the way around. Her wavy black hair was pinned to the top of her head, and her eyes seemed to be a paler brown. Almost amber. The freckles I remembered from high school had paled, making her seem sexy instead of young. She wore a black choker and a sleeveless *Star Wars* T-shirt that hugged her curves. The ripped jeans sitting low on her waist were painted, patched with contrasting thread, and wide on the bottom in a way that was out of style, but somehow right with the red cowboy boots.

"Ella," I said. "Nice to see you again."

"You too."

She was looking at me the same way I looked at her. Taking stock of my face, my suit, with her thumbs hooked in her belt loops, ringed fingers tapping her hips.

Bit of a challenge, this one. Maybe I'd make a deal with her. Maybe I wouldn't. But no matter what my decision was, I wanted her to agree to the proposal. I wanted her to want it as desperately as I needed it.

I said, "You look good."

"Let's not start with bullshit, okay?"

Before I could answer, a man came from the same door. Six-three. Built. Dressed for business and looking right through me.

"Logan Crowne," Ella said. "This is my friend, Amilcar Wilton."

We shook hands and I wondered if the El Camino was his. That would be a kind of relief.

"Good to meet you," he said.

"Same."

He turned to Ella and nodded. "I'm out."

"Yeah?" she answered as if he'd said more than two innocuous words.

"Yeah." He kissed her cheek, and though she and I hadn't agreed to a damn thing, my blood ran a little hotter and my hands tightened into fists as if she was already mine.

"Okay," she said. "I'll call you later."

"See you," Amilcar said to me as he passed.

Behind me, the door closed and we were alone.

"Cool place," I said.

"Thanks. You want to sit?"

"Before I get comfortable, Mandy said you were single. That meant unattached. Completely unattached."

Outside, a car started in the back alley. It wasn't the rumble of an El Camino, but the whirr of a new Camry.

"You mean Amilcar?" she said, eyebrows raised. "No, no. He's a friend. A good friend, but you know… *just* a friend."

"Ah. Right. Just checking."

"Full disclosure. I wanted him here to meet you. He's a first impressionist. It's like a gift. One look and he knows."

Every person who knew about what I was trying to arrange was a potential leak, and if my family found out, I could kiss Crowne goodbye. I didn't know this Amilcar person well enough to trust him.

"You told him?" I asked.

"I said you and I are dating, if that's okay."

"And he gets an impression of everyone you date?"

"I wanted to make sure you're not just trying to get laid."

"I don't need to go to this much trouble to get laid."

"Or maybe you're a serial killer."

"I didn't kill Millie. We just broke up."

She laughed.

"Sit." She indicated a worn couch and two chairs around a chest that served as a coffee table. "I've got a pot of water boiling. Or soda. I have Sprite. But…" She looked me up and down again, and I squinted at her as if that would help me discern what she was seeing. "I can get you a glass of milk if you want that."

Milk?

"Whatever you're having."

I'd be fucked before I let her get milk out of the fridge just for me, because even though it didn't matter what she thought of me as a man, I cared.

5

ELLA

LEAVING Logan in the working side of the space, I crossed to my makeshift kitchen.

Yeah, a guy like that didn't have to work to get laid at all.

The Logan Crowne in my memory was straight-arrow, straight-A, just the cool side of math nerd, and way too handsome to be shunned by the rich beauties who could have anyone they wanted. I'd heard them talk as if I wasn't right there, on my knees, fixing the hems on their costumes. They said Millie must be putting out. They said he'd dump her soon.

But he didn't, and though I'd blushed whenever he was near me, I couldn't help but root for them to make it as a couple.

The Logan Crowne standing in my studio wasn't that boy anymore. He was a full-on man. Old-school, Carey Grant gorgeous. Women probably took their clothes off as soon as he walked into a room.

Not that it was supposed to matter.

"I hear Millie's the theater director at the Ahmanson," I called out.

"She goes by Millicent now."

"Why did you guys break up?"

"She was a little too ambitious for me." Before I could ask him what the fuck he was talking about, he changed the subject. "What are you doing with the big one?"

Trying to catch a glimpse of him through the doorway, I leaned back as I turned off the hot plate under the saucepot of boiling water. He was pointing at the Big Blank.

"Not sure," I said. "It's bigger than I usually do, so I haven't decided what's important enough."

"Did you do the one out front?" He leaned in the doorway. "Break shit?"

I saw the living space the way a stranger did. Mismatched canvases covered the walls. Beat-up concrete floor. Shit kitchen. The bed visible on the other side of the half-wall. He was looking right at it with those damn eyes.

"That was a bunch of us," I said. "The stuff on my own is tiny."

He looked back at me, and I zipped my hoodie, as if that would keep him from thinking I'd take my clothes off just because we were in proximity to a bed. Which—I admit—was a temptation. It had been a while since I'd been around a man I wanted to take my clothes off for.

"So all this..." He waved his hands at the art on the walls. "Some's pretty big. It's not all yours?"

He was looking right at Kira's painting, of course. A woman sat with her robe open as wide as her bare legs, straight blond hair covering her face as she looked down at the nude woman on her hands and knees, eating her pussy.

Great.

"Friends, mostly. We trade, or buy if we can."

He was still looking at it and it was making my neck break out in prickly heat. Did he think I'd bought it? Because I fucking had.

"There's an iPod on the table by the red chair. Pick something, would you?"

"Good idea," he said. "Break the tension around here."

I laughed nervously, grateful he'd acknowledged what we were both feeling.

He unbuttoned his jacket and sat in the shitty chair Nerfy had given me when he moved. I always hoped for free furniture for the studio, because it could get paint on it, but seeing him there, I wished I had something nicer for him to sit on.

"You left Wildwood." He scrolled through my music, making himself heard from the other side of the wall without raising his voice. "No one knew why. It was the biggest mystery of the year."

"Was it?" I called out, because whatever power his voice had wasn't one I shared.

"Solve it for me."

"I smashed my stepmother's car window with a pattern weight."

"Why?"

"Sugar?" I called.

"In what?"

Of course. He'd asked for whatever I was having, but I never told him what that was. Terrible hostess. He probably needed a wife who was better at this.

"Mint tea."

"Yes, then."

"Full disclosure." I put the leaves into the white porcelain teapot. "It's wild mint that grows behind the building. Could be toxic, but it hasn't killed me yet."

"It's fine." He turned his attention back to the music.

As I poured hot water into the pot, I peeked to the other side again. How much did my iPod reveal about me? He seemed fascinated.

He looked up at me with his thumb on the glass. "The window. What did she do?"

"She convinced my father I shouldn't work at Papillion until I got my grades up." I poured hot water over the leaves. "That company was my life. It was my mother's life, and that bitch wanted to cut me off from it."

I crossed to him with the tea tray and two packets of sugar pressed between my lips.

"And getting your grades up wasn't an option?" He put the iPod back into the cradle, then plucked the sugar from my lips.

"Fuck her."

He laughed. "You haven't changed."

Was that true? I felt more beaten down and more defiant than when my father was alive. Maybe the only difference was my volume. I was the same, but more of it.

Blind Willie Johnson came over the speakers. I'd hoped Logan would find something he liked so I could feel him out based on his musical choices, but he'd chosen the list I played most frequently —probably for the same reason.

I didn't know this person. He didn't know me.

How badly did I want to buy back my father's company?

How much did I want to keep my promise to him and get Bianca out of my life?

Because getting married for it was absolutely insane.

He pinched the tops of the sugars and flicked them to get the granules to the bottom of the packets, blue eyes on me, then the chair.

Did I want to obey the eyes that commanded me to sit without saying a word, or the strong, graceful hands that promised so much more without guaranteeing it?

"So, you want to talk about getting married," I said, sitting on the couch. "Why?"

"Mandy said she told you." He was so confident and sure, so dapper and traditional, that this meeting was simply the first step in a reasonable, time-tested process.

"I want to hear it from you."

"The only thing I ever wanted to do was run Crowne Industries." As he spoke, he tented his fingers around the cup's edge. "We all figured Byron would be the guy. But I wanted it, and I was going to be ready to take it. I majored in business. Got a Harvard MBA. Top of my class, by the way. But my brother? I love Byron, but everything's easy for him." He shook his head, drinking pensively. "He split and did his own thing for five years. My chance, right? I busted my ass to prove I could handle it. Five years, and he strolls back into his old office like he owns the place. Like that." He snapped his fingers. "I'm sidelined. And I'm going to stay sidelined unless I get married."

"Is that an official rule or a feeling you have?"

"My father thinks I work too hard. He brought Byron back in so I'd have time to find a wife while he retires to take care of my mother."

"Is she all right?"

"No." He put his hands up to cut off further questions. "And I know what you want. I can execute that for you. We'll start buying up shares after the first six months. The buys could take time, but I'll own enough of Papillion to exert pressure by the time we're done. I'll sign it over to you as part of the divorce."

He made it seem so simple. He was absolutely positively sure that if we did this thing, stuck to it, waited an allotted amount of time, we'd both walk away with what we wanted.

I believed we could walk away, but I wasn't so sure getting us both what we wanted would be that easy.

"So," I said, pressing my praying hands between my knees. "That's it?"

"That's it. The rest is in the details."

"Right. So, where do we start on those?"

"Your house," Logan said. "Your rules."

I liked that. Rules would make the conversation a little less weird. "You get a question, then I get one. Then you."

"What about follow-ups?"

"Permitted. I'm the host, so you can go first."

He sat back in his chair with his cup in his lap and crossed an ankle over his knee.

"I think it's best if we stay monogamous," he said, respecting me enough to get right to the point. "Can you handle that?"

"For how long?"

"Two years."

"One year."

His jaw tightened as if he was holding back a reply.

"I'm an adult human woman," I added. "You and I obviously? Not a thing. We can marry for business, but I can't hold that up for a year."

"One year," he said with a nod. "No cheating."

"For either of us." I put my cup down as if I meant it.

"I'm also an adult."

"I'll take that as a sign you can keep it in your pants."

"That's right. Your turn." He ceded the floor, and I noticed his strong wrists the width of his hand.

I toed a boot off and kicked it to the side. "So." I pulled off the other boot and laid it next to its sister. "You can run an empire, but you're threatened by a woman's ambition?"

His laugh didn't make me feel silly for asking as much as it answered the challenge. "I'm not, but I don't want to marry it."

"Well," I said churlishly, tucking my socked feet under me. "That's good to know right off the bat."

"That won't count for you."

"Which brings me to the big one. Why me?"

"Is that a follow-up, or are you asking two questions in a row?"

"My house, my rules."

He nodded, and I feared he might think I couldn't stick to an agreement. I wasn't ready to give up before we even finished the conversation, but I had a perverse need to sabotage every opportunity.

"There are a hundred women who'd marry you in a heartbeat,"

I said. "But here you are. In my studio. After not having seen me for how long?"

"At least ten piercings ago."

"See? And that's another thing. Am I even your type?"

"Am I yours?"

"Fuck no."

"Right." He put his cup on the table, and I thought he was going to walk out. Instead, he bent forward, leaning his elbows on his knees. "Look, I could dip into the usual pool and be half of a 'cute couple.' But I'm not interested. I don't need a woman nagging me for attention. Bitching about birthdays and anniversaries. I don't have the patience or the time. I'm interested in doing private business with a businesswoman who can keep the business private. Is that you?"

He had me on a string until the last sentence. I was an artist, not some powerhouse in pumps and a jacket with inch-thick shoulder pads.

"What I don't get," I said, "is why you don't hit up an ex-girlfriend or something."

"I've had four long-term girlfriends since Millie. Some better than others, but I work seventy hours a week and I travel. Every one of them resented it. Two sulked. One made an ultimatum."

"They loved you."

"Love makes for messy divorces."

"Wait. That's three. What about the fourth?" I asked.

"Doctor June Mackie. Worked eighty hours a week. She married John Burkis last year. The senator."

"Wow," I said. "You weren't kidding. You literally broke up with her because she worked."

He sighed, and I got the feeling that this was the one woman he'd really loved. "I'd rather jerk off than schedule a fuck every two weeks." He poured more tea in his mug. "You want yours warmed up?"

Was making himself the host a strategy? Was he showing me how nice he could be? Or did he want to be in control?

I peeked in the top of the teapot to check the water level, then I nodded and watched him refill my tea. "You could have worked less, you know."

"That's not what I wanted." He handed me my cup by the handle so I wouldn't burn my fingers.

"Thank you, Logan. You're a full-service provincial asshole."

"Imagine if you married me." He sat on the couch with me, keeping a respectful but crossable distance between us.

"Imagine if it was the nineteen-fifties," I said. "You come home every night at ten from a hard day running the world, expecting your slippers right at the door and the ironing board put away. Dinner hot. Wife in full makeup—"

"That's not—"

"Ready to get on her back and spread her legs at the drop of a hat."

"Okay." He stopped me, hand up. "That, I won't deny."

"Knew it!"

"But she'd be the one dropping hats."

"Oh, really?"

"Totally worth her while, and not just on her back. On her knees, or facing down on the bed with her feet wide on the floor. My wife's gonna be ass up begging for it. She'll wait all day, soaking her panties until I come upstairs to give her everything she wants for as long as she wants it."

A knot the consistency of oil paint gathered in my throat when he started, growing into a sticky, unswallowable lump as if every bit of liquid from my mouth had pit stopped there on the way to the throb between my legs.

Oh, hell no he wasn't talking like that for a year.

"Those are big promises," I said, voice cracking when the knot broke.

He shrugged. "I only promise what I can deliver."

"To your one-day-real wife."

"Who may or may not have my slippers at the door."

And that was the rub, wasn't it? He was shameless in his needs. Everyone close to him must have known what he was looking for in a mate, and every one of them would know I wasn't anything close to his dream girl.

"No," I said. "We'll never sell it. I have friends too. They know I want what my parents had. Same as you. If your side doesn't blow it, mine will and we'll be caught."

His laugh was so deep and authentic, I froze with my tea getting cold against my palms. How could he miss what getting caught would do to his name? I was damn sure of what it would do to my father's.

"What's so funny?" I twisted to face him, swinging a pillow that he caught and tucked behind him when he faced me.

"Anyone else would give me a song and dance about the 'sanctity of marriage.' Or that their whole lives, they dreamed of their wedding day to some Prince Charming, blah blah. You're worried about *getting caught.*"

"That makes us compatible because we're equally immoral?"

"We're surprising. Unexpected."

"We're not a movie!" If I sounded frustrated, it was because my deal-breaker was his dealmaker. How did you get past that?

"Have you met people?" he asked. "They're worse than a movie. My brother got a woman smart enough to do better but picked him anyway. You see it all the time. Mandy? What about Mandy and that fucking—"

"Ugh! Renaldo!"

"Total slimeball."

I grabbed a pillow and screamed into it. Logan laughed. When I picked my head up, I must have been a sight, because he laughed harder.

"Now you tell me," Logan said. "Does that couple make sense? Did Mandy dream of hooking up with a philandering—"

"Manipulating—"

"Controlling—"

"I'm going to scream into this pillow again."

"She didn't fantasize about a guy like that, but we believe it. They're not convincing in spite of being wrong..."

"They're convincing *because* it's so, so wrong."

He tapped the tip of my nose. It was a shockingly intimate gesture, touching me then pulling back into his own space, but I didn't jerk away or flinch. My body was okay with him.

"And think how easy the divorce is," he said. "Everyone gets to say 'I knew it,' and 'I told you so.' We'll be surrounded by psychics who aren't surprised by anything."

"How are you going to make them buy you being in love with me in the first place? We have to show up places together. You know how people in love act. It's disgusting."

"I can act. Can you?"

"Acting and faking it are two totally different things. As soon as you kiss the bride, it's going to be obvious it's the first time."

He tried to put away his smile, but the corners of his mouth wouldn't obey. Even when he tried to obfuscate with a sip of tea, he was irritatingly bemused. "Is that all, Ella?"

"That's not enough?"

"No. It's not." He shifted close enough for me to smell the layers of his cologne.

Anise. Musk. Wealth.

"We're going to kiss for the first time, and you tell me if you're convinced," he said, putting his hands on either side of my face.

I surprised myself by leaning into his caress, resistance melting away in the warmth of his palms and the intensity of his gaze as his thumbs stroked my cheeks. "Convince me then."

The world got so small, so fast that I didn't have a moment to think, only act.

Or not act. Just stay still while he wrapped me in the cocoon of his attention.

If I spoke again, I'd break the spell.

If I breathed, all the pain and uncertainty would rush into the space between us like backstabbing friends.

If I moved, something I wanted to know would be forever unknown. An idea I didn't have yet would be forgotten.

He leaned forward slowly, as if giving me a chance to push him away.

Not gonna happen. He smelled too good. He was too handsome, too well-dressed, too charming for me to refuse. Maybe this scheme would fall through in an hour. Maybe it would be an utter disaster financially and emotionally. But that kiss was a risk I was willing to take.

His mouth found mine willing, and when the tip of his tongue brushed my bottom lip, I went boneless. I tasted crisp mint leaves wet with dew. When his hands moved back on my neck to hold me still, I let my weight drop into the support, giving him more control than he needed but less than I craved.

Time could only be measured in stars while he kissed me. I wanted for nothing and felt nothing but his lips and his hands. I thought not in words, but in dots of moments strewn across the sky and connected by his touch.

But even a billion light years has an end. Gently, he dropped his hands and pulled away. My spine held itself up and my lungs filled with air.

"Now," he said. "That's out of the way."

"It is."

"So?" He laid his thumb on my chin and turned my head to face him. "Do you want to practice more? Because I think we got it."

I couldn't live through another kiss like that and maintain my sense. "You made your point."

"I can make things happen for you. More than just a buyout." He spoke softly, as if offering not a business deal, but personal satisfaction only he could provide.

The tea was cold. I needed to get off the couch and boil more water, but I couldn't. I was locked in place not just by the promise in his words—but by the suggestion in his tone.

"I'm scared," I said, and like a punctured balloon, the smallest opening let out all that I barely held inside. "My father's name isn't just a name. He made it mean something and he gave that to me. It's the only thing I have left. And when he died, he asked me to hold on to it. He said I should use my gifts for it. It's what he wanted and I'm scared. If I do this, and we try to take it over, we could fail. I could lose my connection to Papillion and I'll break my promise."

"He's dead, Ella."

A fact was a fact, but I didn't like it coming out of his mouth right after it kissed me.

"Thanks for the reminder."

The pressure behind his words propelled me up, where I could see a leftover bag of blue crystals glittering through the plastic like a transparent geode.

"I'm a bad choice for you."

I took the cups back to the kitchen before I said something I couldn't take back.

6

LOGAN

ONE MINUTE, I had her. The next, she was rinsing mugs of mint tea in the kitchen.

Unpredictable, that Ella.

Again, not the kind of woman I'd spend the rest of my life with, but I saw the appeal of a partner who always surprised you. Whose heart wasn't easy to see and whose mind was a fascinating tangle of emotion and motivation.

It didn't hurt that she was lovely to look at. Even with the holes in her face and the tattoos peeking from under her clothes.

I could find someone else, but I didn't want to.

Bringing the teapot, I went into the kitchen. "Why?" I put the pot on the counter. "Sell me."

She dumped the tealeaves and rinsed the pot without looking at me. "If I tell you why you shouldn't marry me, what are you going to do with that information?"

"Use it to tell you why you should."

"Or believe me?"

I leaned on the counter, arms folded, watching her profile as she looked into the sink. Her nose was a soft curve, and her forehead looked higher from the side. "Tell me and I'll decide."

"Did you hear about the house in Westlake?" she said, running water into the pot. "The one they demolished? On Benton?"

"No."

"It was all over Twitter." She swirled the water and dumped it. "The *LA Times.*"

"I'm more of a *Wall Street Journal* guy."

She threw me a white towel and pushed the pot into my chest. I took it, but wasn't sure what she wanted.

"Dry."

"Ah." I'd never dried my own dishes, but I'd seen people do it in movies, so I stuck the towel in the pot and pushed it around.

"When they bulldozer-demolished it, it had been vandalized. The inside walls and floors were covered in rhinestones. It was like they opened a geode."

"Sounds... cool?" I wiped the outside.

"After it was down, they gave out the rhinestones. People all over the city kept them like good luck charms." She faced me. The fluorescent light hit the apex of her forehead, making it higher and more pronounced. What was going on under that skull of hers?

"When I was pulled out of Wildwood," she said, "I was put in Fairfax High. I fell in with 'a crowd.' Graffiti artists. Really creative but really wild. Amilcar was one of them. We got busted a lot. They got arrested and I got sent back to Daddy. You know how it is, don't you?"

She'd gotten arrested at least twice, but I wasn't ready to tell her I knew already.

"Not really."

"You sure you don't want to bail and just go back to the boring me?"

"No way."

She sighed, as if gathering a little more strength to lift a heavy load. "One night, we were throwing up a piece on Melrose. That shitty stretch between Western and Normandie everyone drives right past? Cops came. We dropped everything and ran. Blah blah. I was already around the corner when they shot Keenan because —and this is real—he didn't let go of his spray can and they thought it was a gun."

"Ah. I'm sorry."

"We were devastated. He was murdered... and for what? We decided to stop the small-time throw-ups and move to bigger things. We painted Keenan's name over billboards. We plant trees where we're not supposed to. We deface things rich people hold dear. But one thing, one big thing, it took years to plan." She watched my face, reading my confusion like a spreadsheet full of circular references. "You still don't get it."

Was I being thick? Was I being an uptight ass she wouldn't respect?

"You're saying you have a history," I guessed.

"Half right." She took the teapot. "I have a present history."

It clicked. Thank God I wasn't that much of an idiot. "You did the house in Westlake."

"Gold star." She tapped the tip of my nose.

"Okay, so?"

"We're a secret collective. There are maybe two dozen of us, in and out, you know? Everyone does what they can, but no one talks. No one. Like fight club. So if you tell anyone, I'll have to kill you."

Everything I'd assumed about her was wrong. She'd shed another protective layer and revealed someone so captivating and complex, I found myself awed by my unexpected desire.

"And you were never charged?" I needed to hear her tell the truth.

"Once." Her shirt hitched up when she put the pot in a high cabinet. Another tattoo on her belly. "Had to pick up garbage on the side of the 101."

"Bet you stopped traffic."

She bit her lip, and though she turned away so I wouldn't see, I would have bet my shares in Crowne Industries that she was blushing.

"Still want to get married?" she asked. "Because I have a record. I do things people don't like. Illegal things. The internet will destroy my work then eat you alive. I'm a dead weight. I'll drag your family name to the bottom of the ocean."

Her life was too complicated. I needed a simple and believable situation. She was a bad business decision. Too much risk.

But the risk was the attraction. I'd gone from needing her to wanting her, and the want was strong enough to pull everything out of whack. I wanted to fuck her. Tame her. Touch the explosive heat inside her.

My body's desire set off alarms in my mind.

"You're right," I said. "It can't be you."

No matter what choice I made, her or someone else, I would have regretted it, but this tasted especially bitter.

"I hope you find someone," she said. "Or you could just, you know, do what your father wants. Take a break from work. Have a little fun. Fathers have a way of dying. Making them happy isn't such a bad idea."

"I can't be a different person for him or anyone."

"Fake it 'til you make it."

"I hate that expression. Pretending something's real doesn't make it a fact. It's like Anthony Hopkins didn't become a cannibal when he played Hannibal Lecter."

"Maybe he started liking fava beans though." She made the tooth-sucking noise the actor made in the movie, and we laughed.

"Go on," she said. "Get out of here before you change your mind."

———

I'D HOPED to go to dinner with my parents while my lawyer adjusted the agreement I'd had drafted for Mandy.

So much for that.

Ella was right. She was the wrong girl to marry, but in selling her on the idea, I'd sold myself. There was a very small number of women I could approach, and none of them were perfect. I ran down a list of possibilities as I drove to Bel-Air, and they all came up short. Most weren't desperate enough or were looking for a real husband in LA's circle of eligible bachelors.

My parents had just about moved into their new Bel-Air place. It was too big for two people. Too big for ten. But it was the last spec house Byron had built, so when they wanted to move back to LA, they bought it and put the staff in the westernmost wing, then planned the party of the century.

Taking the back entrance on Stradella Rd, I waved off the valet, pulled into the underground lot, and took the back elevator up to dinner. When the doors closed, I saw my reflection in the polished steel and straightened my hair. I was still Logan Crowne. Same guy with the same problems.

I took a deep breath. The doors slid open as I exhaled.

Dad had made dinner sound like a social gathering, but I knew him better than that. My tendency to overwork didn't come from nowhere.

I stepped into the house. Every possible exterior wall was made of glass to take advantage of the three-hundred-sixty-degree views, and the huge interior rooms were made intimate with the use of half-walls and shapes that increased the number of corners.

Following the sounds of voices, I found my father making a drink at a side bar. My mother, brother, sister in-law, and their baby were on the patio overlooking Stone Canyon.

"Dad."

He looked at his watch before shaking my hand, as if checking to see if I was late. I wasn't. Not that he would have said anything, but I knew the man.

"Glad you could make it." He held up an ice cube by the tongs. "One for you?"

"Sure. The Glen Alan. How's the party planning going?"

"Every time I turn my back, your mother adds to the sheer volume of it." He put the ice in a second glass.

"You could set a limit."

"Why put a boundary on happiness?" He plucked the bottle up by the neck, let it go upward, spinning in the air, and caught it on the way down. "You look good, by the way." He pulled out the cork. "Rested."

"I feel good," I lied. "Resting."

"Olivia's up all night with Garret, and Byron's up doting on her. Nice to see a face without dark circles under the eyes."

Dad handed me a glass of scotch. We clicked.

"Like they don't have a staff?" I snorted into my drink and took a sip that chilled and burned at the same time.

Dad sat on the couch, and before I could join him, Byron strode in and went right to the bar.

"The prodigal son returns." My brother flipped a glass in the air and caught it.

"I'm not Colton," I replied.

"If you were, you'd be having more fun." He poured his scotch straight.

"Sit," Dad said. "The two of you."

We sat across from our father. I leaned forward to catch every word. Byron leaned back, spreading his arms and crossing his legs ankle over knee as if he needed more space.

"So," Dad started. "Byron. It's been a little over six months. Do you feel caught up?"

"Yes," Byron said. "Some of the names changed. The numbers shifted, but it's manageable."

Dad pointed at me. "You agree?"

"It's a complicated business." I leaned forward. "We never know what's coming down the pike. The rigs off Macau are operating at eighty-nine percent, and if it drops any more, we're going to lose South American revenue to the Saudis."

"True, true." Dad took a sip and pressed his lips between his teeth to swallow.

"It'll be handled," Byron said. "Don't worry about it, Dad. Just take care of Mom."

Asshole. Byron cared about my parents as much as I did, but he was still being a brown-nosing, playacting asshole.

"We'll handle it," I added. "And whatever else."

"How are you feeling about some downtime?" Dad asked me.

"Downtime?"

"Space." Dad placed his drink on the table between us and leaned forward, mirroring my posture. "Outside. Life. People."

"Fine."

"There's a rumor making the rounds." Dad stood, plucking up all three glasses in his fingers. "About you." He pointed at me and went to the bar.

"That he's a party animal?" Byron joked.

"Shut up," I said.

"Come on," my brother said. "You wouldn't be Logan Crowne if you had a life."

Clink clink. Ice dropped into glasses.

"Dad, really. It's been great. I appreciate it. Going out with friends is all it is. Whatever the rumor is, it's either bullshit or not anything you have to worry about."

Our father stood over us, holding two glasses in his palm. I took the one with ice and sat back as indolently as my brother.

"Apparently"—Dad lowered himself onto his seat—"you were in Harry Winston buying an engagement ring."

Someone had let the cat out of the bag. It was dead, but it was out, and I had to dispose of the body one of two ways.

Deny it, and I could forget about retaking my position by getting married.

Confirm it, and getting a fiancée was do or die.

"Really?" Byron exclaimed, clapping me on the back. "Who's the poor girl?"

Do or die. I didn't give up that easily. Crowne was mine.

"No one you know. And I haven't asked her yet."

I waited for my father to congratulate me, but he sat there, feet spread apart, two hands circling his glass, taking me apart in a way only my father could.

"That's fast," was all he said.

"It is. But not as fast as you think. It's been going on. I'll let her tell you when you meet her."

"When's that?"

When required a commitment to a plan I couldn't execute on my own.

"Is she here?" Byron asked. "Or Canada?"

"She's busy," I said. "You like that in a woman, right?"

"I do." My brother seemed genuinely happy for me.

I wished I shared his joy. My father didn't hide his suspicion. He needed an explanation.

"I'm sorry, Dad. I didn't tell you because I didn't want to get your hopes up. Frankly, I didn't want to get mine up either."

It was becoming obvious—even to me—that I hadn't said her name. If my father hadn't noticed, I'd worry about him. I couldn't talk about it much longer before he brought it up.

"Look," I said, "let her say yes first, okay?"

"You should bring her around some time," Byron said.

"Maybe Crowne Jewels."

"You're not rushing this, are you?" Dad asked.

"No. Absolutely not. This is real. When you guys meet her, you'll know."

"Fine." Dad put down his glass. "Let's talk about the UVX pipeline before your mother finds out we're working."

7

ELLA

THE BIG BLANK was still a huge white rectangle.

I ate noodles from the Vietnamese place around the corner and stared at it, willing a message worth the four hundred dollars in materials onto the primer.

With *Geode House* done and the next project still unknown, I had time to do my own work. This was the moment to produce something important, something with my name on it. It was time to stop making silly little paintings on slabs of wood I found in the garbage.

The couch smelled like Logan.

Anise, musk, and wealth.

The canvas was empty because I was. All those nights breaking into the property, gluing tiny stones, rushing toward a big day that I hadn't been prepared to be such a success—it all left a hole in me. I'd thought it would feel great, but it was awful. The work wasn't mine anymore. I had nothing. No one and nothing. The day would come when all those hours would be forgotten and *Geode House* would fall into obscurity.

My small paintings were shit. Derivative. Boring. Message-free. I hadn't found a vocabulary or a technique in the hundreds I'd produced, and I figured maybe it was the scale. Small gauge for small ideas.

Risk was inside that big canvas, and only that canvas was big enough to fill the hole the *Geode House* had left.

I got to the bottom of the container, with a few curlicue beige noodles and a half-Rorschach of brown sauce.

My water glass still smelled of mint and my tongue remembered his kiss.

I put down the container. My Blind Willie album was on shuffle, and I really should have fucked Logan, just for fun. We didn't have to get married. I could have reached under his shirt. Let him put his hand under mine. Leaned back so he was on top of me. Wrapped my legs around him and pushed against his erection. I could have said yes, I'll be your wife now, for one hour. Let's fake it 'til we make it, then forget it.

My phone jolted me out of the fantasy. It was Bianca. I shouldn't have answered, but it wasn't like dreaming about Logan was helpful.

"Hi," I said.

"Oh, thank goodness!" she said.

"What's wrong?"

"You have an email from Ningbo. They need a pocket placement approval for the Raquel tee tonight."

Bianca didn't know what to look for, so she couldn't sign off. Of course they needed it tonight, or they'd miss their delivery calendar.

And of course I'd approve it. Otherwise, it would take another day to fix it and tick tock.

"I'll take care of it."

"Good. See you tomorrow!"

I hung up and opened my laptop. I found the email and the photo of the T-shirt with the butterfly on the pocket.

APPROVED.

There were seventy-five more emails.

I'd told Logan I was scared to lose what I had.

But what did I have? This shit? This garbage wasn't what Daddy had meant when he wanted me to honor the name.

I closed the laptop.

Where was the risk? In marrying Logan? Or not trying to get the company back?

Logan and I had spoken when we agreed to meet. Was he calling from his office? Home? Cell? I pulled out my phone and found the number. All I had to do was call it.

And get married to Mr. Traditional.

"Fake married," I reminded myself.

My real husband wouldn't try to own my identity. He wouldn't want his slippers out and my legs spread. He'd be a partner in everything, just as my parents had been to each other.

I wouldn't mind if he looked like Logan, talked dirty like Logan, and kissed me with the same intensity. All that. Without the backward ideas.

My finger hovered over the call button when the screen flashed and the device exploded into vibrations.

Logan Crowne was calling just as I was about to call him.

Accept or reject?

I answered it and put the phone to my ear.

"Ella," he said.

I bit my lip, unable to confirm or deny because I was busy adding another real-husband trait to my list. The voice. My real husband had to have a voice as deep and resonant as Logan's, with the same confidence, even when asking a question.

"Ella? Are you there?"

"Yes, Logan. I'm here."

I stood in front of a copy paper-sized painting I'd done two years ago. My parents' wedding photo, but as I imagined it from behind, with the photographer in the background. One of the rear vents in my father's tux jacket opened to accommodate a pair of scissors in his back pocket, and the back of my mother's vest was embroidered with bookkeeping notations. It was terribly on-the-nose, but the way I'd painted his hand on her back, with the thumb just resting on her skin, seemed so real and intimate—such an encapsulation of who they were together—that I'd spent a year trying to recapture that square inch of canvas.

"And yes," I added. "Yes."

"Yes?"

"We can get married if you still want to."

"You need to give up that thing," he said. "The gorilla thing."

"The Guerilla Arts Collective?"

"Past is past, but I can't have you getting arrested or caught trespassing while we're together. It would look bad."

I'd used the GAC as a way to get him to change his mind, but now he was turning it on me. The one thing I enjoyed was the one thing he was asking me to stop doing.

But what was there to do anyway? We were all exhausted from *Geode House*, which had been years in the making. We didn't even have a concrete plan for a second piece.

"Fine," I said, pacing the length of the room. "But I need you to promise me something."

"What?"

"You can't kiss me like that again."

"Like what?"

He knew exactly what I was talking about. He just wanted me to tell him what a good kisser he was.

"What's our timeline?" I asked, changing the subject.

"Tomorrow. Lunch."

"You're nuts."

"I have a feeling, Ella Papillion, that you're a little nuts too."

Having thought of myself as a little immature, but very sane, I almost objected.

Maybe he was right, and maybe that freed me a little to do something crazy.

"Lunch," I said. "I'll be in the office."

He shot out one laugh of recognition for a woman who went into a job she hated on a Saturday. "I'll see you there, Mrs. Crowne."

He hung up before I could take the name change off the table.

8

ELLA

SOMEWHERE IN THE WORLD, people got the weekends off, but with the Crowne Jewels driving the city into a fashion frenzy, everyone showed up to the Papillion offices. Michelle, the receptionist, was juggling a phone ringing off the hook when she held her hand out for me.

"Bianca," she mouthed while pointing at me. "Office."

I waved and bounced up the stairs because... sure, I had time for a meeting before I got married.

———

IN HER TOP FLOOR OFFICE, Bianca stood behind her desk, waiting with her fingers splayed over the glass. The closet containing my father's most beautiful and valuable gowns was half-open, taunting me. I didn't have the code.

I started to close the door, but my stepmother stopped me. "Open door policy, Ella."

The large space that housed the design department was on the other side. Most of the team was out, but a few stragglers had come in to catch up.

"Sit," Bianca said, opening her hand toward the empty chair like a hostess at a car show.

I sat and put my hands in my lap, knowing that—by lunch—she wouldn't talk to me as if I was a trained puppy. "Yes?"

Jean-Claude came out of the closet with a black cocktail dress. He closed it and made sure it was locked with a *beep*. He was my age, with skin as white as a snowfall and big blue eyes that made magazine editors swoon.

"Pardon," he said with a French accent.

"Jean-Claude," Bianca said, "when we're sleeping, what are they doing in China?"

"Making T-shirts." He shrugged, looking at me.

Fucker. I didn't know what this was about, but fuck him for having the code to my father's closet.

"Thank you, darling."

Dismissed, Jean-Claude left with the black gown trailing behind.

"Did you know that, Ella?" Bianca asked.

"I get the spinning of the earth."

"While we sleep, our Chinese suppliers are executing our every wish. And when we wake—ah! Done! Poof. Magic. An entire shipment of T-shirts is now ready for packing, right on schedule. As if we dreamed them into existence. But there's a price for this sorcery, Estella."

She sat finally, putting her hands in front of her and smiling like a schoolteacher whose student didn't know more about the business than she ever would.

She was going to get on my case for not checking my email from home.

Did I have to be nice to her?

"The price?" she continued. "We pay in a language barrier—which can sneak up on us—and we pay in margin for error—of which there is none. Once you approve a pocket and lay your head to rest, it's sewn on while you dream of pretty things, and when you wake, it's too late."

She slid a printed-out email across the desk. I read it.

The Raquel tee didn't have a pocket.

"You didn't check the style number."

"How did they not check?" I protested.

"Raquel looks a lot like Rachel, and the Rachel tee has a pocket, but it's in next month's delivery. Did I mention the language barrier? The one you're quite aware of? Hmm?" Her voice went from fake sugarplum fairy to a growl that was at least authentic. "Because I shouldn't have to."

"I'm sorry, I—"

"Macy's already cancelled. That's a two hundred thousand dollar order, Estella."

"I was busy," I said, fist pounding my knee. "I was in the middle of something. I—"

"We're protecting a name. An idea. A fantasy. Details matter. Basile and I tried to—"

"Get my father's name out of your mouth!" I launched up, hands on the desktop, waist bent over the edge as if I wanted to eat her whole and spit the bones.

She didn't move a muscle. She knew who she was and how deeply I fell within the boundaries of her power. I couldn't win, even to fulfill my father's dying wish, but I wasn't going down easy. I didn't avert my gaze from hers. Didn't submit an inch.

When a light knock touched the open door, she glanced over my shoulder and broke into a trademark phony smile.

"Mr. Crowne," she said with a voice that matched her mask.

I spun. Logan stood in the doorway, smiling at me in jeans, jacket, and a fine gauge blue sweater that hugged his torso and matched his eyes as if they'd been the color standard.

"I'm sorry," Michelle said from behind him with a helpless expression. "He just came in."

"It's fine, dear," Bianca said with a voice so sweet and bright, a person wouldn't know she'd just been ripping me a new asshole. "Come in, Mr. Crowne. Can we get you anything? Michelle, get Mr. Crowne some coffee. Hurry now." Then to Logan, indicating his sweater, "Is that LVM's fall cerulean?"

"I have no idea." He kept his eyes on me. "You all right?"

"Yeah, I... you're early."

"We have some business first." He met Bianca's gaze. "Would you excuse us?"

"Of course," Bianca said. "Let me know if I can get you anything."

"I will."

Bianca shot me a threatening glance before leaving and bumping into Michelle, who reacted quickly enough to get out of the way.

"Your face is red," he said, closing the door.

The room went quiet. I could finally breathe.

"Rough morning." I sat on the couch, rubbing my eyes until I saw stars.

Logan sat in the chair across from me. He reached inside his jacket for an envelope and put it on the table between us. "In a few hours, you're not going to need a job."

"I told you. This isn't a job. It's a promise to my father."

"And I told you. He's d—"

"Stop. Don't say it. I know he's dead. Okay? Just..." I snapped up the envelope. "Just stop before I decide I can't live with you."

He looked out the window and rubbed his chin. The Roman bridge of his nose was visible in profile, and the jut of his jaw was more pronounced. So unfair for such a rich man to be that handsome. He was one hundred eighty pounds of injustice in a size eleven shoe.

I unfolded the contract and laid it out, scanning past the monthly cash allowance (ten grand), the car (whatever I wanted), the diamond ring (mine to keep), and the term (three years).

"You said one year," I said, getting a red pen from a cup on the coffee table.

"It may take longer."

"Nope," I said. "If you can't get what we want out of this in a year, you have no business running that company."

"And you won't have one to run."

He was right, but so was I.

"One year," I said, scratching a line over the term and replacing it with twelve months. I tapped the pen point on a paragraph. "And this? I'm not changing my name."

"You and Olivia are the only women in the world who don't want to be Mrs. Crowne."

"That will never be part of the deal."

Redline. He could call it off if he didn't like it. I stopped reading long enough to catch him grinning at me. His smile had an authenticity to it, as if it was involuntary, and he'd be shocked to learn he wasn't completely stone-faced.

I went back to the contract without telling him.

The next paragraph made my skin tingle. My mouth went dry and my core went liquid with possibilities. Recent test results for sexually transmitted diseases were available, and by signing, I agreed to the same. I was about to ask him what made him think that was something either of us should worry about, when I saw the next paragraph.

"How would there be children?" My voice sounded like a butter knife dragged over cracked asphalt.

"Just in case," he said with an infuriating shrug.

"In case... what?"

"Things happen."

His fingers laced together, hitching the jacket cuff enough to reveal the analog silver watch and brown leather bracelet under it. It made his hands look as if they were the seat of his competence. The leather strap under the timepiece hinted at a side to him outside his dreams on top of Crowne Industries. It insinuated short-term desires that were never fully satisfied. Rich or poor. Handsome or plain. A reminder that Logan was no more or less than a man.

Things happen.

Those hands. Between my thighs. Grabbing my ass. In my hair.

"First of all, I haven't had sex in four years. None of your business why, but... so you can sleep at night knowing your wife won't die of syphilis on your watch, I'll get tested."

"Thank you."

"Secondly, things happen, but they won't. And if they do..." I clicked the pen twice as if that was all I needed to convince myself I didn't want him. "And my IUD fails which never happens..." I crossed out the offending line. "Resulting children are Papillions. Not Crownes."

Dropping the red pen in favor of a black one, I pushed pen and contract to him.

"Initial the changes before you sign," I said.

I challenged him with a wielded black pen, and he flicked his blue eyes from mine to the pen and back again, hesitating long enough to make me think he was changing his mind.

Worry caught hold of me and wouldn't let go.

I didn't want him to change his mind.

My reaction told me more about how much I wanted to do this than any assessment of the risks or benefits.

"Absolutely not."

"You're welcome to find someone else to marry this afternoon."

He considered, working his jaw like a man trying not to say something. "That IUD. It works?"

"Haven't tested it without a condom. But it's the best birth control out there. Look it up."

"Abstinence is better," he said, grabbing the red pen.

Next to the clause about the children, he wrote *To Be Decided* under my red line, initialed in black, then slid the contract and pen back to me.

"You first," he said as if asking me to take off my clothes before he did.

I stood on the edge of the roof with options disappearing behind me and signed my name, articulating every letter so it was clear who I was and what was important to me. When I was done, I handed Logan the pen. Without hesitation, he quickly looped his signature with a huge C at the last name, dated it, and tossed down the pen.

"We should go," he said, folding the pages. "You ready?"

We had hours until lunch, but why postpone the inevitable by living inside a skin you knew you were going to shed?

The net was too far down to see, but it was time to jump.

9

LOGAN

"I'M READY," Ella said with a mischievous flick of her eyebrows that didn't promise a carefully planned scheme to get what was mine, but danger, adventure, and the risk of failure.

I was drawn to her unknowns, but was she the right woman to convince my parents that I'd turned a corner? Or was she the woman I should have met a decade ago, when the stakes weren't as high?

Pushing away my doubts, I took her hand. "Then let's go."

Bianca was right outside, flipping through a notebook.

"So—" she said, but I didn't hear the rest.

Ella turned, leading me to the stairwell, hand in hand down the steps like Bonnie and Clyde, with a threat behind and nothing but possibilities ahead. The speed of the descent knocked caution out of me. The loss of control should have been disconcerting, but we whipped around the third landing so fast, I didn't have time to worry about anything but keeping my feet under me.

Ella stopped on the second floor and we collided. My body disengaged from my mind, tapping muscle memory to use our velocity to push her against the wall and crash my mouth onto hers. I held her by the back of the neck so I could leave my mark on every crevice and plane my tongue could reach.

With a groan, she clutched my shirt, pushing and pulling at the same time.

What was I doing? Besides getting a hard-on the size of a city block, what was I doing?

She jerked her mouth away, but I held her firm, close enough to see a tiny dot on the white of her eye, as if the freckles on her face couldn't bear being constrained to skin.

"You promised to stop kissing me like that," she said.

"Last time was practice."

She let go of my shirt, laying her hands flat on my chest to smooth the fabric.

"You don't need practice." She shoved me away.

"That's your story," I said. "When anyone asks why you fell for me, it was the kissing."

"I was going to say it was your cock."

My dick twitched as if it heard her call. "Don't make this harder than it has to be."

She smiled. "He said."

"Make a note. I fell for the bad jokes too."

"Noted," she said, opening the stairwell door to a warehouse space filled with racks of clothes. "I'm only getting married twice. I have to dress for it."

She spun and ran deep into the racks. I rushed to keep up with her. From what I could see, the racks were filled with cheap T-shirts and denim. Against the opposite wall, she stopped at a locked chain-link cage.

"There's something in here I can wear." She poked the combination into the padlock and clicked it open. As if she knew exactly what she wanted, she reached into the racks and pulled out a plain white dress with a big red tag hanging under the left arm. "What do you think?"

"It's fine," I said, taking the hanger. "We need to go."

"Okay."

We hustled out of the cage. She locked it behind her and I took the lead, getting her down to my limo without kissing her again.

"Loranda," I greeted my driver, who was opening the back door of my Cadillac limo. "This is Ella."

They shook hands.

"Where to?" Loranda asked.

"Civic Center. Judge Reynard."

"Yes, sir."

Once I was in the back, facing Ella, Loranda closed the door.

Ella closed her eyes and took a deep breath. "It's Saturday."

"Judge Reynard came in for me." I hung the dress on the hook over the door.

"The shit money buys." She started unbuttoning her shirt. "Don't look."

She spun her finger in a circle to make a turning motion before she undid another button, exposing the center of her lace bra. The contour of her breasts was just visible above the cup.

"Come on," she insisted. "Turn around, you perv."

I twisted to face the window. The tinting dimmed the streets as they blew by.

"We need to lock down our story," I said, trying to ignore the rustle of clothes a foot away. "Where we met. How long we've been together."

"We have to stay close to the truth. We met at Wildwood."

"But you left."

"And we met again like... what's reasonable?"

Out of the corner of my eye, she wiggled out of her jeans. The temptation to see if her panties matched her bra was overwhelming.

"Four months ago," I said. "How can I ever forget the moment I saw you again, after all those years? Starbucks on La Cienega. I was waiting for an Americano and you were ordering... what's your drink?"

"Vanilla latte." A long zipper hissed as it was undone. "Sometimes."

"I didn't take you for a vanilla latte person." Again I wanted to look, and again I kept my eyes on the passing city.

"And I didn't take you for a guy who'd wait in line for anything."

"When my driver's parked in the red and my assistant's doing her job, I get my own coffee. Best decision of my life. Saw you as soon as you walked in, and I paid for your drink. You filled a place in my soul or something. I didn't recognize you until you came up to me to say thank you."

"This is full of holes. You had to recognize me. A guy like you wouldn't have picked me out of a crowd." I felt her transfer to the seat next to me.

"You're not making this easy."

"It's not my job to make this easy. Can you zip this?"

Finally, I turned around. She was twisted awkwardly to show me the triangle of skin where the back zipper was open. A line of lace bisected it. I could unhook the bra right there.

"A guy like me?" Slowly, I zipped up the dress, enclosing her beautiful skin behind white fabric.

"I'm not spending the next five minutes stroking your ego."

She shifted to her original seat across from me. The long-sleeve dress was low and scooped at the neck and short at the skirt. It hiked up her thighs, leaving only the mystery of a shadow between her legs when she sat across from me. All I had to do was put my hands on her knees and exert a little pressure to spread them apart.

"You will. You're marrying me."

She crossed her legs, and the shadow shifted to where her thigh met the leather seat. Her little booties were red.

"I forgot shoes," she said, leaning back, arms out to each side.

"It's fine."

"So why do I love you enough to marry you?" She looked out

the window. "You're different than anyone I've ever been with. You're..." She turned back to me. "Well, really hot, obviously. But you make me feel safe. Like everything's going to be all right. Like it's all under control."

"Is that what you want in a husband?"

The car entered the Civic Center. Almost there.

"It's what you have to offer, so yeah. I'm not marrying you for the wild times."

"Obviously." The car stopped in front of the courthouse.

"And you're marrying me for what?" she asked.

"For the wild times." I took the small velvet box out of my pocket. "Wear this. We can get it sized if it doesn't fit."

I tossed it to her and she caught it.

"Jesus, Logan," she said when she opened the box. She put on the ring and held out her hand.

The ring had been meant for Mandy Bettencourt. The perfect two-and-a-half-carat square-cut would have suited the socialite just fine, but on Ella, it looked exaggerated and gaudy.

Would that make my family suspicious?

"You love it," I said. "Which is out of character, but you're surprising and that's why I love you, remember?"

"Actually? It's gorgeous and I do love it."

Loranda opened the back door. I got out and helped my fiancée onto the street.

———

JUDGE REYNARD WAS SEMI-RETIRED, an old friend of the family, and was happy to come into his office on a Saturday. His two-room office was carpeted, and the forty-year-old leather chairs matched the drapes. The receptionist had been with him for longer than the chairs, and she rattled through her notary duties without distraction.

Judge Reynard came out in a cardigan and bow tie, big glasses that made his eyes huge, and soft brown shoes. He patted down the few strands of white hair he had left, made kind but perfunctory greetings, and ushered us into his chambers.

I took out the rings. Ella and I made promises with our fingers crossed behind our backs. The judge pronounced us man and wife with a yellowing smile and cheerfully permitted me to kiss the bride.

I intended a short, symbolic peck on the mouth, but as soon as my lips touched hers, they took the wheel, loosening instead of tightening, letting my tongue through so it could taste her. Holding her face as if I didn't want her to move, I kissed her and I didn't know why. Judge Reynard was ancient and had seen it all. There was no one to convince, least of all Ella. But she gripped my jacket lapels and gave me the kiss back so strongly, I felt as if I was another man, living a strange life and doing things that made sense to another man.

I pulled away. The curve of her breasts heaved at the edge of the low neckline.

"Very nice," Judge Reynard said. "I was worried about you two."

"You shouldn't be," Ella said.

"Good, good." Judge Reynard patted down his hair. "Well, I'm off to lunch. If you two want to stay here and chat for a bit—"

"We've got to get going," Ella said.

"There's a couch right over there."

"Thanks but—" She stopped herself when I sat down. "Okay, then."

"The door will lock behind you. Good day." He left, closing the door.

Ella stared at it with her jaw on the carpet. "Did he just leave us alone in his office to consummate our marriage?"

"I think he did."

She looked at the couch, then back at me in her revealing white dress and little red boots. Was she willing?

Was I?

I wasn't made of stone. I wasn't immune to her beauty or the heat that came off her when we kissed. But we were there for a reason that had nothing to do with how much I wanted her.

"Ella," I said.

"Yes? Is that what you want me to say? Yes?"

Oh, it was. It definitely was.

"We have things to do."

She got that mischievous look again. I was going to have to spend a year resisting it.

"Such as?"

"What are you wearing tonight? To Crowne Jewels? You can't wear that."

She looked down at herself. "Yeah."

"I'll get you a gown."

"No, you won't." Dead serious. As if I'd tread over sacred ground.

"It's not meant as an insult. But you're going to meet my family. If we're going to convince them it's love, you can't wear ripped jeans."

"Logan. I have it."

Her tone was pure *don't fuck with me*, so I didn't, but she couldn't stop me from worrying. My mother had a keen sense of the bonds between people. When it came to couples in love, she got what we called "the tingle," and it was never wrong. Without that tingle, she'd be suspicious. She'd tell my father. He'd get suspicious, and suspicion wouldn't get me to the head of the table.

"Fine," I said. "But the earrings. The ring in your nose. They have to go."

"No."

Her job description didn't include making my life easy, and she was sticking to it.

"Just for tonight. When we announce."

Her arms crossed as if she intended to stand by her refusal, but she was a series of contradictions in every way. "Fine. Tonight."

"Thank you."

The moment to consummate the marriage on the couch was gone, so I opened the door and we left the office where we'd lied to a judge, God, and each other.

St. Peter could add it to my list.

10

ELLA

I was married.

Not just married, but the wife of one of the richest, most handsome men in the country.

I'd taken one of Los Angeles's most eligible bachelors off the market. I couldn't even wrap my head around it.

"I have to go back to work," I said as Loranda opened the door of a black Cadillac limo.

"We have to move you into my place."

"Look, I fucked up a T-shirt last night and I have to do damage control."

"Are you serious?"

He didn't get it. Or maybe I didn't. When I was twelve, on my way home from school, the bus was late. I was across the street, getting a candy bar, when I saw the bus pull in. I ran for it without looking and got hit by a car. Blacked out for a second. When I came to, all I could think about was making the bus and whether or not I could still eat the half-open Snickers that was on the asphalt. Maybe this was the same. I'd been hit by a speeding marriage and was still worrying about what I had been doing before I hit the ground.

Except Papillion was my responsibility. Dad had said so with his last breaths, and I didn't need Logan reminding me that he was dead.

"I can take a cab."

He paused, lips pressed together as if calculating the differences between who I was and who he was. "I'll get a cab. Loranda can take you back."

"Thank you." I kissed his cheek, getting in the back seat before he gave me another reason to marry him.

———

AVOIDING Bianca was pretty easy considering she was hobnobbing with Fiona Drazen in the showroom. Fiona needed to change her gown again and my stepmother was in full salesperson mode. I did what I could about the Raquel tee, which wasn't much, and made sure the Rachel was exactly what the stores had ordered.

This wasn't what I'd been trained to do.

Non. Again.

Daddy had taught me how to do everything the right way. No compromises. He'd taken me to a thrift store and told me to find a jacket with the sleeve set improperly. I flicked through the racks, bringing him contenders he rejected, until I landed on a tweedy Jones New York jacket with draglines at the sleeve cap. One, twice, sold for six dollars to the man tapping his foot impatiently.

Non. Again.

It was late on a Tuesday. Or Thursday. Or over a week when I was ten, or the first half of eleven. Definitely after Mom died, but before Bianca started showing up at breakfast. I remember feeling desperate to please him, so I was sure it was in that window where I was sure I could fill the hole Mom had left and terrified he'd leave me too. Which he did, even after I figured out how to set in a sleeve.

Non. Again.

We went back to the sample room with the Jones New York tweed jacket, and he instructed me to dismantle the entire left side and put it back together correctly. I did all that, except for the part about it being correct. Daddy ripped my seams open the way other people cleaned a toilet—with force and disgust. He handed the jacket back with the sleeve removed.

Non. Again.

This went on. And on. Late one night—with Daddy in his design room, draping on a form that squeaked when he spun it— the way a jacket fit together clicked. I forced my little hands to take the turns, pressing the pedal that had been set onto a box.

Non. Again. Non. Again. Non. Again.

What I expected to hear played in my head in a loop as I put the jacket on the form and sat down to find the flaw. It looked perfect, but my instincts were shot. I'd thought I'd gotten it right ten times already. Maybe if I looked a little longer.

I was resting my head for one moment, and the next, Daddy's voice cut through a dream of pre-worn tweed.

Ah! Oui, little peanut.

He was sitting in front of my fitting mannequin. When I stood next to him, he put his arm around my waist and pulled me in tight. He kissed my cheek loudly so a whole empty office could witness his pride. His daughter. His baby girl who'd finally pleased him, and who was nearly in tears because of it.

Oui! See how it fits now? Perfect! Look at the lines. Look what you have done!

The lines. Lines were my job.

I wanted the thrill of making guerilla art in the dead of night, but I dreamed in beading and boning and woke up to thread and interface. Fashion was all I knew, and it was a prison.

Now, with the Crowne Jewels a few hours away, I had nothing to wear.

Ridiculous.

We had rooms full of beautiful things at Papillion, but the stuff nice enough for the party and the surprise wedding announcement was under lock and key. I could borrow something, but from whom? I knew people, but not many who would have something that could stand up to scrutiny.

I'd have to steal what I needed, even if it was already mine.

Jean-Claude had the black cocktail dress in his office. He was knocking it off of course, because he didn't have a lick of real talent, and I'd told him so.

I hadn't regretted my honesty until that day.

I knew the Papillion building better than my own body. I'd mastered the back halls and service entrances during after-school hours, so I got upstairs without being seen.

Bianca was meeting with not one but two Drazens.

I dodged left, but Jean-Claude was at his desk, the black dress on a form next to him and another one of my father's old gowns on a hanger. The mauve one Margrethe of Denmark had worn to her sister's wedding.

Slipping into Bianca's dark office, I listened to his muffled voice through the wall and prayed Bianca or the bathroom called him. Getting the dress off the mannequin required more time than pulling a hanger.

My prayers were not answered. He kept talking and talking. I wished him explosive diarrhea or a long lunch. He could win the lottery or get another job for all I cared. I just needed him out of that damn office long enough to get my father's dress.

Then he got louder, until I could hear the guttural consonants of his French accent. "I said, 'there's something wrong with that girl,' and she said—"

Ducking behind a cabinet, I watched him on the other side of the office window, pausing at the open door.

"The usual. 'She is this, she is that,' but..." He paused to listen, reaching into the printer for a sheet of paper.

I held my breath, wishing him away.

"I know. The cheap supports the beautiful, so…" He went back into his office.

Fuck.

I stepped out from behind the cabinet, into the office where I'd signed away a year of my life. The red pen was laid on the tabletop. It had only been a few hours since I'd used it.

A light went on. I froze as if I'd been caught.

No. I exhaled. It was the motion-sensor lamp in my father's closet, creating a halo around the door. The keypad flashed red.

Jean-Claude hadn't closed it all the way when he'd gotten the mauve dress.

I swung it open to a tiny, empty white anteroom and another door. The hum of a climate control unit hummed from the other side of it.

Something clicked above me.

A little brown moth banged against the light.

"You stay in here, wool-eater," I said to the insect as I tested the inner door.

It opened, and on the other side was a hall of wonders. Racks stuffed with garment bags. Glass-topped drawers filled with jewels, and shelves upon shelves of shoes.

Everything in there would have my name sewn into it.

With the speed of a criminal unencumbered by guilt, I found the perfect dress to announce my marriage, and locked the door behind me.

11

LOGAN

As soon as Ella was out of my sight and out of my control, I regretted not chasing her down. I didn't know what she was wearing or if she'd keep her promise to get the metal out of her head. I didn't know if she was chronically late, which reminded me how flimsy our story was and how likely she was to say something out of earshot that I'd contradict.

All the Crowne siblings had been set up with a suite in the Bel-Air house my sister had coined Crownequarters, and I paced mine as I texted her.

—Don't forget to pack a bag—

—Already in the back of the ElCam—

—No. I'm coming to get you tonight—

—I'm fine—

—I didn't ask if you were fine.
It's common courtesy—

—It's infantilizing—

I considered the possibility that I'd go completely insane in the first five minutes of this marriage.

> *—I'm sending Loranda to get you. Meet me halfway on this or I'm going to infantilize you with your first spanking—*

—First? I don't think so—

Well, well. That was unexpected. I'd typed the threat of a spanking in such a frustrated heat, I hadn't imagined actually doing it. Her answer unlocked the full scene. The weight of her over my lap. Her voice yelping. The sting of my palm as I turned her ass pink.

> *—Hardest, then—*

—Promises, promises—

She and I had already made promises we had no intention of keeping, but this was one I could deliver on. Typing the next message, I let my imagination loose.

> *—Don't tempt me, because once you're over my knee, I'm going to pull your skirt up and spank your ass so hard you turn red under your panties. Then I'll take them down and slide my fingers in your sweet, wet pussy. When you're so close you forget the pain, I'll spank you again. And again. You won't know whether to cry in pain or beg to come, so you'll do both—*

My finger hovered over the send button. I was hard for the second time that day, with no relief in sight. This text was a distracting turn down a road that wouldn't get me where I was going tonight.

I deleted it and sent a short command.

—Don't be late—

———

THE BALLROOM WAS FILLING UP. The glass doors were open to a pool with a web of narrow concrete bridges leading to seating pods that overlooked the dry ravine of Stone Creek. Six-month-old Garrett slept peacefully in Olivia's arms, and Uncle Rodney blocked my view of the entrance.

"Someone said your brother's coming back," he said.

"Which one?" I shifted to see the entrance, and my uncle moved to block my view again.

"Colton," Olivia said.

"They say that every time there's a get-together," I replied.

Colton was the ne'er-do-well among us. A lazy, talentless slob who'd called in our father's promise to provide One Big Thing—a request he might question, but wouldn't deny—took the money, and disappeared into a haze of parties and women. We rarely heard from him outside the tabloids.

With his attention on the baby, I peered around Uncle Rod, and finally—with a mixture of relief and awe, I caught sight of Ella.

She was elevated beyond standard beauty into something more divine. Even if the woman in the silver, sleeveless gown had been a complete stranger, she would have stopped me in my tracks.

Her dark hair was set in a complex braid with a loose curl over her bare neck, ending just where the metallic dress met her skin.

She was radiant in less makeup than most women wore to walk to their car, clutching her matching purse in front of her chest with two hands, and most importantly, a single earring in each ear.

My wife.

Jesus Christ, what good deed had I done to get her to marry me?

When she saw me, she relaxed, and I took my eyes away from hers long enough to see the diamond ring from thirty feet away. It was my signature on her.

For a moment, we seemed a few percentage points less fake, and instead of making me nervous, the sliver of realness pleased me.

But that didn't last long.

Like a smiling fucking vulture in pressed, tan linen and an open collar, Caleb Hawkins swooped in with his trendy jacket and unruly hair, said exactly the right thing—whatever that was—and she smiled.

She was not to smile at Caleb Hawkins or any of his brothers. Anyone but them. Our families had bruised each other for at least two generations. So long, we rarely thought about the original dispute over a stretch of river in the Yukon. But we never forgot, and neither did they.

In school, the Hawkins boys had played dirty, and as men, they cheated in business, took shortcuts, and amassed wealth they hid like thieves.

Which was why they had been invited. Friends close. Enemies closer.

I couldn't hear what Ella said back to him. Maybe it was the distance or the music drowning them out. Maybe it was the rage of blood in my ears.

"Caleb," I said. They stopped chatting and looked at me. "I see you've met Ella."

I almost said, "my wife," but telling him before I told my family was no less than a slap in the face.

"Ella." He bowed slightly, holding her gaze. "Lovely. Is that short for something?"

"Estella. I'm Estella Papillion."

"Latin and French," he replied, wresting control of the conversation from me. "Estella's Latin for star, and it suits you."

"And Papillion," she said, "is French for butterfly."

"Of course." He smirked with a seductiveness I didn't like one bit.

"Ella," I broke into their little flirtation before I broke his face, "this is Caleb Hawkins."

She tucked a dark curl behind her ear, exposing the lovely curve of her throat.

"Pleasure," Caleb said with a smarmy little twang that froze my expression as I watched Ella with veneration and longing he must have observed.

"So. Caleb," I said, putting my arm over my wife's shoulders. "Didn't get the memo about ties? I think the waitstaff has some extras."

"I'm sure," he said. "Well, great to meet you, Estella. Get this uptight prick on the dance floor tonight before the stuffing rips his shirt."

"I will," she said with a wave as he walked away.

"Sorry about him. He's a predator, so hide if you see him again."

"Noted."

"You look…" Gorgeous. Radiant. Stunning. "You look nice."

"So do you." She slid her hand under my jacket's silk lapel for a moment.

"He's right. Your name suits you. Star."

"Just one of many in the sky." She shrugged.

"The dress," I said, trying not to stare at the way her breasts were pushed above the edge of it.

"My father made it for my mother," she whispered. "Princess Sikhanyiso wore a similar one to her brother's wedding."

"I'm sure you look better in it."

"Sure." She didn't believe me, because we were fake, but I was being completely honest.

"Why are your eyes darting around? Are you waiting for the cops to pick you up?"

"Bianca. She'll be here, and I don't want her to see me wearing this. I didn't ask."

"You mean you stole it?"

"My name's on the label," she snarled, then smiled. "But yes."

Even though a stolen dress had the potential to complicate the evening, I laughed. Who wouldn't be delighted at a crime so in character, so justified, and so aesthetically pleasing all at the same time?

I offered her my arm. "Come with me, star."

She smiled and jabbed me with her elbow.

Leading her across the room, I nodded to people I knew, and some I didn't, avoiding all attempts at a conversation until we reached an archway with a velvet rope in front of it. I tilted the pole to let Ella through, turned a corner behind a floating wall of bookcases, then led her up the sweeping stairs that weren't connected to the glass walls, giving the sense we were climbing air.

"How big is this house?" she whispered as if we were in a church.

"Not as big as Byron's original plan." I laid my hand on the small of her back to guide her and realized she was taller than usual. I looked down at her heels. "How are you in those shoes?"

"These?" She kicked one up. I could have used the heel as a chopstick. "They're vintage Papillion. I could walk a mile in them." The shoe clapped down, and I guided her to a roped off stairway with two guards in front. "Where are we going?"

"After the cocktail hour, family and friends are coming to this side." The guards recognized me and opened the rope without saying a word. "She won't find you."

We walked up to the rooftop together, where the view surrounded us on all sides, unbroken by glass corners or limited by a ceiling.

"Wow."

She wasn't reacting to a welcome separation from her tormentors, but the lights set up to draw pictures on the surface of the clouds.

"My parents," I said. "My mother's glad to be near us. And anything that makes Mom happy makes Dad happy."

She looked away from the sky, and me, to the musicians setting up. The rooftop we called the Tower was bustling as the caterers got ready for the VIP guests.

"My parents were like that. Dad let Mom run the business any way she wanted because it made her happy, and any success she had doing it made him happy. It was like a loop."

"My mother got a Master's in English literature and never did anything with it so she could support my father full time. Perfect marriage."

"Of course." She nodded as if it pleased her to know we were incompatible.

"Here." I laid my hand on the curve of her back again, feeling that overwhelmingly satisfying sense of control, and led her to a little table overlooking the pool of webbed bridges with the circular conversation pods. I held out her chair. When she sat, the silver gown pooled over the sides as if it had melted over her body.

"Mister Crowne," Maurice, the head of the catering company, said as I sat. "Can I get you something?"

"I'll have a Macallan. Rocks," I said, then turned to Ella. "Anything for you?"

She bit her lips back, then said, "Sprite with a little of that red stuff on top?"

"I'll have that sent right over," Maurice said, turning on his heel and disappearing.

"It's a party," I said. "You don't have to drink Shirley Temples."

"I don't want to get fuzzy. We have to keep our story straight."

"Right." I spread my legs to opposite sides of the chair and leaned over the table to get near enough to speak with definitive, emotionless force. "Here's the deal. You and I are soul mates. You make me a better person, and I make you stronger."

I put my hands over hers. My mouth hit the gas pedal before my brain put the next thought into gear.

"I'm the only one who fucks you right." A part of me wanted to take it back, but her lips parted and her eyes opened just enough to shrink my common sense into silence. "The first time I fucked you was in my garage. You pulled in. I had dinner reservations, but we didn't make it out of my house. I took you on the hood of my Maserati."

"You have a Maserati?"

"I do now. I made you come so hard every part of your body shook and you wept in my arms."

Her throat rippled when she swallowed, and though she was looking right at me, I knew she was looking into the place in her mind where my words had created a picture.

"Mr. Crowne," Maurice said from above us, "your drinks."

Ella pulled her hands from under mine so he had room to place her drink. The layer of syrup curled into the bubbling soda like fingers exploring their way to the bottom. He left the scotch with its single, perfectly clear ice cube in front of me and disappeared.

Ella placed her fingertip on the edge of the glass and ran it along a half circle. "That was quite a third date."

Behind her, in the warmly lit foyer, people were coming up the stairs. Family first, Mom and Dad, arm in arm. Liam and his son. Byron had Garrett over his free shoulder.

"First date," I said. "It lasted three days."

Byron passed the baby over to Olivia and came toward us.

"What are your parents going to think of me?"

84

I stood and held my hand out for Ella, who let me help her up. "That it was love and it all happened so fast, we're already married."

"Logan," Byron said when he was in earshot, "I thought you'd disappeared."

"Just getting away from your cologne," I said, shaking his hand. "It smells like spit up and diapers."

Byron smiled and faced Ella. "Don't let him fool you. He's turned out to be a real baby whisperer. Garrett refuses to cry when this guy's in the room. Shuts off like a faucet."

"That's kind of shocking."

"Byron," I said, "I'd like you to meet Ella Papillion."

She held out her right hand and they shook.

"Nice to meet you. Can I get you two a drink?"

"I'm fine," Ella said, reaching for her Shirley Temple. "I'm good." She held it up with her left hand, exposing the enormous fuck you on her finger.

Byron raised an eyebrow, then turned to me. "Logan. Anything for you?"

"I'm fine, I—"

"Oh, honey!" my mother cried, pushing past Byron with hands shaky from early stage Parkinson's to kiss me. "Your father was looking for you." She went right to Ella. "I'm Doreen Crowne."

"Ella Papillion." Their shake took four hands. Mom wasn't going to miss the ring. "So nice to meet you."

Then Dad was there, with my brother Liam and Uncle Rodney. Ella managed the introductions gracefully, laughing at the good-natured teasing we flung around. She and I stood close together, not knowing how much pretending was required until Lyric saw the ring.

"Oh my God, Logan," Lyric cried in a mixture of ecstasy and sisterly annoyance. "Is this it?"

"Is what it?"

She took Ella's left hand and held it up. "Duh."

"Lyric," Dad said in a soothing tone, as if reminding a child to use her inside voice before addressing Ella. "There was this rumor that Logan bought *a* ring. Not *that* ring."

Ella looked at me and tilted her head toward my family, lips tight because it was my job to break the news.

"She added two and two and got five again," Byron said while Ella's eyes were locked on mine.

"At least he'd get married before he had a baby," Lyric retorted.

"Okay, boomer," Byron shot back even though my sister was in her twenties.

"Geriatric memeing gives me sadz."

This was going to devolve into a cage match right in front of Ella, who—up until lunch—was trapped by a stepfamily whose cruelty wasn't as good-natured.

"It's a lovely ring," my mother said.

Dad was starting to separate from the pack to talk to Maurice. Guests were coming up the stairs and soon it would be too late to tell the people who mattered most.

I took Ella's hand. She squeezed.

"I have an announcement," I said. "Dad! Come on. Let Maurice do his job."

A few more words passed between them before Ted Crowne gave me his attention.

"This isn't my party. I didn't want to steal my Mom and Dad's thunder, but I'm impatient and..." I looked at Ella. "Someone very important to me thinks it's wrong to keep secrets." I turned back to my family. "So we're about to be very rude, and tell you all, during this party for my parents' move back to LA, that this beautiful woman let me marry her." I put my arm around my wife and pulled her close.

"What the fuck?" Lyric cried.

"How long—" Olivia was interrupted by Garrett putting his finger up her nose.

"Holy—" Lyric was beside herself.

Byron took my hand, then pulled me into a hug. By the time he let go, the Crownes had turned into a swarm of hugs, kisses, and congratulations. Dad asked why I was keeping her a secret, and I said it happened really fast. Mom asked where we met, and Ella said Wildwood while I accepted two flutes of champagne from Uncle Rodney.

Ella took the glass from me, we clicked them together, and I did what was necessary to convince my family we were real.

I kissed her.

12

ELLA

MY QUICKENED HEARTBEAT started with the spanking text, sped up when Logan told me we'd fucked on the hood of his car, but when he gave me a champagne-flavored kiss, my feet left the ground. Surrounded by the elation of his family, filled with the helium of happiness, and grounded by his constant touch, I became a joyful liar. Forgetting I had to keep my story straight, I drank champagne, toasted to our future, and smiled so hard and so long my face hurt.

Leaning over the Plexiglas wall around the upper patio, I pointed at the floor below, where a hundred people danced in the center of a huge blue pool.

"Let's dance!" I cried, pulling Logan downstairs.

I'd forgotten why we were upstairs in the first place, and either Logan forgot as well, or he believed my signal that it didn't matter anymore.

Before we even got to the dance floor, I saw Bianca in a gown of jewel-colored silk ribbons my father designed. Mom had been frustrated by the cost of it, but every season, Dad got to do one outrageous, beautiful thing. Now my stepmother, the knockoff queen, was wearing it.

She was laughing with Jean-Claude and Val Luke, batting her lashes like a milkmaid, turning flirtatiously, until her eyes landed on me. "Son of a—"

"Ella." Logan said with concern.

"No." Connected to her by the insult of her wearing that dress, I threaded through the crowd.

The details of the ribbons were clearer now that I was close. The gold thread and interior seam finishing. My parents had argued over each element while I did homework at the cutting table. They spoke their own language. They were as passionate about their work as they were about each other.

Bianca couldn't defile my childhood happiness. I wouldn't allow it.

"Well, hello, Estella," Bianca said. "So surprised to see you here."

"What are you wearing?" I hissed.

"What are *you* wearing?" Bianca clenched the matching clutch, which had streams of feathered ribbon fringe on the bottom. "Wasn't that in my closet?"

Stolen. It was stolen and it was my right to steal it.

"It's got *my* name on it." My drink was in my right hand, so I jabbed my finger in her direction with my left.

"What do you have there?" She was looking at my ring, then at Logan and me.

"Oh, this?" I said. "Well, Logan and I—"

She'd pulled me into a hug before I could finish. "This is wonderful! You didn't tell me you were involved!"

There wasn't an ounce of suspicion in her voice, but she was a great actress.

"We didn't tell anyone," Logan said.

"You must call me Mother from now on."

"I will."

"Oh, my God, you're Mrs. *Crowne*!"

"Not quite, I—"

"I'm so, so happy! Jean-Claude!"

The designer had been distracted by another guest, but Bianca pulled his shoulder.

"Look!" She pointed at my ring, and I plastered on a smile to show him.

He congratulated me and kissed both my cheeks.

"So, that's how you got invited," he said with a little laugh.

I wanted to slap him for every shitty way he'd undermined me since the day we met. "And how did you get invited? Plus-oneing I guess?"

"Hey," Logan said into my ear, "let's dance."

"But—" The rest was lost in his insistent tug toward the open space, where he put his arms around my waist and held me close.

"Breathe," he said. "Just take it easy. Be nice to my stepmother-in-law."

"I'm sorry. That was childish."

"Eyes on the prize." He spun me out and pulled me back into him. "Just follow me."

"I don't dance."

"I knew that." He dipped me, and I followed. "From the fall dance at school."

"Did you?"

He yanked me up. "That's the official story."

His parents were talking quietly by the rooftop railing. Doreen frowned, watching us.

"I don't think your mother's convinced."

He glanced up at them, then back at me. "Let's fix that."

When he leaned down to kiss me, I put my hands flat on his chest.

Logan wasn't my type. He had things I needed now, but nothing I wanted for the future. I'd die of boredom with him, and I was clearly not what he had in mind when he imagined a happy marriage. But some things needed to be said out loud.

"Wait," I said. "We have to get divorced at some point, and…" I paused to organize my thoughts and failed. "There's a lot of kissing and... it's necessary. I understand. But the thing is..." I stopped myself, meeting the cool blue of his eyes. "I don't want you to get confused."

"About what?"

"We're getting divorced."

Anyone who heard his laughter without hearing what we were talking about would have thought he was delighted with the woman he loved. "Yes, Estella. We're getting divorced."

"No feelings," I said. "Right?"

"None whatsoever."

"Okay. Kiss me."

It must have been the champagne and the music. Definitely the way his arms held me so tightly, rocking back and forth with the rhythm.

No feelings, sure. But Logan kissed like he meant it, and the champagne fizzed inside me, bubbles popping up from the base of my spine, shaking long dormant nerves awake. His hands stayed in an appropriate position, but all I wanted was to feel them stroke lower, deeper, where I shuddered with desire.

"Stop," I said, pulling away.

"You all right?"

"Fine, just... I need a second."

"You're flushed." He brushed the backs of his fingers along my cheek. "That's how I know you want to fuck. Make a note." He spun me away and rolled me back.

"How do I know when you want to?"

"You're in the room."

I laughed. It was such an act. So fake. So over the top, yet when he guided me in the dance with a smile on his face, I let myself live it. For one dance, then two, we were at our most convincing, acting as if there wasn't another soul for miles. He looked at me as if he wasn't faking it, and when he kissed me, I kissed him back as if it was all real.

The music stopped as another round of trays came around.

"Are you hungry?" he asked, running his lips along my neck. "There's a room with dinner somewhere."

"We should mingle. I don't want to make a bad impression."

He looked away, then back at me with a heat I didn't expect. "If they could see what was in my head, they'd be impressed."

"What's in your head?"

"Getting my hand under your dress and finding out if you're wet."

"Logan," I scolded in a hiss. "We just said—"

"We said no feelings." He took me by the chin. "If I took you right now, fucked you raw, gave you a dozen orgasms and came deep inside you, it would mean nothing to me."

My panties were soaked through. "Me neither."

He looked over my shoulder as if he needed a moment to think, then found my hand and squeezed it. "Come."

He pulled me off the dance floor.

"Where are we going?"

We went down a stairway we hadn't before, past a security guard, and into a closed hallway with double doors at the end. He pushed me into a wall with a kiss that wasn't like the others. It was thoughtless, reckless, uncontrolled. It was a cyclone of desire I was already caught in, spinning upward, limp-willed with the force of it, because it was my whirlwind too.

"Let me get inside you," he growled, lifting fistfuls of silver fabric until he could get his hands under my skirt. "Let me take you."

Reaching from behind, he pressed his hand against the dampness of my underwear.

I gasped. "No feelings. It means nothing."

"Just fucking." With his free hand, he shifted a shoulder strap down my arm. "And a little sucking."

"Only a little?"

He pushed the neckline aside to free my breast. "I've wanted to see what's under here." He traced the lines of my tattoo, a butterfly in the center of my chest exploding into smaller ones above and below. He traced them, then ran his thumb across the hard nipple. "It's beautiful."

"Thank—"

You was lost in a gasp as he bent to take my nipple in his mouth while sliding under my panties. When he felt how wet I was, he groaned and my body jolted from the attention. Digging my fingers in his hair, I pushed his mouth into me, and he sucked so hard I went blind with pleasure.

"Take me, please," I begged.

In one graceful motion, he grabbed me by the backs of my bare thighs and hitched me against his hips. I wrapped my legs around his waist so he could carry me as he backed into a metal bar set across a set of double doors to open them.

The garage lights went on automatically. It was jammed with guests' cars. Fifteen. Twenty. I had no time to count because the whirlwind of messy, reckless kisses and probing fingers took me again and I was on my back on the hood of a red car with my knees bent and my beautiful silver gown bunched around my waist.

His feet still on the floor, he bent over me to suck my nipple again, yanking my underwear down over one leg before sliding two fingers inside me.

"God, you're so tight. I'm going to fuck this so deep. Say yes." He jammed his fingers in as deep as they'd go, then thumbed my clit. "Say I can bury my cock inside this until you come."

"Yes, already!"

He unbuckled, unzipped, pulling out his thick erection. "Open your legs for it." He shoved one knee to the side, spreading me wider so he could mount me, then pushed inside.

"Oh, God," I gasped, stretched past where I'd ever been before.

He thrust again and buried himself to the hilt in one shocking stroke. "That's right. Take it."

He slammed into me again, and I exhaled a cry of pleasure.

"Take it all."

He did what he'd promised. Fucked me harder than I thought possible, pushing against my clit with his body, demanding I take all of him and nothing less. He used his cock with cruel efficiency, and I gasped with every thrust, pushed closer and closer to the brink each time.

"Come on my cock," he snarled in my ear.

"Yes." One word. A single affirmation was all I had.

"Let me feel it."

"Yes. Logan."

"Give it."

Shoving hard into me, he buried himself, pressing against my pleasure center for the one, last bit of stimulation I needed; pitching me into a void of disembodied, physical ecstasy. My scream bounced against the high ceilings and concrete walls, mixing with his hard grunts as his dick pulsed with release.

We panted together without speaking. The cold metal of the hood was hard on my skin, and my balance had been kept by no more than the pinion of his dick, and all I could think about was how much I wanted him again.

"That meant nothing," he said when he caught half a breath.

"Right."

We were just a married couple with a story about being in love. None of it was real, permanent, or outside the parameters of a contract.

"Wait," I said.

He straightened on his arms to look at me. "What?"

"What kind of car is this?"

"This? The one I just fucked you on?"

"Yes." I knocked on the hood.

He craned his neck to confirm. "Ferrari 488 GTB."

"We have to change our story."

He seemed to think I'd lost my mind. For such a smart guy, he could be pretty thick.

"The first time we fucked story?" I added. "The Maserati?"

He laughed. "Right. Good call. I'll have to buy a Ferrari." As he started to get off me, he leaned in for a kiss, then stopped himself. "Right."

He got off the car and offered his hand to help me up. I didn't need it. I stood on my own, letting my dress drape around my knees and my underwear loop around my left ankle.

"Here." Reaching toward my panties, he started to get on his knees. "Let me."

"I have it."

"All right." He ran his fingers through his hair, turning away to let me get my underwear back in place.

"I'm done if you want to turn around," I said.

He did, hands in his pockets, eyes on the floor as if he'd been caught raiding the cookie jar.

"That was fun," I said.

"Yeah. Really fun. Thank you."

"My pleasure." I smoothed my dress. "You're going to make someone very happy one day."

"As are you." He offered me his arm. "Shall we?"

I looped my hand in the crook of his elbow. "We shall."

He walked me back upstairs. I was sore and wet, stinking of sex, when I felt a drop of his fluid between my thighs.

"I should probably find a bathroom."

"There are thirty-four." He guided me around a turn. "If we keep going, we're bound to walk into one."

"What did we do those three days?" I asked. "After we defiled the Ferrari?"

"We sat in my living room and I fed you takeout Chinese. Then —and I'm not going to offer this information up unless someone asks—I fucked you again, but slowly."

"After Chinese?" I wrinkled my nose.

"You couldn't keep your hands off me." He stopped at a half-open door with a tile floor and white marble sink on the other side. "Besides, it was a quickie in the garage. You only came once. I had something to prove." He pushed the door open and leaned in to flick on the light.

"Maybe you shouldn't tell that part of the story," I suggested, halfway into the bathroom.

"What about your two—no, wait, I think I remember three screaming orgasms?"

"Keep that part implied."

"Fine, killjoy. Go. I'll wait here."

He stood like a sentry with his hands in front of him, handsome as a god and confident as a king. I closed the door, and as if given permission, his fluids seeped out of me.

I hiked up my dress before it got ruined, lowered my trashed underpants, and sat on the toilet, in the first quiet moment since Logan had broken the post-sex haze with three words.

That meant nothing.

He'd been right, and he'd been right to repeat what we'd agreed. I'd needed the reminder that we were strangers and we had a deal to be no more than friends. If it meant something, we wouldn't be able to split up. We'd be messy and expensive. All the benefits of the arrangement could be compromised by the wrong emotions.

That meant nothing.

Except the best sex I'd ever had.

I cleaned up, straightened out my gown, and was fixing my makeup in the mirror when I heard voices from the other side of the door.

"Just want to make sure you're happy."

That was Mrs. Crowne, my mother-in-law.

"I am happy," Logan responded softly, though his voice echoed in the huge room.

"It's just so sudden."

"Not to me, it's not."

"I told your father you'd feel pressured. I said, 'Hold off but don't tell him why.' I said, 'Let him find someone in his own time.' But he went and told you boys everything in his head."

"Mom, I don't care about the succession. I could marry her now or in ten years, she's still the one, okay?"

"Don't you think...?"

They must have walked away. I had to put my ear to the door to hear Logan.

"Me on this. I didn't know it, but I was waiting for her, and when I finally found her, my life... everything added up. She's... she's the gravity that keeps my feet on the floor. The elevator that lifts me up."

The utter terribleness of that line aside, that was a lot from a guy who had no feelings for me.

His mother's response got lost in the white noise created by the paper-thin space between my ear and the door, as did his. Then I heard heels on the hard floors.

I counted to five, and when I heard nothing, I opened the door.

13

LOGAN

MY MOTHER WAS GETTING frailer every day. Her dress fit but looked as if it were on the hanger, and the muted blue reflected on her skin as if she didn't have any color of her own. The formal twist in her hair and the makeup she'd had someone carefully apply were a merry falsehood.

If she found out I'd lied about this, she'd break. In my grab for power, I hadn't even considered what losing trust in me would do to her health.

"I just haven't had a chance to see you two together." Mom put her shaky hand on my arm to reassure me. "To feel it, is all."

"Are you basing your opinion of my marriage on whether or not you had *the tingle?* Mom, really?"

"I trust you know what you feel."

"You should. You know I wouldn't do this lightly."

"I know," she said. "I think I'm just angry with your father. He shouldn't have made that ultimatum. I told him not to."

"Don't be mad at him. Listen. Let me wait for Ella to get out, then we'll meet you out there, okay?" I kissed her cheek, and she hugged me as tightly as she could. "I love you, Ma."

"I love you too, sweetest," she said. "You're a good boy,"

With a smile seemingly meant to erase her own doubts as well as mine, she walked carefully away, getting smaller in the distance until she was part of the stream of people moving between dinner and the dance floor.

This was bad.

I'd made a mistake I couldn't ever recover from. Not just my reputation as the public face of Crowne Industries. Not only with the people I loved. But my opinion of myself had curdled into a thick, sour mass.

The bathroom door opened, and Ella smiled at me, as preened and beautiful as a siren calling me to be the man no one who loved me thought I was capable of being.

That meant nothing.

When I'd said those words, I wasn't really speaking to her. I'd needed to remind myself that the urgency of our connection had made me emotionally lazy. In the dancing and laughter, the constant buzz of anxiety had bubbled and popped like the champagne I'd drunk, and something else had slipped in.

I'd felt things.

Feeling things meant I'd lost control, and that was unacceptable if we were going to get through this.

"Hey," Ella said, taking my arm. "Sorry I took so long."

"It's fine." I led her back to the party.

"'Elevator that lifts me up'?"

"You heard?" I expected her to mention my mother's doubts so we could plan our next course of action. For the first time since my father's ultimatum, getting the top spot at Crowne wasn't the first thing on my mind. I needed my mother soothed immediately.

"Please say you didn't come up with that line," Ella said. "We'll have to take you behind the shed and shoot you."

"Was it that bad?"

"You were doing okay for a minute. Gravity was a little soft, but ending on the elevator—"

"Was it so bad she wouldn't believe it?" I interrupted.

"I don't think your way with words is going to make her believe you love me."

Great.

I didn't even know how to convince my own mother.

"So"—Ella leaned into me as we entered the crowd—"do I get a ride in your red Ferrari?"

"I never said red."

"It was red... the one we just—"

"I'm not getting a red car," I snapped, attention forward as if I was driving. "If you knew me, that would be obvious."

"Okay. What color then?"

"Black. Make a note."

There were too many people around. Too much laughing. Everyone walking in every direction, and Ella and I had no destination, no purpose, sitting ducks to get caught in the worst kind of lie.

We kept it light. She showed off her ring. People I barely knew congratulated and hugged me. We made excuses about our secrecy, claiming it all happened so fast, we forgot the basics.

My mother always seemed nearby, with or without Dad, reminding me that I'd lied to her and would have to continue lying or hurt her more.

Liam, my younger brother by four years, walked toward us with his three-year-old son, Matt. over his shoulder.

"Liam," I muttered to her. "Be ready."

"Right."

I'd briefed her on my family, telling her as much as I could, but suddenly, I knew it wasn't enough.

"Logan!" Liam said, free hand extended. Matt rested his head on his father's shoulder, thumb lodged in his mouth. "I just heard!"

"Sorry about the secrecy." I shook his hand, lying, lying, lying.

"You must be the newly-minted Mrs. Crowne," he said.

"Papillion," she said as she accepted his handshake. "Ella Papillion."

"She won't change her name," I grumbled. "It wasn't my preference."

But it'll be easier to get divorced in a year.

"What's your secret?" Liam asked her.

"Pardon me?" She put her hand to her chest, exposing the ring.

"How did you get him to look up from his precious P&L statements?"

She smiled and took my hand, leaning into me as if we were in love. "He was pretty good at getting my attention."

I felt her looking at me with a smitten smile. The pressure of the falsehood pushed against a newly-awoken conscience, forcing me to counter with a frown. "I bought her a coffee. And jewelry. So it was easy."

"Logan!" She shoved me as if I'd been joking, which I wasn't. I was only lying.

Liam laughed, but there was no light in his eyes. He'd seen the vein of cruelty in my attempt at humor

"Who's this handsome fellow?" Ella asked, craning to face the boy. "Are you the Matt I've heard so much about?"

He nodded, eyes drooping.

"He's wrecked," Liam said. "Big night, and it's past bedtime."

"That thumb taste good?" she asked, and he nodded a little. "When I was your age, I sucked these two fingers." She held up her right pinkie and ring finger. "I still have a callous right here. See that?"

"Please tell me how you stopped," Liam said.

"I just stopped, I guess." Ella shrugged. "But the morning after my mother died, I woke up with them in my mouth, so I guess I stopped needing it until I did again."

"Ah," Liam said pensively, and a dead weight fell on the conversation.

"We were going to get drinks," I said to Liam. "Can I get you anything?"

"No, no, I'd better get this little guy to bed."

We said our good nights and I pulled Ella toward the bar.

"Make a deal with me," I hissed under the music and laughter.

"Another one?"

"Don't offer up anything to anyone in my family. Ever."

She yanked me back by the hand. "What just happened?"

"You stepped in it."

"How?"

"Liam's wife died almost a year ago." Without waiting for her reaction or even to see if she'd followed, I strode to the bar.

"Logan," she said, coming up next to me, "I'm sorry."

"What can I get you, Mr. Crowne?" the bartender asked, wiping his hands.

"Macallan and"—I turned to Ella—"Shirley Temple?"

Any happiness we'd felt leading up to the encounter in the garage had drained out of her. She stood behind a cinderblock wall of hesitation. "Gin with ice."

"Coming right up!"

The bartender went to make the drinks, and Ella slid onto a stool, chin up with a stone-cold profile to prove she didn't give a single shit what I thought.

"This isn't going to work," I said.

"What's not going to work?"

"This entire thing. It's—"

"Shut up," she hissed. "You shut up right now. This was going to be a tough night and we both knew it. Don't you dare bail just because you forgot to tell me your sister-in-law died."

"I didn't forget," I growled back. "I didn't have time. We rushed."

She faced me with a big smile and a city burning in her eyes.

"We rushed because you needed to, remember?" She placed her

hand on my arm, telegraphing newlywed affection while grinding her teeth. "You want your brother out."

"And you wanted a few million dollars."

Our drinks came. She jabbed her lime down with her swizzle stick.

The ice cube in my scotch had a crown embossed in it. A real family made from a real marriage.

Logan and Ella were an act. A stage play put on for people who never bought a ticket.

"You have everything," Ella said, taking my hand. "Your family loves you. Every last one of them. Even the brother you're so busy fighting. They'd do anything for you. You think I envy your money? No. Not after tonight. Now take that fucking scowl off your face, Logan. You're a newlywed."

I smiled but had to hide it behind my glass when I saw my mother halfway across the room, practically running in her heels.

"Colton!" she shouted.

There he was, my failure of a brother in a backward baseball cap and tuxedo pants that fit like a garbage bag, opening his arms so our mother could run into them as if he were back from a war.

His presence on the earth irritated me, but he'd take some of the attention off Ella and me while we regrouped.

"Is that the Colton you were talking about?" Ella whispered.

She should know that. She should know we watched him spend all his money. That he was an embarrassment to the Crowne name. There was no way she wouldn't fuck this up.

"We need to go," I said.

"It's ten o'clock."

"Let's go. We have a suite on the east side of the house."

She pushed her glass away with a tight jaw and eyes hardened into stones. "I want to go home."

"I'm your home now."

Fuck. The way her face fell made me feel like the one who'd

fucked up, but Colton was a dead weight on my attention. I had thirty seconds or less to avoid him.

I took my wife's hand and pulled her into me, guiding her out with an arm around her shoulder. We didn't speak until I'd closed the suite door behind her.

"I had your things sent up." I pointed at the bag left by the entrance.

"Thank you."

"Ella," I said in a tone that set up a reasonable discussion between reasonable adults.

"I'll stay up here. You can go back down if you want."

"No." I jerked my tie open, and she stood in the center of the suite's living room with her molten silver ball gown and makeup designed for a party. "I don't want."

She passed me to get her bag then walked through the bedroom to disappear into the bathroom. I watched her shadow move across the light under the door, then I sat on a chair by the bed. King-sized mattress. More comfortable than the hood of a car.

God, what had I done?

I should be fucking her on that bed or not at all.

She stepped into the dimly-lit room, arms crossed over her pajama top, sock feet set apart. She'd made a choice—whatever it was—and was sticking to it. I stood up and crossed my arms, because she didn't get to make all the decisions.

"No," she said.

"Did I ask a question?"

"No divorce," she said. "I promised my father I wouldn't abandon his name. And I'm aware he's dead. So don't say it. But the bottom line is, Papillion doesn't belong to me. I can't put a single butterfly on a single shoe on my own. The only way I have to honor his request is to keep my job and fight for his name."

This woman had the business sense of a bent spoon. Fuzzy

goals. No strategy. Tactics that included indefinite, undefined expenditures.

"Great plan," I said. "If by 'great,' I meant 'nonexistent,' which I did."

Immediately, I was sorry I'd snapped at her and shut her out, but the only other option was letting her in, and that would make it all worse.

"Are you taking the couch or am I?" she asked.

"I will," I said, and went into the bathroom. The mirror had a little TV set into it, so a guy could watch the morning news while he shaved and avoid looking at himself altogether.

14

ELLA

IN THE SUITE's living room, I sat on a couch with my back straight and my hands in my lap. The exterior walls overlooked the landscape, and the interior walls were decorated with original art. The cushions were plush and luxurious.

I felt like a tourist, but this was my life now.

Logan and I were nothing more than business partners, but the feelings I wasn't supposed to have were hurt by his insensitivity. He owed me nothing. Not trust in my judgment. Not respect for my decisions or love for the people I cared about.

And I owed him nothing. He was from another universe, where the law was a friend and a judge would work on a Saturday just because he'd asked. He and I had been born on the same planet, but I'd been kicked off early enough to know it wasn't the only one in the solar system.

I couldn't bridge the space between our worlds.

Logan came out of the bathroom in sweatpants. Bare feet. No shirt.

I'd spread my legs for him before seeing the full glory of his body.

"There's breakfast tomorrow with everyone," he said. "We'll brief beforehand."

I wanted to say more, but I had no idea what I wanted to tell him.

"Look," he said, ready to start some speech he'd obviously prepared in the bathroom. As beautiful and strong as his shoulders were, they seemed unable to handle his burden. "About what happened in the gara—"

"I want valid things, Logan Crowne," I said. "I need this deal. So don't try to divorce me because they're not your things."

He seemed so vulnerable in his half-naked state that I had to not only steel myself against a desire to touch him, but also a deeper need to reassure him that everything would be all right. Unable to bear standing that close to him, I went to the door.

"I keep my promises," he said, telling himself a story he needed to believe. That he was a trustworthy and loyal man whose word was a contract. I wanted to believe it too, but our contract was built on known lies and unknowable truths.

"You will," I said. "You'll keep every last one of them."

Before he could answer, I walked into the bedroom, not looking back until my hand was on the doorknob, taking one last glance at physical perfection partnered with emotional shortfall.

I closed the door between us, ending my wedding day.

———

As I lay in bed with the faraway party humming along, I couldn't hear Logan on the other side of the wall. The house was probably soundproofed and too new for creaky floorboards, but I felt him pacing as if the vows we'd taken connected us by more than a signature.

Of course he was worried. His mother had questioned our marriage, and she was absolutely right to do so. We'd anticipated that, yet the reality of those questions right after we had sex had probably caught him off guard. He was competent, but he was also human.

I didn't think I'd be able to sleep, but I did for a few hours, waking after three in the morning to the music of crickets and the chatter of night birds. The party must have ended.

Wide awake, I slid out of bed in my sweatshirt and plaid flannel sleep pants to look into the darkness of the canyon. A deep balcony connected the living area and the bedroom, and at a metal table sat Logan Crowne with his face lit blue by his open laptop. He scrolled, banged at the keys, marked a notebook, and scrolled and banged some more. He'd put on a hoodie against the early morning chill, but his feet were bare in his slippers.

After putting on shoes, I dug around my bag, found what I was looking for, and went outside. "Hey."

"Good morning." He hit the enter key before looking at me. "There's night staff if you want anything."

"I'm good. Here." I held out the fuzzy Christmas socks I'd packed. "These are poly chenille. Warmest ever."

He took them as if he wasn't quite sure what I wanted him to do with them.

"They're one size fits all." I pointed at his feet. "And they're clean. So."

"Santa socks?"

"Yep." I sat down. "Biggest lie ever told for the two biggest lie-tellers ever."

He chuckled and kicked off his slippers.

"So, working late?" I asked.

"It's seven at night in Beijing." He pulled the socks over his feet, stretching the jolly fat man's smile. "And they never go home if there's a fire to put out."

"Is there a fire?"

"There's always a fire." He pushed his feet back into his slippers. "These really are warm. Thank you." He closed the laptop and leaned back.

"You're close to your family," I said.

"Not all of them, but in general, yes."

"I was with my parents, but... you've met the family I have now. It's not the same, obviously. I tried for a while, when I was a kid, but I got tired of being laughed at." I cleared my throat, forcing away the memory of any specific, painful incident. There were too many and they were all unbearable. "Anyway, I don't think I realized how much it would hurt you to lie to them."

"Are you talking about feelings, Ella?"

"Are we not supposed to do that, Logan?"

He smiled, looked into the darkness for a moment, before rubbing away an invisible blemish on his laptop. "Let's talk about facts." He pushed back to a slouch, lacing his hands over his stomach. "Did you ever wonder why I was at Wildwood? I mean, progressive school. Wall-to-wall music nerds. Art three times a week. Kids missing half the year because they were starring in some Marvel movie. Did that ever strike you as weird?"

"No. There were plenty of math kids."

"Sure. Nadia Goodman was in quant lab, adding corollaries to chaos theory, but that's not me. I'm not a creative breakthrough guy. Look at me, and tell me what the fuck I was doing there?"

In the silence, I looked at him in his blue hoodie and my Santa socks. His cheeks were shadowed with the first growth of beard. He was always clean-shaven in school. Always standing straight when everyone else was liquid. Running the entrepreneur society. Playing club lacrosse because we had no team. Dating a girl too ambitious for his traditional values.

"Why then?" I asked. "You could have gone anywhere."

"Right." He shifted in his seat in preparation, then back. "I could have."

"What happened?"

"Once upon a time, in the hilly part of Beverly Hills, there lived a boy," he started. I laughed, and he smiled before he continued. "Our neighbors moved, and the new owners gutted the place down to the studs. The entire property was a construction site. We—Byron and I—could see it over the fence from our rooms. It was pretty tempting, especially on weekends. All those piles of dirt to climb, the digging machines just sitting there. And we figured, why not? Just check it out. Who were we hurting?"

He took a sip of his water and flipped a glass over to pour me some even though I hadn't asked.

"Byron inspected the foundation like a damn city planner. I scaled the house frame to get to the third story they were adding. I could see all the way to the ocean. I felt like I was on top of the world. Anything I could see was mine. The whole city. So I drew a sight line from the horizon to the house. Thank God I did."

I didn't interrupt the pause he took.

"The pool was empty. Just the tiles and a balled up painting sheet over a puddle of tar. Everything was so orderly except for that—the tar and unfolded sheet—so I looked again. It was Lyric, just lying there. She was the sheet. The puddle was blood."

"Oh, no."

"Yeah. I never yelled Byron's name so loud. She had a concussion. Didn't remember shit. Otherwise, she was okay, but my father asked what the fuck—and my dad doesn't drop a 'fuck' unless he's really pissed off. He asked us what the fuck happened?"

"He couldn't have blamed you," I said.

"I'll never know. Because I lied. Like that." He snapped his fingers. "Obviously she followed us, but I said I saw her crawling through a space in the fence from my window, so I grabbed Byron and went over there. My brother backed me up, but he wasn't happy about it. I made him a liar too."

"Logan," I said, "you were a kid."

"If I hadn't seen her from the third floor, we would have gone home and left her on the bottom of that pool. She was two, for Chrissakes, and man, I loved that baby. Mom brought her home and I swaddled her and played with her and held her all the time. Then I almost killed her and lied about it because I thought…" He rubbed his eyes. "God, this is so ridiculous." He dropped his hands onto the arms of the chair. "I've never told anyone this, and now that it's about to come out of my mouth, I want to laugh at myself."

I drank a bit of water to hide my surprise, and he paused. Maybe to collect his thoughts, or to change his mind. He barely knew me, yet he trusted me with a story he'd kept to himself all these years. I wouldn't dare break the spell to ask what this had to do with which school he wound up at.

"It was Christmas break," he said. "Sixth grade. I don't know what that was like for you, applying to middle school?"

"I was at Wildwood from first grade."

"Right. So you skipped it. It's essays, interviews, events. Like college. A lot of pressure, but not a problem. I had it under control. Harvard-Westlake and one backup. I forget which because it didn't matter. But when Dad asked what happened with Lyric, I just... all I could think was that if Harvard-Westlake knew I almost killed my sister, I was sunk. I'd lose control of the whole thing. So I lied. And it was fine. Right? Byron had my back. Lyric was okay. Nothing to see here."

He shifted to the edge of his seat and put his elbows on the table. I leaned into him, because here was the crux of the story.

"But it was all a lie. My essay was about ethical business practice and I was a liar. I couldn't do it. I rewrote it about some generic bullshit and fucked up my applications so bad they didn't even waitlist me. I wouldn't let my parents step in and write a check. Nothing. Exactly what a liar deserves." He leaned back again. "My matriculation counselor found out Wildwood was under-enrolled. Didn't get enough qualifying applicants. So I applied to make Mom happy. Tried to fuck that up too. I wrote the essay in iambic pentameter and they loved it." He spread his arms, facing his palms up to the sky. "Here we are."

Here we were, under a clear sky, with the hum of the pool filter and the squeak of crickets accompanying a story he'd never told another soul. I didn't know what response he was expecting or what he needed to hear. I couldn't tell if he wanted me to soothe him, cheerlead his choices, or if he wanted me to bolster his low opinion of himself.

"So why lie about this then?" I asked. "About us?"

"Because I'm pissed my father put me in this situation. There's nothing like anger to make you feel like you're right to do wrong."

The observation wasn't directed at me or my decision to take him up on his offer, but I felt it like a knife to the heart. I'd been angry for years, and I'd used that rage to justify marrying him.

The moral high ground was narrow and slippery.

"We can get an annulment," I said, letting my heart speak before my brain sorted out the consequences.

"And then what? For you?"

"I'll still be my father's daughter. Still holding down the fort from the base."

He shrugged, hooking his toes around an empty chair to turn it and prop his feet on the cushion. "You're all right. I definitely would have fucked you under other circumstances."

"But you never would have married me."

"Can't say that's a lie."

"Can you can keep it up for a year?" I said.

"Maybe." He leaned his head against the back of the chair to gaze at the sky, then closed his eyes. "I'm too tired to think."

"Me too." I stood, holding out my hand. "Come on. There's an ocean of mattress in there. It's big enough for both of us."

He considered my hand for a moment, then took it, grabbed his laptop, and led me to the bedroom. He put down the computer, and I shut off the light before getting under the covers.

"This is my side of the bed," he said, standing over me and tossing his hoodie over a chair.

"You said that the first time we slept together," I answered, pulling the blanket up to my chin. "Our first date."

"And you pretended you were already asleep."

I shut my eyes, opened my mouth, and made snoring noises. He laughed, and I felt the mattress dip at the center as he crawled over me. When I felt him get under the covers, I thought I'd won the battle for territory until his feet pushed my legs.

"Hey!"

He shoved me to the edge, laughing as I fought back move for move. I was no match for him, and before I knew it, the sheets were a mess and I was halfway to falling off.

"Yield!" he cried, pinning my wrist to the night table.

"Never!" With my free hand, I pinched a chunk of skin under his ribs.

He pulled away, back to the center, giving me enough room to slide back. "Is that how it is?"

He grabbed me and we wrestled, our troubles forgotten in laughter and hand-to-hand combat. I tried to pinch him again, but he was too quick, grabbing my hand, then the other, and holding them together with two fingers.

"You want to play dirty." He reached under my arm and tickled me. I squealed. "Oh, she's ticklish!"

"Cheat—" The word was drowned in uncontrollable giggles. I twisted away, and he rolled with me, getting on top so he could pin my wrists to the headboard with one hand.

"What was that?" he asked.

"That's cheating," I said between gasps for breath.

"You mean this?" He went to tickle me again, but when I tried to roll, he slid between my legs to pin me with his pelvis.

He was hard.

We didn't say a word. We didn't move. We'd gone from dead serious, to playful, to aroused in the space of ten minutes.

"That night," he whispered, letting my wrists go. "You let me have my side of the bed, but not right away."

"When?" My hips pushed into his rod with an involuntarily jerk.

He slipped his hand under my sweatshirt and traced the underside of my breast with his fingertips.

"After we finished our first date." His teasing fingers were cool on my nipple, making it even harder.

"So we're on the same date? Now?"

"Do you want to be?"

"Yes. Do you?"

"Yes."

"Then I think…" I had to stop when he turned the nipple just enough to make me push into him. "It's the same night so…" He gently twisted the other way. "So not a problem for feelings. Right?"

"Right." He pulled my shirt over my breasts, eyes flicking from one to the other as if deciding between desserts before choosing the left to suck. "No feelings."

He slid his hands along my sides and pushed my pants down, his mouth following. When I was bare, he threw the pants aside and held me by the calves, raising and spreading my legs.

"I ate your pussy," he said, kissing the inside of my knee and working up. "And you came, but you tasted so good…" He ran his tongue along my seam, leaving the tip at the head of my clit and circling. "I couldn't stop."

He kissed the nub, and I groaned. When I looked down, he was looking right back at me. Pressing me open, he flicked, watching me as he made me writhe with his mouth, gently pulling my clit between his teeth before pushing his tongue inside.

I came, pushing against the headboard and raising my hips. "Logan! Just wait, I—"

Though he slowed down, he kept his promise and made me come again, twisting with the unbearable, overwhelming sensation of too much pleasure, until he had to stop and I was on my stomach with him behind me.

"Oh, my God," I said. From behind my closed eyes, my face

smushed against the mattress, I felt him take off his sweatpants. "Did I know you were the one right then?"

"I don't know." He put his hands on my hips and pulled them up to get me on my hands and knees. I felt the head of his dick start at my asshole then slide down to my entrance. "You decide that part of the story."

He pushed inside me, three strokes deep, and stopped to wrap his arm under mine and place his hand under my jaw. Then he slammed into me, making me see stars.

"You want it all?" he asked.

"That's not all of it?"

"This is all of it." One hard thrust and he was root-deep, leaving me shuddering against him. He put two fingers in my mouth, the middle and the ring. I closed my lips around them. "Suck while you take it."

I did as he commanded, and he thrust into me again and again, teasing my clit with his other hand. I dropped to my elbows. The harder he fucked me, the harder I sucked. If I wasn't half conscious with the coming of the fourth orgasm of the night, I would have sworn I'd have taken his skin right off.

"Come with me," he growled at exactly the right time.

Humming against his hand, I did as I was told, and he unloaded inside with a deep rumble in his throat. Lying on top of me, still inside, he kissed my shoulder.

"So did you know I was the one?" he asked, rolling off me to the side of the bed he'd claimed.

"Yeah," I replied, getting on the other side. "That's my story and I'm sticking to it."

"Noted."

"What about you?"

"Nope."

"No?" I kicked him.

"I knew from the moment you ordered your froufrou coffee."

"Shut up." I whacked him with a pillow, but the bed was so big, I only got him with a corner.

"Are you looking to get fucked again?" He reached for me, and I skootched closer.

"I'm too tired." Laying my head on his shoulder, I let him put his arm around my neck.

"Not tired enough."

"I'm mostly dead." My eyelids drooped, and I yawned. "Thank you for a great first and last time in the sack."

"Pleasure was all mine."

I had a clever response, but couldn't get the words out before I fell asleep.

15

LOGAN

HOW TIRED and worn out had I been to tell her the story of finding Lyric in the pool?

No one knew but Byron, and he hadn't mentioned it since that day, when he told me I was stupid for lying.

What had come over me?

I should have been anxious as hell, pacing, trying to make myself believe things that weren't true. That I wasn't repeating old mistakes and I was fine, fine, fine.

Instead, I was lying awake, naked except for a pair of silly Santa socks, wearing Ella's head on my chest and her drying juices on my dick.

In a few hours, we'd move her into my house. With every step, I pushed us deeper into a lie I was less and less sure I could maintain. Knowing how she fucked, how she slept, and how she took her coffee wasn't a substitute for love. Getting our story straight wasn't the same as living it.

We'd made a business decision, and yet—when she'd suggested an annulment, my reaction had been visceral. I'd had to peel that back to give her a less emotional reason to stay married.

In the dark with her, I didn't panic. The anxiety was usually worse at night, but not that night. Somehow, it stayed locked in its cage while I put the pieces in place.

Our families.

Our business.

My feelings.

Without the voice telling me I was losing control, I could see my feelings for her clearly.

They existed as a soreness where I was hard. Tenderness. Potential.

If in our year together, they grew past the confines of what I could hold, they would be dangerous, and if they grew then dissolved into boredom or distaste while hers didn't, that could be worse. I didn't know what she was like when she was really angry, but she had little to lose making my life hell.

I should have panicked and spent the following few hours strategizing a way out.

Instead, I fell asleep.

I woke with the sun peeking over the horizon and no solution for the risk she posed.

———

LIKE EVERY OTHER room in the house, the gym overlooked a pool and opened to a view that didn't disappear until the horizon faded into haze.

Colton was already benching. Surprising, since he was the only late sleeper among us. He saw me and dropped the weights into the rack.

"Yo, yo," he said, sitting up. "Good morning."

"Morning." I draped my towel over the handle of the treadmill and set my run uphill.

"You split last night." He shook my hand, then tried to lead me into a finger hook fist bump thing I had no interest in.

"You split with your money years ago."

"You mad?" He got onto the treadmill next to me.

"Don't care." I started my run as if his actions didn't concern me.

"Cool."

"Mom was devastated, so fuck you."

"Yeah." He ran next to me. "Fuck me. So, you got a wife, huh? I'm gonna meet her at breakfast or nah?"

"If you show." I kept my eyes on the expanse of Los Angeles. Colton was a pain in the ass and he was turning my sour mood bitter.

"I'm back for good," he said. "Gonna make it right with the 'rents."

"You mean you spent all the money."

"Man, you haven't changed." The belt under his feet shifted and he ran with it. "Never cut a guy a break."

"You got enough breaks." I could see his stats. He was lazy and careless, but he was a fit fuck and already running faster than me. I tapped my panel until my pace matched his.

"Yeah, well, break time's over. I'll be hauling pig slop ten years before he flicks me another dime. That cool for you?"

"Not my problem."

I had enough problems. I loved my brothers, but Colton was unmanageable, much like Ella, who I wasn't allowed to love.

Which I didn't. I didn't even want to like her.

But the sex. The alternating tenderness and ferocity had softened me. I'd told her things I hadn't spoken about to anyone. I'd wanted her to know me, the real me, the part that wanted to crawl under her skin when we fucked and lose my identity inside her.

Colton and I ran in silence long enough to lull me into thinking he'd stop talking, but no.

"So you fell in love, huh?" he asked. "Didn't know you had it in you."

"I guess I do."

But I couldn't love Ella. We were on a timeline. Losing myself in her wasn't possible, nor was it wise.

"All the girls you brought around." *Tap-tap.* His belt tilted uphill. "I was always like 'why's he even with her?'"

"What's that mean?" Instinctively, I added to the grade, because if he could run this fast uphill, I could too.

"Dude. The doctor?"

"June."

"She was totally hot. Smart as fuck. Never once in two years, *neh-ver* did I look at you guys and think, 'Yeah, he loves that chick.' And Mom didn't—"

"My mother doesn't run my relationships."

"Not saying that. Just... you were a stone-cold motherfucker, dude."

"Can we just have a run? Or do you want to sit and talk about *your* past?"

"Whatever." *Tap-tap.* Faster, and fuck him for it.

I added to my speed. Maybe we'd be too breathless to talk.

"Good morning." Byron's voice came from behind us. "Colton. It's good to see you, brother." He slapped Colton's back.

"Yeah," he replied, jogging too fast to run his mouth.

"Olivia says she knows your new wife." Byron got on the treadmill on the other side of mine.

I was fucking surrounded. "Oh, yeah?"

"She fit Olivia's gown from last night," Byron said, setting his run, then checking mine.

"Great."

"Speaks highly." Byron upped the grade and started. He'd scale a wall just to beat me. "Very talented. She was surprised Ella's not running that company by now."

"Her stepmother got control in the will."

"Apparently. How's she feel about that?"

"Ask her."

"I might." Byron's belt picked up speed.

I made a note to warn Ella it would come up. We had to craft a response. I didn't want any red flags popping up before we started buying shares. Then it was going to get real adversarial, real fast.

My body was so engaged in the run, I forgot to steel myself against the pleasure of the story of us taking back what was hers. Doing something just and right, together. The pitfalls, the wins, the eventual, indisputable victory of putting her back where she belonged.

Ella was a fighter, and I was her champion.

Byron cut right into the fantasy. "Did you see the new bid on the pipeline?"

"Yeah."

"It's interesting."

"Let's not bore Colton with business."

"Not bored," the brother on my other side said.

"Good," Byron said. "If you want to work at Crowne—"

"What?"

"He needs a job," Byron said. "And you know Dad. He'll find something for him to do."

I knew Dad fine, but I knew Mom better. She was the one who'd put a net under Colton. Dad would teach you to swim by throwing you off a pier and rescuing you if he thought you'd drown. Mom would jump into a kiddie pool to make sure we were all right.

"Nah," Colton said. "I'm cool."

Byron leaned over to look past me at Colton. "It'll be good for you."

"Gotta find a place to crash first. Got a fat 'no' from Pops about staying here."

"He'll bend, just give it time." Byron wasn't even out of breath. Meanwhile, I had a crushing weight on my chest.

Byron pulling me down was bad enough, but now he was dragging in Colton of all people.

Fuck this.

I shut the machine.

"Had enough?" Byron asked.

"This gym's too crowded."

"See you at breakfast," Colton called back.

———

ELLA HAD PUT a hoodie over her pajamas and was pacing the suite's patio with her phone to her ear. Her hair was pulled up in a bun that sat high on her head, exposing the curve of her ears and the length of her neck.

She waved when she saw me, pointed at the phone, and mouthed, "Bianca."

"You can be mad I took it but you can't just fire me." She listened, looking in the middle distance with the mountains behind her.

I threw myself into a chair and turned my emotions down to a low, rolling boil.

"I know 'you're happy but,'" she said, sitting across from me to rest her elbow on the table. She rubbed her temple as if her stepmother was giving her a headache.

"Honey!" I said so Bianca could hear. "I'm home."

Ella smiled and gave me a thumbs-up. "I have to go," she said. "Fine." Pause. "Yes, I believe you." Pause. "Okay. Bye." She tapped off and tossed the phone on the table. "Fuck."

"What happened?"

"She fired me. Fuck. I shouldn't have taken that dress. 'Darling,'" she said, imitating her stepmother's affect. "'You know I love you dearly, but even if I overlook the mistake over the Rachel tee, I simply cannot send the message that stealing one of Basile's dresses is acceptable.'"

"Why do you care about a job? How much do you make? I'll—"

"Don't you dare," she objected with a defensiveness to match the overt accusations in my voice. "I promised my father on his goddamned deathbed. I said I'd take responsibility for the name. That I'd stay connected to it." She launched off her chair and crossed the distance between the table and the sliding glass doors with her arms crossed, spun, then came back. "She can't do this. She can't cut me off like a... like an employee." At the edge of the table, she pointed at me as if I were Bianca, grinding every word through her teeth. "I am Basile Papillion's only child. Do you hear me?"

She was a warrior without weapons.

A princess who needed a champion.

"Hell hears you right now."

She threw herself into the chair and used another to mirror my reclined posture. "We're going to rip that company from under her, I swear to God. I want her to beg me not to, then I'm doing it anyway."

"Vindictiveness isn't good business."

"That office has been my home since I was a kid. I don't know what I'm supposed to do with myself."

"You could just be my wife. If you take that on full time, it'll make us credible to my family."

She slid down the chair and crossed her ankles. In profile, there was something missing from her face. A lost piece from that side, specifically. I studied her as she spoke, trying to place it.

"The nineteen-fifties called," she said. "They want their culture back."

Found it. The nose ring was the missing piece. She hadn't put it back in yet, and in casual clothes, she didn't look right without it.

"It's just a job," I said, sticking to a point that pissed her off because I was right. "You've still got your name, or mine if you want it."

"Never."

"Why not?"

She took her feet off the chair and faced me. "When my

parents got Christmas cards, some of them were addressed to Mr. and Mrs. Basile Papillion. I asked my mother if she'd changed her first name too. She said no, but some people are old-fashioned and that's the way they did it. When my dad got remarried, you know who the cards were addressed to? Mr. and Mrs. Basile Papillion. Same. My mother was just replaced. Poof. Like she never even existed."

"I don't want to erase you."

"You just want to prop up our story. I know. Sure." She twirled her hand as if she was weaving my words from the air and throwing them back at me. "You're in this world but not of it, right?"

"I'm not—" I stopped myself.

What was I?

I was a man who wanted her to look the way she was supposed to.

I got up and went to the bathroom. There were two countertops, each with their own mirror, and two sinks. My stuff was on the vanity where I'd put them the night before. Her stuff was on the other. I scanned it for little boxes, shiny things, trays with jewelry.

"What are you doing?" she asked from the doorway, just as I saw what I was looking for in an open contact lens container.

"Sit." I slid the stool from under the sink and pulled the seat to its highest setting.

She sat.

"Look up." I held up the nose ring. "Let's see what we're dealing with here."

"I can put it back in," she said, pointing her chin toward the ceiling. "It's not a big deal."

"I know." I stood over her as near as I could, between her legs. "But I want to."

After sliding the narrowest end through the hole in the crease of her nostril, I closed the ring and took her chin so I could look at my work. "Better. Now you look like you should."

"Like a jobless temp wife?"

I leaned down to whisper. "Like *my* wife."

I felt her suck in a breath, drawing me closer as she put her hands on my neck.

"Thank you," she said, even though I hadn't done much but slip a ring into the hole in her nose.

"I want..." I paused to give myself a moment to change my mind—as if I hadn't already decided what I wanted from her. "I agreed to help you get what's yours, but right now, it's not about the contract. I want to."

I knelt on the tile between her legs and ran my hands up the length of her thighs, to her waistband. "We're going to wait a few months to settle in, then we're going to quietly start the buyout."

"How long will it take?"

"As long as it does." I tugged down her yoga pants. "Six months at the outside."

"What if it's longer?" Another tug, and she lifted her bottom off the seat so I could slide the elastic over her ass.

"Then it's longer."

"You can't renegotiate a deal between my legs."

I got the pants all the way off and tossed them in a corner. Her bare legs met at a seam, and when I pushed them apart, the shadow opened into slick, pink glory.

"Logan," she said.

"Yes?" I spread her open until I could smell her hunger.

"I don't think we—"

Her thought melted into a moan as I kissed where she was tender, licked where she was wet, and sucked where she was swollen. She clamped her legs around me, arched her back, and pushed her cunt into my mouth so I could breathe her orgasm.

I wiped her juices off my chin.

"You're something, Logan Crowne," she said, leaning against the wall, breathless. "Really something."

"I've been told that."

"There are things I wanted to say." She pulled up her pants, and I stood. "Then Bianca called, but now I really think I should say them."

When her waistband was in place, I held out my hand to help her up. "Say them."

"Last night, or this morning—whatever—I started to have…" She shook her head as if rearranging her thoughts. "Feelings."

"We agreed not to."

"That's the problem. You're… I like you. And if we keep it up, it's going to be really hard to do… the thing."

The divorce. I could see in her face that she didn't want to say the word.

That was a problem.

She was right.

I could still taste her on my tongue. Still wanted to crawl inside her.

She was right, and I wished she wasn't.

"You're right. But, Ella." I took her by the chin so she'd look at me. "We still have to act affectionate in public."

"I know my job." She smirked and took my hand away. "And touching me when you don't have to isn't going to help me do it. So, hands off."

"Noted."

She turned on the shower. "And you're still in here, because?"

"Colton's going to be at breakfast. Let me upload his story while you get ready."

"Fine." She unzipped her hoodie. "Turn around, Mr. Crowne."

I faced the towel rack and listened to her take off her clothes.

16

ELLA

As I changed into jeans and a T-shirt, Logan told me as much about Colton as he could, figuring we hadn't been together long enough for me to know everything.

We went down to breakfast together. He had his arm around my shoulders and I kept us hip-to-hip—because that's what people in love did.

"I'll sit next to you," he said. "We'll hold hands. When one of us is saying something they shouldn't, squeeze."

"Got it." My stomach rumbled with the smell of bacon, reminding me of how much we didn't know about each other. "I should warn you. I eat."

"Everyone eats."

"Just don't look surprised when I ask for seconds."

I didn't have time for more. Doreen and Ted came within earshot just outside the open dining room, holding hands.

"Good morning!" Doreen said cheerfully, releasing her husband's hand to give me a hug.

"Good morning," I said.

She seemed frail in my arms, like a leather bag full of shaking sticks.

"How did you sleep?" she asked.

"Great."

"Logan's snoring didn't keep you up?"

I looked at my husband. Did he snore? I'd been so relaxed and satisfied the night before, a ten-megaton bomb wouldn't have woken me.

"No," I said, offering nothing else.

"I don't snore," Logan added.

"We could hear him across Crownestead," Ted added. "Boy after my own heart."

I was supposed to know this. The entire way forward was lined with booby traps.

"I'm a really deep sleeper," I said, taking Logan's hand. "Like a dead thing. Right?"

"You're gorgeous when you're asleep." He pulled me close, and we all went into the dining room.

A long cherrywood table had been set with white porcelain plates, polished silver, and clusters of crystal glasses.

"Did he tell you about the time he and Byron had to share a hotel room in Brussels?" Doreen said. "There's a recording. I wonder if he still has it?"

Half a dozen people in white shirts and black vests descended on the table with pitchers of coffee and tea. They poured champagne into flutes half-filled with orange juice to make mimosas.

"I had a cold," Logan protested, holding a chair out for me.

I sat.

"It was a series of roars." Ted held out a chair for Doreen, but she ignored him and took the place next to me, leaving Logan to sit across from me, where we couldn't signal with a hand-squeeze.

"There could be an actual lion in the room eating me," I said, slipping off my shoe under the table. "I wouldn't wake up."

"There are six places," Logan said. "Who's missing?"

"Lyric's still sleeping," Ted said, sitting at the head of the table as his coffee was poured.

I straightened my knee until my toes reached Logan's foot, intending to signal that way.

"Dante's actually going to spend five minutes with us," Doreen said. "Matt woke up with a fever, so Liam took him to the doctor. Byron and Olivia are eating in their room. Colton's—there you are!"

Colton Crowne threw himself into an empty chair, wearing low-crotch sweatpants and a ribbed tank, ass on the end of the seat and legs sprawling under the table. His beard was unkempt and his hair was hidden under a backward black cap. He bounced and tapped as if his mind was a nightclub.

"It's so good to have you back," Doreen said. "If we hadn't just thrown a party, I would have thrown one for you."

Trays of eggs, potatoes, and bacon were brought around.

"Nah," he said. "I've done enough parties. And Byron and this guy getting married is the shit you throw parties for."

"Watch your mouth," Ted grumbled. "There are ladies present."

"Right. Sorry, Ma." He looked at me with eyes that were a lighter blue than his brothers'. "Sorry, Mrs. Crowne."

He was half joking. Maybe all the way joking. I didn't know him well enough to judge.

"You can call her Ella," Logan said.

"They'll make you an omelette if you want," Doreen whispered to me.

"This is perfect," I said, accepting a second scoop of eggs. "I'm starving."

A woman put a latte at my place.

"Oh, thank you."

"It's vanilla," Logan added.

The woman nodded and disappeared.

"So," Doreen said, "Logan hasn't had a chance to tell us anything about you. Your father was Basile Papillion?"

"Yes."

"He made a dress for me for the Met Gala that was… I couldn't believe how beautiful."

"Stunning," Ted said before eating a potato.

"I still have it. I was so sorry to hear of his passing. We lost a great talent." She put a shaky hand over mine and squeezed it, looking at me with clear blue eyes that were windows to her heart. Whatever Doreen thought of me or my marriage to her son, her words about my father were sincere.

"Thank you," I said. "He was a great man."

"Talking about me again?" Dante Crowne blew in, perfectly put together and taking up more space than even his six-foot four frame should have.

"Hardly," Logan said.

Dante stood beside me. "You must be the new Crowne in town." He reached out for a handshake, but when I returned the gesture, he kissed the top of my hand.

I decided not to correct the name. Not again today.

Dante took Doreen's seat at the foot of the table. "Colton." He snapped open his napkin and laid it on his lap. "You're back."

"Don't look so happy."

"Run out of money?" Dante asked, turning down the food he was offered.

"Dante," Ted growled.

I glanced at Logan. His jaw was set and his expression demanded my silence, even without his shoe pressing on my foot.

"Ella," Doreen said with an elbow on each side of her plate and her fingers laced together, "tell us. When did you two decide to get married?"

"All unbeknownst," Dante added casually.

"Um," I started, catching Logan's gaze to make sure the story was the same. "About a minute after we met again."

To give myself time to think, I shoveled a huge forkful of egg and potato in my mouth,and chewed fully before continuing.

"It was just obvious, you know," I said. Logan nodded slightly. I was fine. Fine. I just had to hew to the truth. "Then yesterday he walked right into my office and asked me to marry him."

"I couldn't wait another minute," Logan added.

"And we were talking about dates, and I said, 'why not now?' and he said—"

"I said, 'I thought you'd never ask,'" Logan finished, winking at me across the table.

"Yeah, and so we did. And here we are."

"How romantic," Doreen said. "I wish I could have seen it."

"It felt just… right." I took another forkful of eggs.

"Well," Doreen said, "we have to have another party."

"That's not necessary," Logan protested.

"Better him than me," Colton said.

"Why not? Afraid you might enjoy yourself?" Dante turned to me. "I hope you're teaching him how to have a good time."

"Not your kind of good time," Logan shot back with a subtext I didn't understand, but I would have known if we'd been together four months.

I looked at my plate so I could pretend I knew exactly what he was talking about.

"He taking you somewhere?" Colton asked me. "Or's he being all efficient? Like a work trip on an oil rig off the coast of Greenland or some sh—" He cut himself off mid-curse.

"That sounds fun actually." I scraped the last of the food on my plate.

"Ella's got her father's talent," Logan said. "And a sexy work ethic."

Colton pointed his fork at each of us. "You're the same kinda crazy."

"Now I see it." Ted laughed, taking his wife's hand on the table. "Can't you, honey?"

They looked at each other deeply, as if having a conversation without speaking.

Logan swallowed hard, then drank his coffee as if he wanted to hide behind the cup.

In the moments that passed, Doreen didn't answer.

Dante broke the tension with a question. "I hear you're working for your father's label?"

"Since I was a kid." I glanced at Logan, and he met my eyes with anticipation.

Eventually, I would have to tell this story. Better I do it in front of my husband than where he couldn't hear it. "Until this morning actually. My stepmother…" Insulting her wouldn't look good, even if she deserved it. "She and I had a falling out. My fault actually. Anyway, we thought it would be better if I moved on."

"Your own thing, yeah?" Colton suggested.

"Maybe? I don't know. I think…" Could I even say it out loud?

"Ella can do whatever she wants." Logan's foot rested on mine.

"I'm going to spend a while just being with my husband. You know, making sure he has everything he needs full time."

Logan nodded slightly, and I smiled at him in victory from the top of the mountain of things I'd never, ever wanted for myself.

Doreen—the one we were trying to persuade—let out a short scoff.

"That sounds exhausting," she said, smiling at Ted.

"My wife needs to rest after last night," Ted said. "I think a week in Cambria will do us some good." He winked. They laughed together as if sharing a private joke.

"What's in Cambria?" I asked.

"Ted wanted to get away from the rat race," Doreen said. "The boys were all grown. Lyric was in college. So we bought this house up there and it's just lovely. Deep in this wooded area. Miles from the nearest road. You can hear the ocean and see it even, from the top of the hill."

After taking a sip of mimosa, Ted said, "When Lyric moved out, right about then I had my first midlife crisis."

"Your first?" Logan asked. "I didn't even know you had one."

"I was sick of everything. What was the point of the rat race any more? I wanted to get away—and I mean *away*. Your mother went along with it and we bought this house way out in Cambria. Totally off the grid. No internet. No phone. It's one-hundred-percent solar."

"Remember the time the water tank was empty?" Doreen giggled.

"Your showers were too long."

"We lasted two weeks." Doreen put her trembling hand on my arm. "And I said, 'Enough.' I needed to talk to *someone*."

"That was when we compromised and got our place in Santa Barbara." Ted pointed his fork at me. "You should go up to Crownestead sometime."

"Not Cambria?" I asked. "Sounds kind of cool."

"Dante's the only one who can last in the Cambria house longer than a week." Logan said.

"I don't need to natter all day and night like you," Dante said.

"A toast." Ted held up his mimosa. "To my son and my new daughter-in-law." Everyone raised a glass, and Ted directed his attention to Logan. "I always told you that when you met the one, you'd know right away." He tilted his juice in my direction. "Welcome to the family, Ella Papillion."

The Crowne family toasted with juice and mimosas.

"Ella," Doreen said, putting her cloth napkin next to her plate, "I want to show you something."

I glanced at Logan for direction. Concern sat on his face like a rigid mask.

"About what?" he asked with a much too defensive snap.

"Don't you have business to mind?" Doreen said, standing. Everyone followed her lead.

"Ella is my business." He put his arm around me and kissed my head. "You can have her later. I planned to take her bowling after breakfast."

"Bowling?" I asked.

"There's a full-sized alley downstairs," he said.

"And it'll be there later." Doreen took my hand and tugged.

I had a choice. Going with Doreen was risky because without Logan present, I could say the wrong thing. But if I didn't go with his mother, she'd think I didn't want to be part of the family.

The first option was safer, but we had more to gain if I looked committed to not just him, but his life.

"I'll cream you after lunch," I said, letting go of Logan. "Go do some work or something."

I kissed him quickly and let Doreen loop her arm around mine to lead me out of the room.

———

My mother-in-law made a wrong turn somewhere, and we laughed at how easy it was to get lost.

"You need a map," I joked.

"Byron did one," she replied.

"A literal map?"

"He printed it for guests. Full color. He labeled mine by hand with some special object so I'd always know where I was. Red Velvet Pillows. Glass Floor Lamp. Blue Mondrian. Dad's Persian—for the carpet his father bought in Morocco. But of course I always forget to carry it around. Especially when Ted's with me. Ah, here we are."

She pushed through a set of wooden double doors that opened into a massive suite that was a building all its own. The center space went up two stories to the glass ceiling. The two levels between were rimmed with terraces.

Every inch of wall space was taken up with books.

The stark whites and clear glass weren't a match for the thousands of spines, but obviously the residents didn't care.

"Wow," was all I could say.

Doreen waved away my awe. "We're trying to cozy it up a bit. It's not really who I am… all this. But it'll do. Come."

I followed her through another double door, into a massive closet. She turned on the light even though it had windows high above eye level, and turned a corner, into a deeper section with rows of shoes.

"You need a map for the closet," I said.

She laughed. "And I told my husband, how many things can I wear at once?"

The end of the road was a door with a keypad and humidity-control gauge next to it. She entered the code and it beeped, opening with a hiss.

She flicked on the light. The space was bigger than it should have been for a closet-within-a-closet. Three full mannequins lined the room, each wearing an exquisite gown.

"Holy—" I stopped myself.

"Shit?" Doreen said, finishing my sentence.

"This is a Jeremy St. James," I said, eyes wide before a wedding gown with two-inch wide seams that curved around the body, undulating with the form under it. The seams were impossibly perfect and flattering.

"I don't think I could fit into it now," she said. "Six children will do that."

"And this?" I pointed at a column gown that looked simple but wasn't. "Barry Tilden?"

"It stands up on its own. Wore it to two presidential inaugurations." She sighed, touching the sleeve. "By the time I wore it for the second one, I wanted to burn it."

"Did you not like the president?"

She laughed. "Nothing like that. It was…" She tilted her head. "Ted and I were having a hard time. The children, I always wanted a full house, and they were my life, but it was hard. I had all the help a mother could want, and I still felt… well, I was angry with him. He had a life. A purpose outside the house. We were just one more thing he had to do and..." She shook her head. "I already said I was angry. But I chose that life, so I couldn't complain, right? I knew how Teddy was and I married him anyway."

I knew what she was getting at.

She was a smart woman.

"Logan's like him," I said.

"He is."

"How did you stop being angry?"

"I had a secret."

I wanted to cover my ears and shout *la-la-la-la*. If she was sleeping with the pool boy or snorting meth, I didn't want to know.

"When did you wear this one?" I changed the subject, but she didn't take the bait.

"I have a Master's in literature. Poetry was my first love," she said. "But I never presumed to have any talent. I started writing poetry and submitting to journals under a pen name. I did it out of spite. To just claim something, anything for myself. And you know what?"

"He found out?"

"After two years of submissions, one was published. I. Just. Exploded. All that anger... it came through my pores. Ted came home after dark and I threw the letter and the seventeen-dollar check across the counter and said"—she waved her arm with a flourish—"'You don't own me, Theodore Crowne!'"

Even though I knew the ending, the drama held me. "What did he say?"

"Well, he picked up the letter." She pantomimed her husband by looking at her palm. "Then the check." She switched to her other hand. "And he said, 'How long have you been doing this behind my back, Doreen?'"

I gasped. "He did not."

"He did. And I told him that I had to because *he'd* turned his back on *me*."

"Good answer."

"And he put the check down, then read the letter again. Carefully. And he said, 'According to this, you're a breath of fresh air. Warm. Authentic. An original voice speaking universal truth.' And I said, 'I read it, Ted.' And he puts the letter down, and says, 'I thought the woman I married was gone, but she's not. A bunch of strangers see her. And I—'" Her voice cracked. "'I miss her.'"

"Oh my God," I said, putting my hand to my chest. "That's... amazing."

My feelings deserved a better word, but I had nothing less generic to offer.

"Cry for the work we had to do afterward. Marriage isn't easy."

I was sure she was right, but Logan and I wouldn't get to the "not easy" stage. "Did you keep writing poetry?"

"To this day." She put her hand on my arm and led me to the last mannequin on the right. "This one is my favorite. Do you recognize it?"

Though the lines were familiar, I'd never seen anything like that gown before. It had a simple strapless bodice, and a floor-length skirt that flared gently below the waist and outward to the floor. What made it exceptional were the tightly-packed butterfly wings sewn into the entire thing. They were so carefully hand-painted, they looked as though they'd take off.

"Is it my father's?"

"It is." She must have seen my hands twitch. "You can touch it."

Gently, I raised one of the wings to see the stitching that held it in place. The single stich was so delicate, I was amazed it was enough to hold the butterfly in place. My father had worked magic.

"I wore it for my tenth wedding anniversary party."

"It's gorgeous." I peeked under the top edge to admire the way it was finished.

"It is."

"Thank you for showing it to me," I said as if I was done

looking at it, but I could have inspected Basile Papillion's genius for hours.

Doreen went behind the mannequin and unfastened the back to reveal the deep pink lining and a label inside, next to the one that said Papillion, where custom gowns were tagged with the owner's name.

NORA WARREN

"My husband's idea, putting my pen name there. He calls it my true identity. Our secret." She closed the back. "Now it's yours too. And I want you to remember it when being a Crowne feels like all you are."

"I—" I stopped in the middle of saying something irrelevant. I wasn't taking Logan's name, but her point wasn't about what I let the world call me. It was about what I called myself.

Why was she telling me this at all?

Doreen Crowne couldn't care about me. She didn't even know me. She didn't have to trust me with anything, and the truth was, she shouldn't trust me as far as she could throw me. I was an interloper. A liar in their midst. Any reasonable woman would have barely acknowledged me. But Doreen wasn't reasonable. She loved her son recklessly enough to trust his judgment over her own instincts.

Her love was directed at Logan, but I got to warm myself by a heat I hadn't felt since the day my mother died.

"Thank you," I said. "I'm honored to keep your secret."

"Good," she said, heading for the door. "I'd better get you back before Logan starts wondering if I got you lost."

I guided us back to the center of the house without making a wrong turn. The instinctual part of my brain was free to work navigational magic while the rest of my mind tried to figure out a way to earn her confidence in me.

Logan stood with his father at the edge of the overlook, hair turned angular in the wind. When he saw us, he waved. Ted came to us with arms outstretched for his wife as if she'd returned from a long journey.

Logan put his hand on my back and watched his parents, his face relaxed and receptive in the bright sun. Nothing was hidden. Not his admiration or his love. I got it, just then. I understood what he wanted from a marriage and why I wasn't the one to provide it.

Ted and Doreen's children had been loved consistently and strongly their entire lives. No interruptions, no hard stops. They'd never had cause to question it.

Did I envy him his parents? Did a little rage bubble up when I thought of how mine were gone before they'd finished raising me?

Yes to both. But his mother's acceptance had taken all the heat out of it.

Logan and I would divorce, but I would make sure that the intervening year was as painless for Doreen Crowne as possible.

I'd do that by making her son happy.

17

LOGAN

THERE HAD BEEN a time when I spoke to my father freely, without worrying about a slip of the tongue or hurtful revelation. I realized, after my mother took my wife away and Dad guided me outside to look over the view, that those days were over.

"You should consider getting a Cambria," Dad said. "Good for the soul. You and Ella."

"I have everything I need."

"And a lot of things you don't."

I shrugged, letting my hands drape over the railing. The concrete slab jutted over the precipice of the canyon, adding a few degrees of unfettered view.

"What I'm trying to say is," Dad said, "you're giving up a lot for a business that's only going to disappoint you. There aren't any solutions. But getting deeper in—sacrificing your life to it—will get you into the same crises I did. And they're not so easy to solve."

"Ah. I get it now." I looked out over the ravine.

"I'm not calling you a liar," Dad said. "Or Ella. But I need you to know there's more to life."

"It's sudden. The marriage. I know. And... current circumstances being what they are, I understand your suspicion."

"We hadn't met her."

"There wasn't ever a right time, and then we just did it."

He nodded, looking out over the morning. I could reassure him endlessly about the business, but I knew my father. He wasn't concerned about who ran Crowne. He was concerned with my happiness and my character.

"She's really great, Dad," I said. "She's talented, and independent, and a little unpredictable."

All true. Not what I was looking for in a wife, but all very real and very charming.

"She seems lovely. I don't doubt that."

"What do you doubt?"

He laughed to himself. "Everything but you."

The one thing he should have doubted was me.

"Thanks, Dad."

"Listen. I'm going to go back on my word. I need you to stay partnered with Byron for a while."

"I was going to say..."

Did I want to fail?

No. I didn't. I wanted to run Crowne as much as ever, but I didn't want to tear up the world doing it. I'd rushed the marriage. Now I'd take my time convincing my parents I was happy.

"I was going to say," I restarted, "that we should keep him on. I want a little time left over in the day for Ella."

"Good man." Dad put his hand on my biceps and gave me a confident squeeze, then looked over my shoulder at the house. "They're back."

———

As I drove Ella to her illegally occupied warehouse on Highland, we went over everything that had been said that morning, making sure we were creating a solid story. We were partners in a game, swaddled in secrets, weaving a comfortable intimacy between us, until she got to the part about the closet and a dress her father had made.

"And the rest, I can't tell you," she said.

"What do you mean?" I asked, making a turn onto Sunset. "How are we supposed to coordinate?"

"As far as you're concerned, she showed me a dress my father made, but the rest? Never. She swore me to secrecy."

"I don't approve."

She laughed as if I'd nailed the punchline of a long joke.

I turned down a side alley and parked the BMW next to her dark blue El Camino. In the daylight, I could see the cracks in the paint and the rust spots on the chrome.

"I'm getting you a new car," I said, getting out before she could argue. I went around to open her door, but she was already out and jingling her keys. "What kind do you want?"

She opened the steel door. "I don't know."

We entered her studio. She grabbed a box from a pile, tossed it to me, and grabbed another. She led me to the other side of the building and her bedroom.

"What do you like then?"

"I don't know." She opened the dresser and plucked through her underwear, flinging things into the box.

"How do you not know?"

The tangle of lace and cotton piled up in the box. Bra cups, balls of socks, and a single, surprising black stocking over the side. I picked it up, bridging its length between my palms. Soft. Worn at the heel. A little lace top with a little silicone to keep it on the thigh.

"I don't know what I'll want after this is over," she said, opening another drawer. "I guess I'll have to run my father's business."

"But what do you want *now*?"

142

Picking through, she left the ripped jeans in the drawer and tossed two nicer pairs into the box.

"Now?" She looked at the space, the paintings on the walls, the drafting table, and the unmade full-size bed. "I want Bianca out of that office and I want to be a good wife."

"I meant car."

Ella pulled the stocking away slowly, making it slide over my palms. "I don't want a car. I want to get through this and I want it to be clean at the end." She dropped the stocking into the box. "We'll have separate rooms, right?"

She could refuse to have sex with me any time, for any reason. But I had an instinctual resistance to ceding control.

"If you want," I said.

"I need that."

One year, separate rooms. Functionally separate lives. A box full of sexy things I wanted to see her in before I shredded each one. Why was she packing it if she wasn't going to wear it?

"If you're not fucking me, Ella, you're not fucking anyone."

"That goes both ways."

I ran my fingers under my nose. Her scent was already gone, but the memory of getting inside her lingered. One year of hard-ons. Great. This was going to be tougher than I'd thought. As if reading my mind, she tossed a handful of underwear in the box and put her hands on her hips.

"Do you want to get caught cheating on your wife?" She threw open a purple-painted armoire and picked some hangers from the pole. "How's that gonna go down in Crowne Town?"

The rhyme made me smile, as did the fact that she was right. I was a grown man, and cheating was an unnecessary risk for me.

"No other women," I said, looking her over. The warehouse's draft had hardened her nipples enough to dent the T-shirt through her bra. I hadn't spent enough time with her tits. Hadn't discovered the limits of what she liked.

"Deal." She turned to flick through the hangers in the closet.

It was a crime to not fuck her, but I didn't have much of a choice.

———

HOURS LATER, her El Camino pulled into the driveway of my house in Hancock Park, next to my black BMW. The boxes and duffel bags of clothes she'd brought took up only a corner of the rear bed.

She yanked out a duffel, and I grabbed it before she had to bear the full burden. I slung the bag over one shoulder. She took a box by the flap, ripping it.

"I have people to help with that."

"I got it." She gathered the box in her arms. It was full of hardcovers.

Putting my free arm under the weight, I lifted it. "One less trip."

She let me have the box and took another.

My place was modest by Crowne standards, but the way she stopped and looked around made me aware of how big it was. How high the ceilings. How pristine and professionally designed.

"Did I get lost the first time I came here?" she asked.

"The next morning—after our first date. You wound up coming into the kitchen through the backyard." I dropped the duffel at the foot of the stairs and slid the box onto a table. "Give me that." I took her box and put it on top of mine. "You have choices to make."

"Do I?" A flirtation flicked across her lips and quickly straightened as if she'd gotten control of it.

"We're not sleeping in the same room."

"Yeah." She tried to get control of a smile, but wound up biting her lips.

"So, my bride, let me show you option one." I led her through the foyer, then the kitchen, and out to my backyard.

Eight-foot hedges surrounded the space, with a grass patch between the patio and pool, a built-in barbecue and wet bar, and at the rear edge of the property, a two-bedroom guesthouse.

"You can use a code or a key," I said, punching in my numbers to open the front door. I let her in first. "It's got furniture already, but you can replace it if you want."

She didn't hesitate to look around the kitchen, peek past the shower curtains, open closets, or sit on the bed. She bounced on it and ran her hand over the texture of the duvet. How long would it take for me to not think of fucking her whenever she sat on a bed?

"Do you ever have guests stay here?" She leaned back.

"Friends from college, when they're in town. Spillover family, but now that we have Crownquarters, they'll stay there."

I sat next to her as if I was at the end of a semester on Not Touching Ella 101 and this was the final. Multiple choice.

You're sitting next to Ella on a bed. She's half reclined. The afternoon light makes her skin glow and reflects in the irises of her brown eyes, making them sparkle with what could be either adventure or danger.

Do you:

A – Put your hand on her knee

B – Kiss her without warning

C – Say something suggestive and gauge her reaction

D – Keep your mouth clean and your hands to yourself

"It's nice," she said, then sprang up as if it were her final too, and she chose D. "I like the kitchen." She left for the center room and I followed. She stayed on the other side of the island, talking fast. "The warehouse is a commercial space, so I'm not allowed to have a stove, so this would be really cool."

"Good, so—"

"What's through this door?"

I opened it and swept my hand in her direction. "After you."

She went into the unfinished three-car garage with its high wood-beamed ceiling and clean white walls. The floor was new concrete, and the lighting was soft and indirect.

"Wow," she said, pleasing me more deeply than I expected.

"You can use this for a studio," I said.

Her attention snapped from the ceiling to me. "For?"

"Whatever you want. Clothes. Art."

"The Collective is finished for me. I'm out."

"What about your own thing?"

She sucked in her cheeks and crossed her arms. Somehow, I'd stepped in a pile of shit I should have smelled a mile away.

"I have a studio."

"In a condemned building you have no lease for."

"It'll be there longer than this marriage."

"If it doesn't fall on your head first."

We regarded each other across the space I'd built a year ago for no purpose whatsoever, and wanted for her as if I'd known she was coming all that time.

"What's option two?" she asked.

"The main house." Instead of going back the way we came, I unlatched the barn door and swung it out, hoping the way the light streamed into the space might sell it. "This way."

Hands in the front pockets of her ripped jeans, she followed me, taking one last look back at the open garage.

"Was it always supposed to be an artist's studio?" she asked.

"I had no plans for it. Or maybe I subconsciously knew you were coming."

We entered the house through the kitchen entrance. If she thought the guest kitchen was nice, she made no indication that the main one was any better at three times the size.

We climbed the stairs, where four doors stood around a main hall. Ella's eye caught a drawing I'd bought at auction.

"Christo," she said, reminding me of the artist's name. "You have good taste."

"Coming from you."

"Coming from me, what?"

"It means a lot." I stepped toward her. Not close enough to

touch, but my body didn't want hers standing in an opposite corner.

"Don't let it go to your head." She came another step closer. Still not near enough to reach. "So, where's your room?"

"The double doors." I tilted my head toward the master suite.

"And where's mine?"

"Behind you."

She spun around and pushed her way in, standing at the foot of the bed with her hands on her hips. The walls were drenched with light from the glass doors that led to a balcony. All things considered, she was just as fuckable here as the guesthouse.

"What do you think?" she asked, then looked at me. "Which one?"

"Well." I crossed my arms and rocked on the balls of my feet. "We're not fucking. But this room connects, and if you're here? Late at night, I might need more distance between us."

The mischief flashed again and disappeared just as quickly. "Just you? Why am I the willpower in this arrangement?"

"Do you want to test mine?"

With a flick of her eyebrows, I knew that for a moment, she did. But she went to the window and pushed the curtains open a couple of inches. The backyard, the pool, and the guesthouse were below us. Was she doing what I was? Calculating the distance between us? How many steps. How many nights.

"But if family visits?" she asked. "What's our story going to be?"

"You're using the studio. They can get a hotel."

"You want me out there then?"

When did I cross the room to stand over her, looking out the window to where we were imagining her sleeping?

My body wasn't my own when she was near. My mind hadn't been in control since day one. Staying away from her would be that much harder on day one hundred, and impossible on day three hundred.

"It's safer," I said, putting my hand on her shoulder as if I needed to do that to transmit my earnestness.

As if I was being honest with myself.

Earnestness barely made a blip on my radar.

I needed to touch her to soothe an ache that the contact only made sharper.

"Okay, Logan. You win." She nodded and let the curtain drop, looking up at me with warm amber eyes, close enough for me to see the renegade dot on the left one. "We play it safe."

Reluctantly, I let my hand fall from her shoulder. "Good. I think that'll make it easy in the end."

"Yeah."

I was about to suggest we pull the car all the way back so we could move her stuff into the guesthouse. Then maybe dinner. Lock down more of our story. Review a schedule of events I had coming up.

But the doorbell rang.

18

ELLA

WHEN HIS HAND SLID AWAY, my shoulder went cold. I wanted him to touch me again, fold me in his arms, tell me how I wasn't losing my life and everything I worked for, but gaining space to start fresh.

But it would have turned into more than that. The night before, an overwhelming passion had landed us on the hood of a car. It was still there, crackling between us.

The guesthouse was the right choice. Once I moved my stuff in there, it would be easier. Day by day, we'd cool off.

Then the doorbell rang.

"Are you expecting anyone?" I asked.

His house was open to the street. Any Jehovah's Witness or political campaigner could ring the bell.

"No." He took out his phone and checked the doorbell camera. "Shit."

I peered at the glass and recognized the man in the backward baseball cap, bouncing as if the cars passing thrummed a baseline and the birds tweeted EDM.

"Well," I said, "are you going to leave him standing there?"

———

"I'm, like, real sorry, man. It's just for temps, until I save some cash for a place." Colton had both feet on the floor and half an ass on a kitchen stool, rocking it back and forth on the edges of the legs.

Logan's face was tense, waiting for Colton to crash onto the tiles. If Colton stayed too long, he was going to take years off my husband's life.

"How much cash?" Logan asked, pulling a bottle of wine from the glass-doored cooler in the center of the refrigerator.

"Nah, nah. Dad said no handouts from you guys."

"Oh, did you think I was going to offer you money? I was asking about time."

"Give me, you know... a month or two. I figured I'd house-sit while you're on your honeymoon."

"Honeymoon's on hold until next year," Logan said.

I was about to ask Logan which glasses to use, but as the lady of the house, I could get whatever I wanted. I pulled down three wine glasses and made eye contact with Logan, who nodded as he drove the corkscrew.

"Cool, cool. I'll stay out of the way. I'm not trying to witness all your"—Colton waved his hand from me to Logan—"newlywed shit."

"Not our kink," Logan replied before yanking the cork with a *pop*.

"Did he just, like, make a joke?" Colton asked me.

"You didn't laugh."

"Still." He pushed one glass toward Logan. "Fill 'er up, brah."

———

LOGAN STOOD behind me at my bedroom window, looking at the guesthouse. Colton had all the doors open and the lights on, walking around the pool with the phone to his ear. We'd unloaded his car into the back and taken my things upstairs.

"Well, good thing I kept my studio."

"Good thing." When he spoke, I felt his breath on the back of my neck.

"How long do you think he'll be around?"

In the window's reflection, Logan shook his head, watching Colton kick off his shoes and sit at the edge of the pool to splash his feet.

"We're in virgin territory here." He touched the base of my neck, and the skin under his fingers came alive with such force, I had to close my eyes. "You're going to have to wife it up when he's around."

There was no telling how often that would be, but I'd made a promise, and I was going to keep it. "Slippers and a martini waiting for you when you get home."

"That doesn't sound so bad."

"I'm going to be the best wife ever," I said, turning. "But we're locking that door. The one between our rooms."

"I have all the keys."

"You won't use them." I laid my hand on his chest and gently pushed him away. "Not if I don't want you to."

He smirked. "I know what you want." He took my hand off his chest and kissed it, then let go. "I'll see you in the morning."

Downstairs, Colton laughed.

PART II

SIX MONTHS LATER

19

ELLA

I'D GOTTEN my husband a pair of slippers for his birthday. It was a joke only Logan and his mother laughed at, and when I'd set them at the door the first time, we laughed again before he went to a dinner meeting.

Byron was still in the picture. Logan had fulfilled his part of the deal by getting married, so he was in charge. Finally at the head of the table with Ted in an advisory role. But his wedding had happened so quickly and unconvincingly, his brother hung around so that Logan was able to "enjoy his marriage."

Logan was doing his job. My job was to spend a year being perfect.

I filled six months' worth of days with Logan's life, his plans, his demands. He doled out his companionship in teaspoons, still working every hour, and I was the perfect wife for a guy who was never around. My art was a "hobby," and my friends were available for lunch. Papillion survived without me, as did Bianca, who called on holidays.

Life was perfect and fine, and I was bored to tears, unfulfilled, uncomfortable, and invisible.

I was a landmine he brought closer to detonation every time

we were in public. He brushed my skin with the backs of his fingers, kissed me for show, held my hand, and gently stroked the back of my neck. Sometimes, even when we were alone, he moved a lock of hair out of my eyes or put his arm around me.

At Doreen's birthday dinner, he'd kissed my neck and I'd shuddered so hard I had to close my eyes.

I thought it would get easier. I'd get bored of his touch, his little affections, but it had gotten worse by the halfway mark. Without a job outside our marriage, I could barely distract myself from the thought of him and the memory of the way he'd moved when he was inside me. My body was basted together and the stitches were slipping. I was going to explode before this was over.

Every morning, we met in the kitchen. As usual, Logan was already showered, shaved, and wearing his work clothes when I came down. I didn't know when he actually slept. If he snored, I never heard it through the door, but then again, I slept like a dead thing.

"You're up early," he said. "Coffee?"

My morning drink changed from day to day. He knew to wait before pouring mine, and I knew he wanted to get it right.

"Black, two sugars."

He handed me my cup, properly sweetened and lava hot. "Sleep well?"

"Yeah, what time did you get in?" The *Wall Street Journal* was open to the stock ticker. I scanned down to the PPON.

"Late."

"Papillion's down," I said.

"Not enough."

That was his excuse every time. He was going to wait until Bianca drove it into the ground with her shitty T-shirts.

"What are you doing today?" he asked as if it was ever anything interesting.

"Lunch with Mandy at Scopes."

"Say hi for me." He stood at the island, hands circling his cup as if he could crush it.

He had something to say. I knew him at least that well.

"What?" I said. "Say it."

"The Malones are going to be in town."

Mike and Twyla Malone owned a swath of land in Tennessee that the Crownes wanted to lay pipeline through. They were in a constant state of almost-but-not-quite making a deal. The last time we'd seen Mike Malone at a business event, he'd gotten drunk and—when Logan's back was turned—suggested I looked sexually frustrated. He offered to help me out with that. He was right about my dissatisfaction, but that was beside the point.

I hadn't told my fake husband about it until the next day. It had taken all morning to convince him not to burn down the Malones' house.

"You said Malones plural," I said. "Twyla too?"

"Yes."

"So you need me to do a thing?"

"Dinner. You don't have to."

"I'll go. Just don't leave me alone with Mike."

"Like hell," he snarled before changing the subject. "I was going to have Selma Quintero join us."

I almost spit my coffee.

"I take that as a yes?" he asked.

"Why would you do that?"

"She's an art dealer. You're an artist. What's the problem?"

"I'm not ready."

"It's dinner."

"What the fuck, Logan? What if she wants a studio visit? I have nothing! I'm absolute shit!"

He took me by the shoulders and bent down to look me in the eye. His face was strength, confidence, the pure willpower to spend six months behind a locked door knowing he had the key.

"You're Ella Papillion, and it's just dinner. We have six months to make you all the connections we can before we break up."

"Before you what?" Colton's voice came from the back doorway. The fucker was like a cat.

Logan let go of me.

"Aren't you supposed to be wearing the cowbell we got you?" he asked.

"Dude." Colton swirled the coffee around the pot. "This coffee or mud?"

"You have a kitchen."

Colton had lasted two months before begging for a job. Ted and Logan put him in the mailroom. I'd warned Logan it didn't pay enough to get his brother out of our guesthouse. Not with rent in Los Angeles being what it was. He replied with typical rich-person ignorance. How could that be true when the current staff had places to live?

He wouldn't budge. Neither did Colton. Six months after showing up, Colton was still in the back house, but now instead of sleeping late, he'd been coming into the front house in the morning to go to Crowne with his brother.

I enjoyed Colton, but Logan worked eighty hours a week, and morning coffee was the only time I knew I'd see him, and Colton's presence during that time of day added a level of complexity. Logan and I couldn't exist as we were normally. We couldn't just be friends fighting sexual tension. In front of his brother, we had to playact at being married. More touching. More kissing. More reminders I was living with a man who had agreed to never love me.

"I gotta get going." Logan drained his coffee.

"Me too," Colton added.

"Take your own car," Logan said. He put his hand on the back of my neck and looked me in the eye for only a moment.

Fuck Colton and his new morning routine. I was trapped in Logan's gaze because of him. He was saying he was sorry he had to do this, but not sorry. Not sorry at all to grip the hair in the back of my head and pull me close. Or kiss me tenderly with lips that lingered. He was so sorry this was harder than it had to be, and not sorry one single bit.

"I'll see you tonight?" Logan whispered, still close enough to kiss me again.

The question was for Colton's benefit. He wouldn't get home in time to see me.

"Sure."

He kissed the pierced side of my nose.

Colton slurped his coffee like a filling toilet tank.

20

LOGAN

EVERY MORNING COLTON was in our kitchen, I kissed her goodbye.

Every evening event, every gala, every birthday and family dinner, I showed her the affection of a loving husband.

Every day I did the same thing with her I did with every woman I'd ever been with—I went through the motions. Except with her, it was different.

Every day it got harder to lie to myself about why I was touching her. When we were alone together, I reached for her and pulled back. Unless I didn't. Sometimes what I wanted wasn't aligned with my body's interests, and I touched her in spaces where no one needed to be convinced.

The last time had been only a week before. Morning coffee. She had black ink on her fingertips like a Victorian-era poet. I reached for her hand without thinking and stroked her palm open to see the faded gray splotches.

"What's this?" I'd asked.

She'd shuddered, then jerked her hand away. "Nothing. Ink. I'm working on a thing. It's terrible."

Six more months, give or take. In the corner of my computer screen, I kept a countdown of the days until we filed for divorce.

Ostensibly, in the front of my mind, it was a countdown of the days I had to buy up Papillion stock. But the 174 days were the interval before she wouldn't be a temptation. I wouldn't have to stay in the office to avoid a constant hard-on. Every time I walked in my house, I wouldn't feel the rush of her heady jasmine scent.

She'd be relieved. She didn't want me touching her anyway. Once we were done, she'd have her dead father's fucking company and the job of running it.

I checked the stock ticker.

Maybe it was time to tell my broker to start buying.

Byron rapped on my open door. "You in?"

"Yeah. What's up?"

Byron dropped onto the couch on the other side of the room, propping his feet on the table. He never sat in the chair on the other side of my desk. That would imply he was in an inferior position and Byron was never, ever the subordinate.

I sat in one of the chairs across from him.

"So," he said. "You seem happy being a married guy."

"Yeah. And?"

"Deal was, you'd be in charge and I'd back off."

"I am in charge."

"What you don't know is, Dad asked me to stay on."

I wasn't surprised at the deception "for my own good" or the fact that Byron was telling me. The circumstances of the marriage weren't ideal. I had time to make them so.

"Mom loves Ella. He'll come around."

"But no tingle still."

"Don't get me started on that shit."

"I know, I know." He took his feet off the table and crossed his legs, putting his arm over the back of the couch so he could take up more room. "We're gonna close this pipeline deal soon."

"You're an optimist."

"I'm an opportunist. We bought a lot of land to lay that pipe on, and some of it is very, very viable for other uses."

"Such as?"

"Residential."

Jesus, he was going to throw risk on top of risk because he had nothing else to do.

"Hear me out," he said, reading my mind as only a brother could. "This is going to be the safest pipeline ever built. It could leak in ten places, shit, it could crack in half and not a single butterfly would die. It's safe to live right on top of it, so why not?"

"What's Olivia say?"

She was an environmental attorney and wasn't the type to pull punches.

"She agrees."

"And Dad?"

"I came to you first."

That had never happened before. Byron liked to come to me with our father already sold, which meant I had to work twice as hard to unsell him. The only reason he'd switch it up would be because he didn't think he could get Dad to say yes.

"Why?"

"Because..." He uncrossed his legs and leaned forward, rubbing his hands together between his knees. A real Ted Crowne gesture. "I want to build shit, not move numbers around. And Dad's the same as you. Doesn't like risk, and building's a risky business. So I propose this." He rubbed his hands faster, then stopped. "I lease the land from Crowne under my own corp. Release you from liability. Build shit."

"That's not going to work if you're an officer."

"I'll back off the pipeline." He sat back again. "There's plenty else to do around here."

Byron was a live-in nemesis and a shrewd businessman who bent the truth whenever it suited his goals. He couldn't actually think this was going to fly with our father, even if I advocated for it. He would have to choose between this scheme and running the business with me.

"What are you thinking?" he asked. "I can smell brain cells burning."

"Trying to work out your angle."

"My angle's personal. Olivia's sick of me frowning. I'm a lot more use to her and Garrett if I'm doing something I love."

Olivia was a wise woman and he was smart to listen to her. They knew each other well. They could nudge each other toward happiness. Encourage decisions for the good of the family.

What was good for Ella and me?

It didn't matter. First and foremost, I had to get rid of Byron. Getting behind this meant he'd have to go. Once he was out, I could do for Ella what he was doing for Olivia. Make her happy. Give her what she wanted.

"All right," I said, standing. "Let's talk risk."

I went through the motions of hashing out the details, but I was phoning it in. The puzzle I was really solving was how to nudge Ella toward happiness.

———

MALIBU WAS a wreck of traffic at lunch. Supposedly, it was impossible to get a table at Scopes, but I'd never had a problem. The parking lot of the trendy Asian fusion place was full, but the valet guy promised to find a safe spot for the Merc.

I looked for Ella and Mandy at the communal tables, but found them sitting at one of the few separated from the crowd.

"Logan!" Mandy cried when she saw me, standing with her arms out. "What an awesome surprise!"

I hugged her and—out of habit—bent down to kiss my wife, forgetting I didn't have to pretend in front of Mandy. Ella must have forgotten too, because she kissed me back.

"Oh, you guys," Mandy said, pointing from one of us to the other. "I almost believe it."

"What are you doing here?" Ella asked, ignoring our friend as I took a chair.

"I have news, and I was hungry."

The waitress came. I ordered something while she poured water for me.

"Okay?" Ella said. "So what's the news?"

"Byron's going to be out soon," I said, picking up my water glass. "I give it a month before Crowne is mine."

"Yes!" Mandy exclaimed, lifting her wine.

Ella followed suit and we toasted.

"Congratulations, boss. You did it. You got what you wanted," Ella said sullenly.

Her tone hit me like a brick. She sounded like that a lot, and I thought it was just how she was. Forty-five percent cynic. Thirty-five percent pessimist. Twenty percent product of Los Angeles.

For the first time, I realized she wasn't at some benchmark of happiness I could improve incrementally. She was miserable, and I had the feeling it wasn't the fact that Papillion wasn't hers.

"What?" Ella asked me when I'd stared too long.

"Nothing," I replied. "Am I interrupting a girls' lunch or something?"

"Mandy was about to tell me something."

My friend's smile turned as bright as her yellow blouse. "Well, I'm glad you're here. You both get to hear it." Mandy sighed and gazed lovingly at the industrial ceiling vents. "I'm not supposed to tell you." She looked down, drinking her wine.

"Well, in that case—" I said.

"Renaldo's getting a divorce."

"Really?" Ella exclaimed.

"He get caught?" I asked.

"No! Don't look so shocked."

Who could blame me for being surprised? I managed to stay monogamous even though I wasn't fucking my wife. Renaldo had a gorgeous wife he could fuck and he still couldn't keep it in his pants. Guys like that weren't motivated to leave their wives unless they're pushed out.

"I'm shocked and happy for you."

"Me too!" Ella said, grabbing her friend's hand over the table in a touch so sincere, I envied her for it.

"He's coming to Paris with me for the fabric show," Mandy said. "God... travelling with him? Not having to hide? It's going to be orgasmic." Her eyes rolled as if the orgasm was actually happening in front of me, over lunch, then she went rod straight as if her idea woke her from a trance. "You should come! Both you guys! You"—she pointed at me—"never took her on a honeymoon, and you can finally meet Rennie."

I tried to meet Ella's gaze so she could read my mind. Us, in Paris, on a romantic holiday, smiling for the cameras, kissing for show, sleeping in separate rooms.

Instead of looking back at me, she pushed out her chair. "Excuse me, I have to go to the ladies'."

She walked away without another word.

"What?" Mandy asked. "Bad idea?"

"I don't know." I shrugged. "I'll check our calendars."

"What's going on?" she asked, pushing away her salad. "Everything okay?"

Was everything okay?

Sure. Everything was fan-fucking-tastic. Ella was doing exactly what I wanted a wife to do. Socially, she was at my disposal. She was devoted even when no one was around, making sure I had everything I needed, asking me about my day without nagging about my hours, never having a single trouble or concern of her own. Exactly what I always wanted, without the sex. She asked for nothing. Perfect helpmate. Perfect in every way.

"She's unhappy," I said.

"She told you that?"

"No. I can see it. Has she said anything to you?"

"About what?"

"Hating me. Being miserable. Anything?"

"No," Mandy said.

"So she loves her life and she just *looks* like she wants to die?"

"What's the difference? She sold you a year. She knows that. Now you just have to pay up."

The Papillion buyout could have started any time. I'd told myself I was waiting for the stock to go down, but it kept dipping and I kept telling myself that if I waited a little longer, I could get it cheaper. Ella conceded that cheaper was better, but she didn't know the timeline the way I did. She thought it would take a week. I knew better and still stalled.

"It's better for me if she's happy."

"Why?" Mandy leaned over the table with an expression like a laser bright enough to cut sheet metal.

"Just is."

"Do you have feelings for her?"

"I do." I leaned back to let the waiter put my drink in front of me. "She's my friend. Same as you."

Same except without the need to connect our bodies with a touch, or the kisses I had to peel myself away from.

"So." Mandy sat back and crossed her legs, lips twisted in a knowing smirk. "What would you do if you thought I was miserable?"

"You'd tell me you were unhappy and what you wanted me to do about it. That's the difference." I yanked my napkin off my lap and tossed it on the table. "She's like a locked box with a big smile painted on the front. She blames it on the art she's doing. She says it's shit and it's distracting her. And I believed that for a while, but now? No. I don't believe it. She looks like a trapped animal and I'm the fucking zookeeper."

"Look, Logan. Here's the honest truth."

"Thank God. Please. Tell me the honest truth."

"Her art isn't going well, that's true. But she also misses

working. She's bored. She cares about you as a human being and a friend. She doesn't blame you."

"There has to be something I can do."

"Just let it go. In six months it'll be over."

Like hell.

My wife was mine to care for. Mine to satisfy. Mine to spoil with trips and money and whatever else she didn't know she wanted.

When Ella returned, she was fifteen percent less sour, but I was one hundred percent more committed to nudging her.

"Have you ever been to Paris?" I asked.

"My father took me. If you want to go, we can go."

"But what do you want?"

"Whatever," she chirped before sipping wine.

"You know what?" Mandy said, standing. "My turn to go to the ladies'."

She left as if her ass were on fire, leaving Ella and me alone.

"I just want a straight answer," I said.

"I don't care is a straight answer." Her chirpiness was gone.

I actually preferred the hint of a growl. It was real, and I wanted more of it. I wanted her so mad she told me how she felt, or hit me, or walked out in a huff.

"Pick yes or no," I demanded.

"Fine." She dug around her bag. "You have a quarter?"

"What?"

"Straight answer."

"You know I don't carry change or small bills. Why?"

"Never mind." She pulled a penny out of her purse. "Heads we go to Paris. Tails we don't."

"We can't decide things on the flip of a coin."

"If neither one of us cares, then we can."

I cared. I cared a fucking lot and I was sick of being told I didn't.

"Flip it." I pointed at her. "Heads, you suck my dick, tails, I fuck you blind."

What was she thinking for the eternal length of that pause, with her mouth twisted to one side and the penny balanced on the pad of her index finger? Was she hoping to suck my dick or get fucked blind?

The penny fell on the tablecloth.

"Tails," she said. "Paris can wait."

"Ella."

"I can't be the only one maintaining this relationship. Like... fuck this." She stood in one motion and slid her bag off the back of the chair. "If we were married for real, I would have divorced you already."

With that, she strode out the door just this side of running. I caught up to her on the sidewalk.

"Ella!"

"Go back to work!" she called over her shoulder.

I got in front of her, blocking the way. "Don't make someone call the cops on me."

"Then get out of the way."

"Talk to me."

"Why?"

Because I can help you.

I can make you happy.

I can give you what you want.

"Look," I said, "we'll start the buyout. Tomorrow, when markets open, we'll start."

Her shoulders relaxed, but her expression tightened to hold back what she wouldn't say. She didn't believe me. She thought I was lying to shut her up.

"Swear it," she said finally.

That was all she'd wanted. The deal. No more. I should have been relieved. Instead, I felt like a man who'd grasped for some precious unknown object, only to find it was never there.

"I swear." I held up a pinkie.

"Fine." She hooked her pinkie in mine and pulled, but I didn't let go.

"Are you sure that's all you have on your mind?"

"Let's go back before Mandy freaks out, okay?"

We pulled our pinkies apart.

———

AFTER LUNCH, I went back to Crowne. Ella went to her studio, or home. I knew now she didn't want to be at either.

When I got back to the house, Ella was in her room behind a door we kept closed.

I took off my shirt and undid my belt, stopping at the door between our rooms. It had never been opened. She'd set the boundaries and I stayed on the right side of them. I existed in my own space as if that door wasn't even there... until she told me to fuck myself with the flip of a coin and Byron told me he was giving up his place at Crowne.

If she was awake, I'd knock.

Close to the wood, I listened for the sound of her computer keys, or the TV, or her talking to a friend on the phone.

But nothing. Was she even in there?

I put my ear on the door, cutting out the white noise between us, and I heard her breathing.

She was there. I could knock.

Just as I was about to pull away, her breaths turned into a moan. A stab cut my chest.

Was she alone?

Fuck, she'd better be alone.

I closed my eyes, listening for a second set of breaths. A second voice. A bed creaking under two bodies.

She moaned again. Just her. She was alone.

Laying my hands flat on the surface, I envisioned her naked, upright on spread knees with her hand between her legs, butterfly tattoos all over her body, and was rewarded with her breath getting sharper and her moans rising.

I shoved my hand down my pants. My cock had already produced a bead of pre-cum. I used it to lubricate my hand, imagining her thrusting hips, her free hand twisting her nipple, her lips silently shaping my name.

Fucking my fist to the rhythm of her *unh-unh-unh*, I came with her final, long moan, squirting against the doorjamb without an ounce of shame and no regrets whatsoever.

I wasn't allowed to satisfy my wife's hunger. Maybe I could fill her soul.

ELLA

"TALK TO ME," Logan had said on the sidewalk a few hours before.

I almost did. I almost told him things I hadn't even dared to say to myself.

That I looked forward to seeing him in the mornings. That when he was away, I missed him. That I felt neglected in a way I didn't have a right to.

That I wanted him with an indefinable longing.

I still had *feelings*, and not having sex with him wasn't killing them. Denial was only feeding them.

But he was Logan, and he did what Logan does. He'd assumed it was about business, saving the yearning of my heart from slipping out of my mouth. I made him promise to start the buyout because I couldn't bear his refusal to promise what I couldn't even define.

He'd walked me to my car, and when he kissed me on the cheek, I could tell there were things he wanted to say and couldn't either.

What a mess.

I went to the studio.

The Big Blank still leaned against the warehouse wall, and I went there a few times a week to stare at it while I sketched possibilities, filling black-bound books with pasted headlines, broken thoughts, and disjointed ideas.

Amilcar and Tasha came soon after to kill a few hours between her school dismissal and the opening call for the musical.

"Just throw a paintbrush at it," Amilcar said. "Break that shit up."

He rocked in the swing I'd hung from a ceiling beam, curating his playlists while Tasha sat on the floor, surrounded by her thick history books.

"Don't listen to him," she said, flipping pages and making a note. "You gotta plan what you want to say."

Amilcar made a *pfft* sound.

Tasha was probably right, but I had no plans. I was dormant, and I hated it. All the time and money in the world couldn't buy me a purpose. I sat back on the couch and threw open a sketchbook, finding a blank page I could fill with meaningless garbage.

I was drawing arrows all over it, rendering them in fine detail, when Logan texted me.

—*Home at six. You?*—

"Bullshit," I muttered.

"What?" Tasha asked. She was curious and stubborn. She never took "nothing" for an answer.

—*I'm going to be out*—

"Logan thinks he's going to be home at six. As if."

Tasha shook her head as she took notes. "Men ain't worth it. Give them your name and you get grief back."

"Stop talking about us like that," Amilcar said. "I'm right here."

"You're not a man. You're a teddy bear."

He threw a pillow at her. She put up her arm to deflect it just as Logan dinged me.

—*Where?*—

"You almost done?" Amilcar asked his sister. "We gotta stop at Liddy's before the play."

"Give me five." She flipped a page.

"How is Liddy?" I asked.

Liddy was a GAC member, from way back when the Collective was the only meaningful thing in my life.

—*Going to see a friend in her high school musical*—

"We're doing a piece by the river and we're checking out—"

"What?" I bolted straight in my seat, sketchbook snapped closed in my lap.

Amilcar and Tasha glanced at each other, then she went back to her work.

"A piece?" I might as well have been clutching my pearls in horror. "With who?"

"Come on, Fance," Amilcar replied. "You know the crew."

"But... I thought the Collective closed."

"No, you ran off to marry some rich guy."

Logan texted me back, but I didn't look at it.

"You're saying I abandoned you?"

"Not what I said."

"So what are you saying? That I closed the GAC and now you all are saying fuck you, Fancy, we'll do shit without you? At the river? The LA River? What is it?"

"You know how it's called Frogtown over there—?"

"And who's financing it? Where are you based? Who's handling logistics? What if you get caught?" The raw energy of betrayal brought me to my feet. "Why did you leave me out?"

"Are you fucking with me? No, no, you have got to be fucking with me."

"I started it! I put everything into that crew!"

"And you left! We didn't all drop dead," Amilcar said.

"I didn't think that."

"So what did you think? We couldn't do it without you? Or what? We wouldn't want to? You're the big inspiration? You leave and we all flop down like those balloon men? Turn the fan off and we stop waving our arms or some shit?"

"No! I—"

"You need to check yourself, girl."

"Stop it!"

The vehemence of my protest was a tell for the fact that I hadn't given a thought to what I thought the rest of the crew would do while I was on hiatus. I'd put myself in the center of a group of people with their own dreams and desires. They had enough talent and the capability to surpass anything I'd done with them. I'd known that, but at the same time, I hadn't let myself believe it.

"Done!" Tasha cried, slapping her book closed and packing it all away.

"Amilcar," I said, "do you guys need anything? Money? Space?"

"Nah."

"You sure? I have so much."

"We'll get you the deets. You can come see it. The crew would be cool with that."

"If you get into trouble, will you call me?"

"Look, I appreciate everything you've done. But we got it. We don't need you coming in like Batman to save us. Just check us out, okay? It's gonna be big. People are gonna pay attention to this one."

He wasn't going to tell me what it was and I couldn't blame him. I'd just be some outsider inserting myself into their project. I'd throw money at them and I'd feel as entitled as they felt obligated.

I had made a bigger life for myself, with more people, more money, and more freedom. But I was no closer to finding out who I was. My face tingled and my nose got a wet tickle inside it. I sniffed.

"Fance, come on, man."

"They will pay attention." I wiped my eyes with the heel of my hand. "And I will. I'll be there, cheering you on."

Tasha slung her bag over her shoulder and hugged me.

"No white lady tears," she said, holding me tight.

I laughed. "I miss you guys is all."

She let me go. "You're coming to see me tonight, right?"

"Of course!"

"I have a car now. I can come by any time."

"That is not a safe vehicle," Amilcar mumbled.

Tasha kissed my cheek.

Amilcar shook my hand, then pulled me into a hug. "We'll see you later."

"Get out," I said. "Before I cry again."

They closed the door behind them. In the back, the headlights of Amilcar's Toyota flashed through the back window, blinding me. They got smaller as he backed up, swung left, and disappeared into the city.

My phone chimed again.

—*I'll come with you. What time?*—

—*Ella? You there?*—

So. Fucking. Demanding.

I had to drop everything because he had a few free hours. Fuck him.

"Ella," I said to myself, "he doesn't owe you anything besides a few million dollars."

—*Seven. Be home at six or I leave without you*—

—*Okay*—

Okay. Sure.

I put away the phone and slumped in the chair.

Alone with the Big Blank, I pried open a can of red enamel. "I can be whoever I want."

I pushed a three-inch brush into the center of the flat crimson circle to the base of the bristles, let the excess drip off, and flung the brush at the Big Blank. It landed flat on the white primer and

CD REISS

dropped to the clean tarp, leaving a puncture wound in the center of the canvas.

I still didn't know what to do with it.

———

AT FIVE THIRTY, I was in the shower, washing off the day's disappointments, when Logan's voice echoed off the wet walls.

"Honey, I'm home."

"Jesus, you scared the shit out of me."

I wiped the fog off the glass. He was leaning on the counter with his arms crossed as if he belonged there at all.

"Sorry."

He wasn't sorry.

"You're early."

"Not sorry."

At least that was honest.

I shut off the water and snapped the door open a crack. He didn't move.

"Logan?"

"Yeah?"

"I'm naked," I said.

"Good thing, since you're in the shower."

"Is there a reason you're standing there?"

"You never mentioned a friend in a play, and I don't want to be late, so you can tell me all about them while you're getting dried off."

I stuck my hand out of the shower. "Get me the towel then."

When I felt the terrycloth in my hand, I pulled it inside and clicked the door shut.

"You remember Amilcar?" I rustled the towel over my hair.

"The first impressionist?"

"Yes." I dried myself from the top down, conscious of Logan's body so close to my skin, separated by a thin glass wall. "His

176

sister's a senior at the performing arts school Downtown, and she's in *Les Mis*."

I could leave the stall naked. He'd just go on about his business, because that was all we were. Business with a touch of friendship. He didn't want me. That was how he could just walk in on me in the shower.

"And?" he said.

"And I think she's a great person. I want to support her."

"The guy. Amilcar. What's going on with him?"

How could he still be uncomfortable with Amilcar? I could bust his balls about his friendship with Mandy or any other woman in his orbit, but that would have missed the point. He was transparently jealous.

"What do you mean?" I wrapped the towel around myself, knowing exactly what he meant.

"How often do you see him?"

"A few times since we got married." I opened the door and stepped onto the heated marble floor. "Why? You think I'm breaking our agreement? Is that why you haven't bought a single fucking share of Papillion yet?"

"No."

I brushed past him to peer in a mirror unfogged by the steam. Some rich person's way of avoiding the inconvenience of condensation. "Good."

"I admire you for waiting until after the divorce."

Was he serious?

I looked right at him.

He was dead fucking serious.

"I've known him a long time," I said. "He's a good man who's dealt with more shit since last Tuesday than you've dealt with your whole life. And I'm not fucking him. He's my friend and he always will be. Period."

His eyes drifted from my face to my neck and down to where my towel was knotted over my breasts. I wanted to believe my nipples tightened because they got cold, but I couldn't lie to myself. It was the way he looked at me.

"Does he know?" Logan asked. "About why we're married?"

A tendril of wet hair fell out of place, dropping over my eye. He gently brushed it back, and I shuddered at his touch.

"No. I told you. Just Mandy."

"About Paris…"

"You want me to flip the coin again?"

"I want you to want to go. If you don't want to, we can go somewhere else."

"Why?"

His laugh was short, subtle, and silent. "No reason."

What was going on with him? If he wanted to fake a honeymoon to convince the world we were real, he'd just say so.

"Then shoo." I pushed him away. "Go put on something normal."

He lingered long enough for his gaze to brush against every inch of my exposed skin, then he went to his room to get out of his stuffed shirt.

22

ELLA

THE AUDITORIUM at the school for performing arts was huge and packed with parents, friends, and the odd Hollywood agent looking for a diamond in the rough. Logan looked like one of the latter in jeans and a blue polo shirt that made his eyes look supernatural. Even in normal clothes, he stuck out like a sore thumb.

"What?" I said as we sat with our programs.

"What, what?"

"You're jumpy."

"Not my usual crowd."

"You mean regular people?"

"In what world are you regular, Estella *Papillion?*"

"Shush, you." I slapped him with my program. "I can see normal from where I am. I can talk to normal about normal problems. You're a satellite looking at dots and blobs."

"Metaphorically interesting, yet objectively incorrect."

The lights went down.

"The thing about being a satellite is you think you're looking at the big picture," I whispered. "But it's just the weather."

"You push that analogy any further, you're going to send it out of orbit."

"They're starting." I put my fingers to his lips, and he surprised me by pushing my hand against his mouth to kiss my middle and ring fingers.

Though I'd experienced Logan's affection before, that touch was different. It wasn't a thing in itself, done to be seen, with its own beginning, middle, and end. It was a flirtation. A promise of more. An aperitif before the best meal you ever had.

Or I was imagining it.

It was possible that when he dipped a hand into my lap to knot our fingers together, it was code for "someone's looking," or when his body keened toward me, it was to relieve an ache in his back.

He held my hand on the armrest. No one who needed to see that could see it, but he did it and I couldn't figure out why. He didn't need to fake for Amilcar, who was sitting ten rows up. The nearest GAC person in the audience was Irma, who he didn't know he had to fake for anyway, but I liked it too much to move away.

The lights came up for intermission, and he didn't take his hand off mine. It felt good and right, but distracting. Like a rock in my shoe exactly where the sole itched.

"Wow," he said. "They're kids."

"And amazing."

"Were we that good? At Wildwood?"

"You don't remember?"

We stood to let people in the row out, and he tugged me to go with traffic.

"We were that good," I said when we got to the aisle. "And we had everything. Alexis had voice coaching Tasha doesn't get. More money for tech and costumes."

"And you." He put his arm around me. "They had you."

Yeah. They had me until Bianca took me out.

I let it go. We were having fun and I didn't want to ruin it with old grudges.

"You buying me a Coke?" I asked, pulling him into the refreshment line.

"Since when do you drink Coke?"

"I'm in the mood for it."

My shoulder tucked itself right under his arm and my hand reached for his pocket as if we were sized to wait in line side-by-side. I felt as if I could slide under his skin and become one person.

"Why'd you come home early?" I asked.

He shrugged as if it wasn't the first time in six months he'd left work before dinner. "I was in the mood."

"Don't bullshit me, Crowne."

He smiled, looking at me as we got to the front of the line. "I missed you."

"Stop lying and order me a bev."

He ordered my Coke and a water for himself, taking his arm away to reach for his wallet.

The lady behind the counter couldn't change a hundred, because of course that was all he had, so I rolled my eyes and paid.

"When you have kids," he asked as we walked back to our seats, "you sending them to private school or public?"

"I doubt I'll have a choice. You know what private schools cost in LA?"

"No."

Of course he didn't. Why bother tallying it up when you could buy the entire school?

"But," he continued, "what if we had kids?"

"How's that even possible?"

"Let's say."

"Let's say there was truth and justice and the moon was made of American cheese."

"Green cheese."

"Let's say the earth was circled by a ball of dairy product and we had babies."

We sat in our assigned places and waited for the lights to go down again.

"Seriously. Do you want children?" he asked. "Or are you too wild and independent?"

"We should have fake discussed this before we were fake married."

"We did." He cracked open his water. "It's the only TBD in our contract."

"Right, you wanted to make sure you stamped your name on nonexistent kids."

"Are you going to answer?"

"Yes. I want one. Maybe two. But if I can swing it, I want to adopt."

"Hm." He drank from the bottle.

"What? You want me to assure you that if we accidentally adopt, they'll be Crownes?"

"Just asking."

"No follow-up?"

He hadn't shaved before we went out, so when he rubbed his chin, I could see the stretching shadow. "Adopting. Why? You don't want to be pregnant or something else?"

"When I was a kid, I took my parents for granted. When my father died, it shook me so bad. I felt abandoned by both of them, and I was eighteen. Practically an adult. Can you imagine being a little kid and feeling like that?"

"No, I can't."

"Okay, then can you imagine being the person who doesn't abandon them?"

He screwed the cap back on his bottle and stuck it in the circle at the end of the armrest. "You're a good person."

The lights went down and the show started again.

———

AFTER THE LAST bow was taken, we joined the flow of bodies walking out, arm in arm so we wouldn't get separated. Loranda waited right out front, illegally parked. She smiled at us and waved, opening the back of the Cadillac. Some stared, some ignored it, but everyone had to change their path to get around it.

Logan stopped in the center of the front courtyard. The breeze blew his hair out of place as he faced the Cadillac.

"What?" I asked.

"Let's take the bus."

"The *what?*"

"It'll be fun."

He made it to Loranda in five long steps. By the time I got to them, his driver was closing the back door.

"Logan," I said.

"Where's the bus stop?"

"Do you have a Tap card?" I asked. "Or cash even? Like dollar bills. They don't change hundreds and I spent what I had on a soda."

He looked down, instinctively patting his pockets. I expected him to turn them out. "How much is the bus?"

"I have it," Loranda said, reaching for her wallet.

"No," I said. "No, no, no, no. No. No."

"It's not a big deal," she said. "Really."

"My wife doesn't really want to take the bus." He turned to me with a smirk. "Not so regular, are you?"

"I have cash," I said. "But no quarters. I'm going to overpay for you. You're welcome."

"You sure?" Loranda asked. "I think he's good for it."

"I'm sure." I nudged my husband toward the end of the block. "We'll see you later."

"Tomorrow morning!" Logan cried.

Loranda waved and got in the car.

The crowd had thinned. Across the street, a group of men laughed loudly, and in front of us, three young women belted out the refrain of "On My Own."

"The songs are catchy," Logan said.

"They sure are. So." We stopped at the corner with the singers, waiting for the light. "Which bus?"

"Which..." He looked around and didn't find a sign that said "Logan's House" or "Hancock Park," so he pointed at a bus rocking down Grand Street. "What about that one?"

"You're going to Long Beach? I guess that could be fun."

He turned to where Loranda had been parked, but she was long gone.

The light changed.

"Poor satellite," I said, hooking my arm through his. "Come on."

I led him across the street, following the three women to the west-flowing side, who had moved on to "I Dreamed a Dream," and stopped under the bus awning.

"Just because I don't know which bus to get on in a strange neighborhood doesn't mean anything."

"Okay," I stopped under the bus awning with the singing trio as a bus pulled up, brakes squeaking. "What's the nearest bus to your place?"

The doors opened with a hiss and a clap. We lined up behind the trio and I got out my wallet.

"The orange one."

"They're all orange. And I'll end your suffering now." I got up on tiptoe so I could whisper, "There are no busses to Hancock Park." I got up on the first step and looked down at him. He didn't know where he was going or how to get there, but he looked completely in charge, even below me. Damn him. "I hope those are comfortable shoes. We have a long walk."

We got seats next to each other, facing forward. He let me in first so I had the window.

The driver was a woman who laughed loudly with a regular passenger. A guy in front had so many bags at his feet, he blocked three seats. The couple standing nearby didn't ask him to move them.

"This isn't so terrible," he said when he was settled and the bus lurched forward.

"I don't think Loranda's going to lose her job any time soon."

"See?" He put his arm around the back of my seat and leaned into me to look out the window. "I employ people. I pay taxes. I'm not so bad."

"No one said you were bad, and you better pay your taxes or the people you employ won't be able to get to work. On the bus. Which is partly paid for with... da da da... you get it."

His gaze was still out the window, but he was looking inward, as if I'd put together pieces of a puzzle he'd thought was solved.

"Hey," I said. "Do you want the window? Sunset's pretty cool to watch go by."

"I wouldn't have an excuse to lean over you."

"True." I twisted away from the boulevard lights. "Did I tell you about the time I took the bus up to Griffith Park?"

"It couldn't be more fun than this."

I poked him. "No. It sucked."

"Tell me, Ella." As if he knew the importance of the story, he gave me his full attention.

"I was fourteen, and it was my father's wedding day."

"To Bianca," he confirmed.

"Duh. So. My mother was dead barely two years, and Daddy married her. She worked at Papillion—in merchandising—so he'd known her awhile. That was his excuse. Anyway, she ignored me at the office and the house the same. I thought it would change after they were married, but I realized on their wedding day that no, Bianca didn't want to teach me anything or know me at all."

"Her loss."

"Sure." I turned to face him fully, and he leaned closer. "Dad stayed at his best man's house the night before the wedding so he wouldn't see the bride. Bianca was at the house with me and, like, a billion bridesmaids. Thomas Dworkin—have you heard of him?"

"No."

"Famous fashion photographer. Got a curly moustache like Salvador Dali? Anyway, he'd set up the living room to get the pre-wedding bridal shots. And I'm ready. Hair up. Shoes on. Got this precious little powder blue dress. And Bianca comes down the stairs in her white gown and one of Daddy's cleaning ladies holding up the train. Bridesmaids behind like a bucket of giggling pale blue paint spilling down the stairs."

"Giggling paint?"

"Whatever. So they all pile into the living room, and there's this sliding door. Dworkin's about to close it when he says, 'You coming?' and I realize, no. No, I'm not coming. I'm not taking a picture with my stepmother and her fucking gaggle. I'm just not. I don't know what I'm going to do instead, but then I see my father's office in the mirror. And up on a high shelf, behind me? My mother's urn. Her ashes, and it just makes me mad that she's got to be up there, watching this whole performance."

"You look mad thinking about it." He touched my chin with the pad of his thumb.

"I don't think I am, but maybe. I don't know. So I tell Thomas my father needs me and I have to go. I'm getting Roger—Roger was my Loranda—to take me to Daddy, and I'd be in the reception pictures. Part of me wanted to see if Bianca even noticed. The other part didn't even care. And you know what Thomas says? He says, 'Basile is never wrong,' which we always said, and I believed it until Bianca showed up. Then I knew he got shit wrong. He was needy and weak, and he let her poison him."

"You're turning red," Logan said. "And you haven't even gotten to the bus yet."

I smiled, looking away. My disappointment in my father had been hard-earned and well-hidden. I tried not to think about it, because my face gave me away. I didn't like who I was when I was angry at him. I enjoyed the company of Loyal Ella more than the bitter ranting of Disillusioned Ella.

"When he closed the door," I continued, "I took the urn off the shelf, and—I don't know if you know this, but I found out—ashes are pretty heavy. I ran upstairs, changed into jeans, and took the bus to Griffith Park. I dumped my mother's ashes at the Observatory, where Pluto is closer to the sun than Neptune, which—shit, this is our stop."

I pressed the tape to alert the driver, and she stopped in time. Logan and I leapt out the back doors onto Beverly Blvd, and the bus rumbled away. The air was crisp, and in the moments of silence between cars whooshing by, you could hear crickets.

"Come," Logan said, holding out his hand. "I know the way from here."

I took his hand, and we crossed Beverly into the residential zone, with its massive, hundred-year-old houses set behind long, grassy front yards.

"What did your father say when he found out?" Logan asked.

"He never did. I put the urn back, put my dress on, and waited for the wedding to end."

"Were they worried?"

"I called from a pay phone. Told the staff I went for a walk and got lost. But I was fine. They told my father I was home."

"He believed you got lost?"

"Probably not. But I missed the wedding. He never forgave me for that."

"Never?"

"Basile Papillion wasn't a forgiving guy."

Before I reached "forgiving," I realized the treachery of what I was saying and lifted my voice to a jokey pitch. Because, so what? Was this supposed to be a big deal? Was my father's inner life any of my concern? His forgiveness wasn't withheld to make me suffer. It made him suffer more.

Right?

After the wedding, I'd gone bad. I stopped coming home. I got into trouble. I cursed and smoked and broke windows because of Bianca, not Daddy.

It was her fault. All hers with her snooty little voice and the way she pointed her pinkie when she drank her fucking tea. Tears of rage formed, but I didn't wipe them, or Logan would turn to me and see them. I didn't sniff, or he'd hear. I didn't speak, or he'd know I'd run headlong into a brick wall separating me from a pain I couldn't look in the face.

"Hey," Logan said from high up in his orbit, snapping his fingers. "Star. You with me?"

"My mother called me Star Child." I turned away to look at an obscene Tudor in case Logan faced me and saw the tears that fell when I blinked.

"But your satellite just thinks you're the star, Estella."

"Stop that," I said at the red light.

There were no cars, but Logan stopped at the corner and faced me, bending to make level eye contact. "What's wrong?"

What could be wrong? We were three blocks from home, if home was a place where you slept alone and pretended you didn't. If home was living with furniture you didn't pick and a stranger you agreed can't ever, ever love you.

But there was a truth inside his house. An honesty about who we were and what we wanted. Between us, there was no lying, no regret, no grudges.

"How about this?" I wiped my cheek with the back of my hand. "Last one in gets locked out."

"Wha—"

I took off before he finished, running along the smooth sidewalk with long strides, barely slowing at the corners to check for cars. With the wind in my ears and a cramp forming at my side, I ran to safety.

But your satellite just thinks you're the star, Estella.

No. He wasn't allowed to say stuff like that. He didn't circle me. I wasn't the center of his universe. We were lost planets from separate systems, looking for different suns.

I collided into the front door and was surprised when his body crashed into my back, reaching around me to hit the door code. It opened and we tumbled in. He slammed the door and came to me in half a stride, putting his hands on my arms and his lips level with mine.

"Stop!" The word bounced off the high ceilings, taking on a life of its own.

I didn't know what I was doing or what I wanted but the security of his arms around me. I wanted to give into the impulse to let him have me, but I wouldn't.

I'd promised myself I'd be good. And I was going to be.

Spinning on my heel, I ran upstairs before my cry to stop finished echoing. I burst into my room, and he thrust himself in after me.

"Ella!" He cupped my jaw in both hands, bending again, so I could see the tenderness he should be reserving for another woman.

"Just stop. No pet names. No more"—I pushed him off me—"touching. Don't lead me on. Don't care about me. Don't offer me anything but what we signed off on. Okay? Can you do that? Can you just help me be good?"

He opened his lips to answer. To agree to anything I wanted. That beautiful mouth was going to make a promise I didn't want him to keep. I tightened the muscles of my face and the walls of my heart. That was the right thing, and he was going to do it.

He was going to say yes.

Please say yes so I can be good.

"No."

23

ELLA

No.

Just no.

I didn't expect it or know how to respond. I was frozen in place when he came to me, put his hand at the base of my throat and—with a steady, gentle, and unrelenting pressure—pushed me until my back was against the wall.

"No," he repeated in my ear. "I will not stop caring about you. I will not limit what I want to the terms of the deal. I will not help you be good." His lips drew a line across my cheek, stopping when his nose was astride mine. "I'll agree to one thing only."

With his hand on my throat, I swallowed so hard I heard it. "What?"

"I won't touch you."

His palm bent, and his thumb stroked the length of my collarbone. It was suddenly the most erotic place on my body, pulling the breath out of me, eyes fluttering.

"Say that's what you want," he said. "Say my feelings are mine, but not your body. Tell me never to put my skin on yours. Say I should never lay my hands on you again."

He took his hand off my neck but kept his body an inch away, and his lips close enough to brush mine. I wanted those lips and the tongue behind them. I wanted the teeth and the breath, the jaw and the hunger.

"Say it, Ella."

If there was a future past this moment and a place past his body, it had nothing to do with me.

"Yes," I said.

"Yes, what?"

"Touch me."

He pulled back far enough to look into my eyes. "What happened to being good?"

"Fuck it," I said. "Let's hurt each other. Let's hurt each other so bad we walk out of this thing on broken legs, screaming in pain. When it's over, I want to be praying for death and wishing I could do it all over again."

He pushed me into the wall by the sternum and held me in place as he unbuttoned my jeans. I didn't have any fight left in me. Resisting what I wanted had been exhausting, and letting him hold me down and have me was a blissful relief.

I'd regret it. I regretted a lot of things, but they were my things.

He pushed down my waistband, kissing every butterfly tattooed on my belly, and stopped, looking from my bare skin to my face. "I want you to be sure. Because I am."

My body was a hungry mass of liquid fire, like lava rolling down a hillside, scorching reason and sense in unstoppable destruction.

"Break my heart, Logan."

"I'm going to break more than that."

He threw me over the bed, face down, and pulled my jeans down to my knees. He was rough—demanding that I cede control to him, and I did out of an arousing habit, pushing away the little voice that wanted to remind me it could all go wrong.

"You know what happens to bad girls?" he said.

I looked over my shoulder. He kneeled on the bed and undid his belt.

"They get punished?" I said, savoring the word.

"Some do." He opened his fly. "Do you?"

"I do. I want to be. Yes."

I could have thought of a hundred more ways to agree. Logan ran his hand along my ass, squeezing me, teasing the seam between them.

"How did I keep my hands off you this long?"

"It's hard to be good."

He nodded and pulled my hips to the side of the bed so my waist bent over the edge.

"This is for not talking to me." He slapped my ass so hard I yelped. "This is for pretending you were happy." He slapped me again, then ran his fingertips along my wetness, then added another slap. "That's for being a shitty actress, and the rest, my star, are for letting yourself be miserable." *Slap.* "For treating yourself that way." *Slap, slap.*

He kept hitting my bottom, over and over, until I was crying and gasping, eyes and cunt wetter than they'd ever been.

"Do I stop?" he asked, bending over me to kiss my cheeks. "Because I have one more."

"Give it."

He pulled off my pants and turned me over, standing at my feet.

"The last six months," he said as he peeled off his clothes. "They've been hell. All I can think about is getting inside you and what a mistake it would be. What a fucking mess." Naked, he knelt on the bed and pulled my knees apart. "If I hurt you, you could come after me. Expose me. If you were unhappy, that was just the price for a clean divorce."

He ran his hand between my thighs, eyes between my legs as if he could see how I ached for him.

"I was hurting you anyway," he continued, barely touching my clit. "And in the end, I'd do it without getting something I wanted." He slid two fingers inside me, and I moaned, overwhelmed as all my senses shut down except where our bodies met. "Tell me you wanted it too."

"I did."

"You were a good girl."

"I was."

He took his fingers out, and before I could react, he slapped my pussy. Pain and pleasure fought for dominance. Pleasure won.

"Oh, my God!"

"That was your punishment for being good."

I laughed. "Now I don't know if I should be bad or good."

"Be both." He slapped again, bringing me close to climax, but no. It was gone, leaving me unsatisfied, as if he'd given a starving woman a peanut.

"Take me, Logan. Please."

"But I can do this all night," he said, putting my right leg over his shoulder.

"I'll kill you dead."

"I like it when you're demanding." Kneeling while I was on my side, he rubbed his head on my clit. "That's how I know you're not bored."

"I'm not. Just... do it."

"I've waited too long to rush."

"Fuck me. Please."

"Are you begging?"

"Yes!"

He slammed into me, burying his cock and taking my breath away. He growled, pushing deeper, then pumped his hips against me. My leg bobbed over his shoulder next to his face, which was fierce with lust and an expression that entered me deeper than his dick.

"This what you wanted?" he asked, pushing me against the mattress, twisting me like an object.

"More."

He pushed against my clit with his fist, rubbing the hard knuckles along my swollen nub. He was cruel and careless with my body, and I loved it, winding with pleasure until I was on my hands and knees and he drove me from behind, spreading my cheeks open so he could get even deeper. I grunted as if he'd pushed all the air out of me.

"You all right?" he asked.

"Don't stop."

He wrapped his arm around me, flicking my clit with the tips of his fingers. With every stroke, he slapped away the barrier between the waiting orgasm and me.

"Make me feel how hard you come," he said. "Give it to me."

I wanted it deeper. Faster. Harder. But words wouldn't form, only a blanket of insensate blackness that sent me out of myself where I heard myself cry out, saw the bursts of orange behind eyes shut tight, and felt his fingers as if they were doing their cruelly pleasing job on someone else's body. Over and over, on an undulating wave of overwhelming sensation, I came with him until his name on my lips fell into sighs.

"I don't know if I can take six more months of that," I said when he rolled off me and I could form a coherent thought.

"You're taking it for six more months."

"I might die before you buy a single share of Papillion."

He got on his side and turned my face to his. "I'm putting it in the contract," he said with a kiss. "I know you. You'll live just to see the end of it."

He thought he knew me. Funny thing to think when I wasn't sure I even knew myself. He touched my jaw and cheeks with frightening tenderness, appreciating every bone in my face. A minute ago, I'd begged him to break my heart, but in the afterglow of sex, the armor against hurt clicked back into place.

"You're on my side of the bed," I said with a push.

He got on top of me and pinned my wrists above my head. "This is my side."

"I mean it," I said. "We need sleep."

"I'm not tired." He kissed me, and I felt him harden against my thigh.

When his tongue tasted mine, I arched, ready again. "Me neither."

He let my hands go, and I put my arms around him, wrapping my legs around his waist. He entered me again. We made love slowly, mouth to mouth, breath to breath, touching tender place to tender place.

I was in a tunnel, and he was the oncoming train. He'd crush me or he'd put on the brakes. I was too deep in the shaft to run.

"Logan," I whispered when I was close. "Yes."

Yes, to what I felt.

Yes, to him.

Yes, to us.

"Yes," he replied, tightening his hold on me.

I didn't ask him what he was agreeing to. It didn't matter. I was at the end of the tunnel, stock still, waiting to learn my fate.

"I'm..." I lost the rest in a gasp.

"Mine," he said, closing his eyes. "You're mine."

I lost sense as the orgasm hit me, dying for a moment in his arms.

24

LOGAN

WHEN OUR STICKY bodies pulled apart, Ella got out of bed, shirt hiked over her magnificent tits, bottom still pink where I'd spanked her.

"You need to put something on your ass," I said, sitting up. "Let me."

"I have it." She pulled her shirt down and headed for the bathroom.

I stood. "I want to."

"If you start manhandling my ass with lotion, you're never getting out of here."

"Would that be so bad?"

"What if Colton sees us in this room in the morning?"

"He has no reason to come up here."

"He's going to ask questions." She laid her hands on my bare chest. "Keep your bed messed up. Let's not blow it."

We'd invested a lot of time and energy into making sure he thought we slept in the same bed in my room. She didn't turn her lights on when he was around, and her door stayed closed. Sure, we could make a ton of excuses for why we'd slept in a guest bedroom, but she was right. Any change could crack the dam of lies.

"My room next time then," I said.

Her hands slid off me and she looked away, as if she had to process the idea that there would be a next time.

"Sex is one thing," she said. "I don't want to get used to you being next to me in bed."

She was afraid of being hurt. As much as she'd begged for the pain, she wanted to limit it, and all I wanted to do was inflict it. A decent man would have felt a tug of guilt. All I felt was the pull of desire.

"I'm not finished with your body, Ella."

She smirked, covering up the flash of uncertainty, and stepped away from me.

"Tonight, you are." She crossed into the bathroom and turned on the light.

I plucked my things off the floor while she watched. "See you in the morning, star."

"Good night, satellite."

I opened the door between our rooms and stepped through.

"Hey," she said. "I thought that was locked."

"It was never locked."

She smiled, and after she closed the bathroom door, I closed my door.

My room was empty, and the bed was too big. An ocean of mattress. A clean wood floor. Hard edges and sparkling surfaces. A space devoid of her.

If anyone saw this, they'd know we didn't sleep together.

On her side, the shower went on. She was cleaning me off her, rubbing away the places I'd touched her. I found myself standing by the door the way I had the night I heard her masturbating, envisioning her hands on herself and the paths water took down her body.

The shower stopped. The towel over her tits, between her legs, rubbing her hair damp. I didn't need to hear it to know what she was doing, but I put my ear to the wood anyway. I could hear the scrape of a toothbrush, drawers opening and closing before the rustle of fabric as she put on pajamas and got under the covers.

I should do the same instead of eavesdropping. I stuffed my clothes in the hamper and got into sweatpants, brushed my teeth, got my laptop, and went to my side of the empty bed. Emails needed to be answered and an output report needed going over.

At about two in the morning, I got tired and closed my laptop.

Same time as always, but she was on the other side of the wall. Something more pressing than a distraction, she was a gravity, and the wall between us blocked my orbit.

She was right about us sleeping in the same bed for all the reasons she professed, but there were more. We were the same kind of crazy. Revolving around each other meant giving up our priorities. I'd sent her off course already, and falling for each other would only make it worse for her.

But I wasn't kidding when I said I wasn't finished with her.

I didn't want to hurt her, but I would. All I could do was mitigate the damage.

———

SHE CAME DOWN unshowered but fresh-breathed for coffee the next morning, same as always, with fuzzy socks and hair down over her shoulders.

"Good morning," I said, pouring her coffee.

"Same to you." She sat on a stool by the island. "Just cream."

"How's your bottom?" I got the cream from the refrigerator.

"I'm sitting, aren't I?" She took the cup I handed her. "You have to work harder than that, satellite."

When she blew on the coffee, she looked at me suggestively.

"Interesting," I said.

"What's interesting?"

"You. Us. We never talked about the people in our past, so I had no idea what you were into."

She laughed. "Dude. I'm not *into* anything. Just... I figure going with it when you're in bed with someone is more fun than being weirded out."

I sat next to her. "But you've been spanked before?"

"Yes." She shrugged, breathed in a little coffee and put down the cup. "You want to know more, don't you?"

"Show me yours and I'll show you mine."

"Not much to show, but I'll play." She pressed her hands between her knees as if to warm them. "I was with James for four years. He was my first. Sixteen to twenty-ish. Give or take. Pulled my V-card after three months and in all that time I had one orgasm."

"One?" I confirmed.

"With him. One. I had plenty when he wasn't around."

"With other guys?"

"With mother fist and her five daughters." She held up her right hand. "He went off to New York to make it as a writer and I went... well, I dated a lot for a few years. None of it went far. One woman named Becca. She lasted three whole months, but she wanted to play house and I got so bored with it."

That explained a lot of what I suspected. She wasn't weary of me, but the life I offered.

After a pause for coffee, she said, "I guess I met Malcolm about four years ago. We lasted four months or so, which was, like, a record for me. He was the worst. I mean the absolute most terrible person. So of course I was obsessed with him. He edited porn video trailers, which is actually a thing."

"I didn't know that."

"Good. Because they gave him ideas about sex that were fine, if you knew what you were doing... which he didn't."

My grip on my cup tightened. I'd been fine up to the suggestion that someone had hurt my wife. "Tell me."

"Like, spank me. Make me crawl. Talk dirty all night long. All that shit is fine, but he always took it a little too far. And I didn't know better so I figured, since it turned me on, then maybe he wasn't going too far. But one time?" She shook her head. "He ties me up and blindfolds me, which was normal for us. And there's this weird pause where he says he's going to get something. He leaves, and then he comes back and he's real quiet. I feel him get on the bed, but it doesn't smell like him. He doesn't breathe the same and he's about to do it, when I just said... no."

She paused while I prepared myself to launch into a void of rage.

"He didn't back away, so," she said, matter-of-fact, "I scream loud enough to bust an eardrum. Just this '*Aaaah*' and the guy on the bed? He doesn't sound like Malcolm when he curses me. And so I scream 'rape!' over and over until Malcolm runs in and takes the blindfold off and yeah. His buddy from the editing gig's got a shriveling hard-on, trying to get his leg in his pants."

"Jesus." One word. A prayer for calm in the face of a past horror I felt the unproductive need to rectify. I could get Cooper to find this guy. Ruin him. Twist his hands off at the wrists and leave bloody stumps that would never tie another knot.

"Jesus was not in the room, trust me. Malcolm was all, 'I thought it would be fun, baby,' and 'Don't you know your fucking safe word?' His buddy's putting his pants on, like, 'You said she was into it.' So now Malcolm's real mad, talking about beating my ass raw... while I'm tied up... and he doesn't untie me until I threaten to scream again. And this is when he calls me a crazy-ass bitch. And I know I am, but—"

"No, you're not."

"Wanna try me?"

"Never."

"Good. So I get dressed and get the hell out of there so fast, the blindfold's still around my neck when I get home. And I cried for, like, three weeks."

"He should be the one crying."

She shrugged. "I took care of it."

"How?" Unless he was dead in a ditch, she didn't do enough.

"Got a guy I know to hack into his editing bay. You'll be shocked to know there was child pornography on there. We tipped the Feds. He's doing twenty in Chino Men's and I haven't dated since."

Four years.

This stunning, wonderful woman had been celibate four years because of that asshole? Nothing about this was fair or right. Incarceration was his punishment and he'd earned it, but her punishment was the prison of fear. She didn't deserve it. Not one minute of it.

"Ella." I took her hands. They were ice cold despite the warm cup. "I won't do anything like that. Ever. You can trust me."

She leaned into me and spoke in a low, serious tone. "I know."

"Are you sure?"

"I am. I don't know why. I didn't trust my judgment for a long time, but—I don't know. Maybe it was the big, fat diamond or the proposal, but something about you lulled me into complacency."

Between the two of us, I'd been the complacent one. That was over. I was going to make everything right for her. She was going to walk out of this marriage not just rich—but whole.

"I want to kill him," I said.

"Kiss me instead."

Slowly, with an appreciation for every second our lips touched, I kissed her.

I tried to heal her with that kiss—seal wounds with my lips, soften scars, and pry open the armor she'd built around herself.

Ella was broken, and I kissed her to make whole, even if I broke it all again.

25

ELLA

THE MORNING after my husband spanked me, my ass was pretty sore. But I didn't want Logan to think I was soft. A girl has to keep up appearances after all. Wouldn't do to let him think he didn't have to bring his A-game next time.

Next time.

Yeah.

There was going to be a next time. When I said, "fuck it, let's hurt each other," I meant it. The idea was terrifying, but I was powerless to stop myself. I was a spring-loaded switchblade of pent-up lust and he'd pushed my button. Getting cut was an inevitable risk.

My studio had once been a haven of creativity. Now it was a dead weight of options. A big canvas I was too terrified to choose a subject for, unfinished work that had nothing to say, a living space I didn't live in but would return to soon enough.

For now, I was in stasis. The art could wait. I had a dinner with Mike and Twyla in two nights and I was tired of every article of clothing I had. I didn't feel like that person anymore. I could buy whatever I wanted, but the thought of shopping was almost as boring as the act of shopping itself.

Opening my purple armoire, I ticked through the hangers and came to the silver dress I'd stolen from the locked closet at Papillion a million years ago. I pulled it out. Too dressy for dinner, but a gorgeous thing. The beauty was in the fit and fabric, but the concept was tame. It wasn't daring at all. It lacked.

I'd never seen my father's clothes as anything but perfect. Maybe I was grumpy. Maybe I'd missed something.

A dress form in my size sat in the back of a closet, and I wheeled it out then slid the gown onto it. The fabric fell like liquid, fitting over the curves without a drag line or pucker, dropping into impossibly even flares below the waist.

It was perfect, and yet, decades after he'd mastered fit, he hadn't done much more.

From the couch, I stared at it.

What would I have done differently?

Embroidery? Beads? Applique?

Nope. Nope. Nope.

What do you add to something perfect yet uninteresting?

The answer was nothing. Perfection was an end in itself. It existed silently in a world where the traces of burn on my bottom were reminders of damage, wounds, brokenness. The raw sting of Logan's hand on my ass celebrated imperfection. It was ours alone and needed nothing more.

Rifling my supply drawers, I found Daddy's tailor shears. I kept the ten-inch blades razor-sharp, and clapped them open and closed, asking myself if I was really going to do this.

I slid a blade under the shoulder strap.

His work was squirrelled away for museums and historians. This gown was the only one of its kind, and the only one of his I'd ever have.

I snapped the scissors closed. The strap fell.

———

"WHERE WERE YOU?" Logan demanded, sitting on the back patio with Colton, tie undone and shirtsleeves rolled up.

I never got home after him, and I always answered his calls. But I'd shut off the phone, and time had gotten away from me. I got back to the house past ten after a drive home that was interrupted by frequent sketchbook stops.

"Studio," I said, throwing myself in a chair. "I did a thing."

"What thing?" Colton tossed me a beer.

I caught it, noticing the roll in his cuffs, where it fell on his ankles, the proportion to the width of the knee. "I don't know yet. Or long story. Both."

"Describe the thing in one word." Logan took my beer, opened it, and handed it back with a suspicious look—as if he wanted to know if he needed to call a lawyer.

"Yeah," Colton said. "Quick before he takes off for a conference call."

"Destruction." I took a swig of beer. It was lovely. Cold and bubbly with a souring blossom of hops. I looked at the label as if I could discern why it was so wonderful from the name or ingredients. "Man, that's good."

Both of them stared at me as if an exotic animal had just strolled out onto the patio.

"What's going on here?" I asked. "You guys talking about something?"

"Ma's doing Ma," Colton said with a shrug.

"Is she okay?" I asked, tensing for potential bad news.

"It's not just us for the anniversary party," Logan said. "It's now extended family and friends. It's what she does. Plan small, then invite big. Drives Dad nuts."

The beer wasn't going to be exactly the right temperature for long. Perfection was temporary, so I tipped the bottle into my mouth, taking big swigs to enjoy it before it was gone forever.

"You sure you're all right?" Logan asked.

I took the bottle away from my mouth with a satisfied sigh. "I'm fine."

"Yeah," Colton said. "You got this, like, wild jump-outta-your-seat kinda look."

He was right. I felt like a cheetah running across the plains at a herd of gazelles, wanting to eat every one of them.

"You do," Logan said. "Nice bath would do you good."

"You're right." I put down the bottle and stood. "I'm going to do that."

Logan grabbed the bottle by the neck and handed it up to me.

"Take it," he said. "*Our* tub has room for it on the ledge."

Our tub?

He could only mean his tub. In his room.

I took the bottle. "Good call."

Logan grabbed my arm. When I looked at him, he nudged up his chin and pulled me down to him. I kissed him, intending a little peck for his brother's benefit, but I lingered, unable to pull away. His lips were cold from the bottle, sweet with drink, indulgently soft.

"See you guys later," I said when we parted.

Logan looked at his watch and sighed. "Twenty-three minutes."

The door closed behind me as he called out the time. I figured I had twenty-two minutes to ask him about it.

————

AFTER GRABBING MY STUFF, I went through the always-but-actually-never-locked door and into his suite. His laptop was open on his desk, with a big clock on the screen counting down to something. The room smelled like him, and I smiled, allowing myself to enjoy it for a moment before running a bath.

The water was delightfully scalding and the tub was heated to maintain the temperature and agitate the water so the bubbles stayed bubbly. Fucking rich people really knew how to live.

Logan came in and sat on the edge of the tub just as the pads of my fingers were wrinkling. "You sure you're all right?"

"Yeah. Just a good art day."

"Ah." He laid his hand on my knee. "You going to show me?"

"Nope." I sucked in a breath when his touch inside my thigh went below the water.

"Why not?"

He opened my legs, and the rush of hot water on my folds made me gasp.

"It's not ready. I have to protect it."

"But I'm your husband." His fingers found another kind of wetness. "You're safe with me."

"Am I?"

"Probably not."

When he pushed inside me, I slid down the tub, resting my head on the porcelain with my knees up, groaning his name.

"Star," he said, thumb circling my clit, "I've wanted you all day."

"I'm already naked."

He got off the edge and kneeled at the side of the bath. His arm was so deep in the water, his rolled cuffs were soaked. Bubbles rested in the ridge of the fold, and I was watching them pop when he took his fingers out of me and—leaving his thumb on my clit—pushed deeper.

"Get—" The sentence ended in a gasp as he increased the pressure.

"Get what?" With that, his finger entered me, and my back arched in pleasure.

"Get in here."

He pulled his finger out halfway.

"Don't," I squeaked. "Don't stop."

Slowly, he slid back in, then out again in a gentle rhythm, kissing my parted lips. "All I could think about today was getting inside your cunt, getting my cock wet on it. Slowly. All the way. So deep in you I touched your name. Making you come so I could feel you throb for me."

"I'm going to come."

A vibrating chime came from his bedroom. He pulled his hand away.

"Hey!" I said, sitting straight with a splash.

"Time's up. Conference call."

"How long's that going to last?"

He tossed me the towel and—still smirking like the devil—grabbed a small hand mirror before leaving me throbbing and dissatisfied.

"Asshole," I grumbled, draining the tub.

The bathroom door was open and I could see clear into his room, where he was at his desk, tapping into his laptop. I started to close the door between us, but he held a hand out for me, still looking at his work.

"Come," he commanded.

Faces popped up on the screen, and Logan turned around to me.

"The camera's covered." He indicated a little strip of black tape atop the screen, where the camera was.

I came to him, still wet and still naked, a map of bubbles sliding over my skin.

"I can't see you," the older Asian man said. In the window behind him, it was broad daylight.

"Me neither," the white woman said. "Logan?"

"I'm here," he replied, pinching my nipple with that same devil of a grin. "Camera's busted."

He was really terrible, evil, bad to the bone—twisting my nipple so hard it hurt in exactly the right way with one hand and putting his index finger to his lips with the other.

I nodded, consenting to his wickedness. His eyes lit up and he took his hand off my tit.

"So," Logan said, staring at me while unbuckling his belt. "George. You saw the liability report for Q1."

With my lips, I mouthed, "You're bad."

"Yes," George said. "I wanted to talk about the scatterplot in Section 24."

He mouthed back, "I know," then said, "Hold on."

He took out his erection with one hand, while the other opened a window of charts, stopping on a bar graph.

If he wanted to be bad, I was the girl for it. I kneeled between his legs.

"Yeah," Logan said when I licked the length of him. "I see it. You have it, Joanna?"

"Yes," Joanna replied.

I took him in my mouth and sucked as I pulled out.

"So," George said from above, "here's where I think the data is—"

The rest of his complaint blended into a hodgepodge of nonsense as I focused on the dick in my mouth. Logan rested his hand on the back of my head, and while he was talking about insurance claims, I looked up at him and opened my throat, taking him deeper.

He stopped talking mid-syllable, eyes closed.

Yeah, buddy.

This is how you do bad.

"Sorry," he said to the team. "What I was saying was, there's a way to manage this that"—he gripped the wet hair at the base of my neck, pulling me back a few inches—"can better stand scrutiny. Deeper"—he pushed me back down, hard, and I opened my throat to take all of it—"if you will."

George went on. Joanna said things. I sucked Logan's dick until he jerked me up. I stood, wiping my mouth with the back of my hand while he scrolled through some shit in a separate window and his colleagues looked on into blank space.

"Right." Logan looked at me and turned me by the hips to the screen and two people who couldn't see my nakedness. "That's mitigated in section seven."

With his foot, he pushed my legs open while describing section whatever to the two people on the screen. That was when I saw the little hand mirror leaning on the side of the screen.

Logan Crowne was more exquisitely naughty than I'd ever dreamed.

He pulled me back to his lap, one leg on each side of him, lining his dick up against me, not missing a beat on the call.

I was so wet he was completely inside me in one thrust. Leveraging my hands on the armrests, I fucked him.

"I want to show the board this," he said over my shoulder as he reached around me and spread my lips, displaying my clit and the fullness of his cock in the mirror.

Naughty was the wrong word for Logan. He was a completely and wonderfully debauched demon.

I moved his hand to my clit, and he rubbed it as I fucked him. He increased the stimulation between my legs and covered my mouth as I went tight, eyes scrunched shut, clenching every muscle against where our bodies met as if I wanted to lock us together. His arms pushed me down, and he pressed his face against my spine.

When I opened my eyes, the laptop screen was black with a green digital clock in the center.

"What happened?" I asked, looking at him over my shoulder.

"Call ended." He shrugged. "Crisis averted."

"Have I told you how evil you are?" I twisted until I was curled in his lap with my head on his shoulders.

"And how much you like it?"

"And how much I like it."

He kissed my nose. "I should bring you to bed."

Holding me tight, he stood and carried me to his bed.

"That way," I said before he could lay me down, pointing at the door to my room.

"You're really hell-bent on this."

"Hell. Bent. That's a funny expression."

He carried me to my own bed. King size. Too big. Too lonely. But all and only mine. For now.

I got under the covers and was asleep before I could miss him.

But I did, and I wasn't allowed to.

I watched the light under his door, and when it went out, I closed my eyes, falling asleep while pissed at myself for caring.

26

LOGAN

ELLA and I had things to talk about, but all I wanted to do was fuck her.

The morning after our multitasking session, she was distant and I couldn't understand why. Maybe it was all the things we were avoiding. Our impending breakup, moving out of the house, acting pissed off at me was going to be even harder now.

"You're coming to dinner tonight?" I asked.

"Yeah." She pulled down a loaf of bread. Her hair was up in a little ponytail and her fuzzy socks had a spring pattern. Rings and studs dotted the edge of her left ear, all the way to the top. Still not my type. Still sexy.

"Mandy's going to be there. She'll buffer Mike."

I'd set up a little surprise for her. Not Mandy. Something better that might make her happy. She needed it.

"Great." She plucked out two slices. "You want toast?"

"No, thanks."

She didn't usually eat until after I left. The change wouldn't have concerned me except for the sleepy, distant tone of her voice.

"We should talk," I said.

"Oh, yeah?" She put the bread in the toaster.

"I can start the buyout."

"Cool."

"We need to plan the breakup."

A small but loud part of me hoped she'd try to negotiate an extension. Maybe an arrangement where we'd stay together.

"Infidelity's the easiest," she said with the same flatness.

What the hell had happened overnight?

"I'm not fucking anyone," I replied coldly. My right hand had spent six months getting a workout before I got her into bed. I didn't *want* to fuck anyone but the one woman I shouldn't.

"I'll be fucking someone then."

Was she kidding? Was she talking about pretending to have an affair? Or really doing it?

"You have someone in mind?" I didn't mean to growl, but I did.

"Are you jealous of a man who doesn't exist?"

I had no business in this conversation. I dumped the last of my coffee and left the mug in the sink. "I'm not jealous."

"Okey dokey."

I stood next to her, arms crossed, as she watched her toast brown. "Do you have something you want to say to me?"

She didn't answer right away, but she bit her lip, and I knew she was thinking about it.

"When we split up…" She looked at me with eyes that weren't distant at all. "I don't want to say bad things about you. I don't want to hurt you."

"You won't."

"If it's too amicable, it'll look like it was fake from the start. But now, see what happened? I care about you, and I don't want… I can't leave you and make it look like I don't give a shit. So it's up to you. You have to be the one to hurt me."

I didn't want to talk about this anymore.

"We can make it work so no one gets hurt." I touched her bottom lip, watching the tiny creases flatten as I stroked my thumb across. "Let's discuss it later."

The toast popped and she turned to it.

"I'll get on your schedule." She plopped the toast onto a plate.

Leaning down to whisper, I smelled a jasmine that was hers alone, mixed with last night's sex. "Not tonight." I ran my fingers along the curve of her neck. "After dinner, I'm taking you home and getting inside you."

She paused, frozen with her hands on the butter knife.

"Logan." My name was a breath. "Why is this so hard?"

The back door slapped shut, and Colton shuffled in. "Hey, lovebirds. Ready for another day at the mill or nah?"

"Ready!" Ella chirped, scraping butter on her toast.

"Wanna hit me with a coupla slices?"

"Sure." She put in two more pieces. "I'm headed into the studio early. So butter them yourself."

That explained why she was eating breakfast before I left.

"Cool, hey, Loge, my buddy and I were playing volleyball and lost the ball on my roof."

"Your roof?" I went to the island, leaving Ella where she was.

"Like, over on that side. Maybe one of your guys can grab it when they're up there? Gardeners or whatever?"

"You can ask them where the ladder is and go yourself, or you can wait until the gutters are cleaned."

"Damn, dude."

"Tough being a Crowne," Ella said, patting his shoulder as she passed.

"Got that right, sister."

She went upstairs with her breakfast without kissing me goodbye.

I didn't think about her all day, except during the morning drive when the thought of kissing every stud in her ear gave me such a hard-on, I almost rear-ended a delivery truck. And the morning status meeting with London, when I spaced out on the quarterlies because someone in the room wore the same perfume as her. And lunch. And the rest of the afternoon passed in a blur of fantasies. Ella on her back. On her stomach. Naked. Fully clothed. Everything in between. I jerked off in my office bathroom before my afternoon meetings.

She'd asked why this was so hard.

Good question.

She wasn't happy being the wife I wanted, and I couldn't be happy knowing she was faking it. I had to wonder the same thing myself.

Why was this so hard?

———

I WALKED into the sixth floor of the club early for the reservation. The bar was crowded, and the club area was full of professional creatives making small talk and big plans.

The graffiti reminded me of Ella. Everything did these days.

Mandy was already there, wearing jeans and a yellow sweater. I greeted her with a hug.

"Take this tie off," she said, tugging it. "You look like an uptight bore."

"I am an uptight bore." I undid the knot.

"Everything all right at Crowne?" She crossed her legs and sipped something made with cola and lime.

"It's busy."

She swirled her drink and I ordered mine.

"What's the face?" I asked.

"I should have married you," she said sourly.

Imagining the plan with Mandy as a partner was certainly neater, but less fun. Not that it was supposed to be fun. That hadn't been important, nor had it been the point.

But somehow it was the most appealing part of my arrangement with Ella.

"Why?" I asked.

"Renaldo was supposed to come tonight and he totally bailed.

He never used to cancel on me, and now? Since he left his wife, he's done it twice."

"He's not for you, Mandy."

"What if he's got someone else?"

"You'd be surprised?" The first sip of scotch was the best one. The shock of the cold on my tongue and the dry heat spreading over my chest.

Just like the way Ella looked at me. Cold and hot at the same time.

"You're actually saying 'I told you so'?"

"I'm saying you should mitigate your expectations with him."

"You, Logan Crowne, are the most unfeeling prick I've ever met. The most oblivious to how people really are. We're not computers. We're not spreadsheets or whatever. Things where it all adds up, okay? We're messy and I knew he wasn't mine. I knew the whole time I'd never have him, but I love him and I'm human." She yanked her bag off the back of the chair. "I'm going to the ladies'."

"Mandy—"

"I'm fine! Just give me a minute."

She walked away with her hurt feelings, and as I watched her, wondering if she wanted me to follow her and apologize, I saw Ella coming out of the elevator.

My wife was a blazing presence in the dimly-lit room. She wore a short silver dress gathered at the bottom, with leather straps and belt. It was shredded and fringed with the loose threads, detailed in destruction, but the way she wore it was what was stunning. It was a skin, not a mask.

Only when I saw her smile did I notice she was talking to Mike Monroe.

Smarmy little fuck in Gucci loafers and a Tennessee accent. Trimmed beard and big silver belt buckle. The guy didn't know who he was or where he belonged. No wonder he thought he could hit on my wife.

"Mike," I said, meeting them between the elevator and my abandoned drink.

"Logan." Wide smile. Narrow handshake.

"Where's Twyla?" It came out like an accusation.

"Headache. Y'all know how it is."

"I don't," I said, putting my arm around Ella's shoulder and laying my hand on the back of her neck. "Tell me about it."

"You got a few hours?" he joked with a light punch to my arm. "You need a drink?"

"I'm good."

"Ella?" He raised one eyebrow at her. I wanted to rip it off and gag him with it.

"Gin and ice. Gunpowder Irish, if they have it."

Mike gave her a nod I liked about as much as the raised eyebrow and went to the bar.

"Take it easy on him," Ella said.

"I am taking it easy on him."

"Then stop talking like Darth Vader."

I looked down, not cowed but searching for a new topic of conversation, and my eyes found the place where her breasts met her neckline. "That dress—is that the one you wore to Crowne Jewels?"

Her smile lit all of Downtown. "Not anymore. You like it?"

"I'm not a fashion critic," I said, "but I like you in it."

"Thank you." She swung her hips to make the skirt twirl.

I pulled her into me so I could speak softly, to her alone. "And it's going to look better when I pull it up to spread your legs."

"Logan"—she nudged me—"we're in public."

"What do you have under it? Because I'm destroying anything between you and my cock."

She covered her mouth, cheeks erupting in pink.

Selma Quintero appeared from the elevator in a flowing jacket and layers of beaded necklaces that clicked when she turned to us.

She'd had short salt-and-pepper hair when my parents had her for dinners years ago. Now she was totally gray.

When she came toward me, Ella gasped.

"Logan." She offered her hand.

"Selma, this is Ella."

My wife had a deer-in-headlights look I'd never seen before.

"You must be Mrs. Crowne."

"She's—"

"Yes," Ella said, letting Selma use the wrong name. "I am."

"Pleasure."

My wife shoved me away to shake Selma's hand, then threw eye-daggers at me.

What the hell? I'd invited Selma for her and she seemed mad about it.

Mandy reappeared. Mike came back with drinks. Everyone was there. I followed the hostess to our table, feeling as if I'd dodged a bullet only to wind up in front of a firing squad.

27

ELLA

SHREDDING my father's dress had gotten easier as the days went on, and somehow I'd let my confidence with it build up enough to wear it. But as dinner went on with Selma Quintero to my right and Logan on my left, I felt as if I'd brought Basile Papillion along for a ride into failure. Then it got worse.

"Logan tells me you're an artist," Selma said to me as the plates were being cleared.

"Not... no." I heard my nervous laugh as if I were a separate person, cringing at the high pitch of my insecurity. "I just tinker around."

"Oh, dearie," Mandy said with a sway and a slur. She'd been at the martinis since we sat down. "She's Basile's daughter, so you know—" Mandy waved at me as if she was about to mention what everyone could see. "There's some talent under the hood."

No pressure.

Mandy was trying to be nice, and I appreciated it, but I also wanted her to shut the fuck up.

"I was so sorry when I heard about your father." Selma put her hand over mine.

I believed she was being completely sincere, but I also didn't want to talk about Daddy while I wore his destroyed dress.

"Thank you." I searched for a change of subject, but everything led to my father.

Logan must have been reading my mind. He draped his arm around the back of my chair and leaned toward Mike, cutting the line of the conversation across the one that was making me so uncomfortable.

"Mike," Logan said, "I heard you guys got an office in Memphis."

Faced with something interesting, Mike put down his phone. "Sure did! Let me tell…"

"Papillion hasn't been the same since he died," Mandy said with a lower voice, now that the men were engaged in a parallel conversation. "Bianca had me in to look at the high price points, and well, even the last six deliveries…" She made an exploding gesture with her hands and a crash sound with her mouth.

Two seasons, three months each, one delivery per month. Half a year since Bianca cut the last cord to her husband—me.

"Well, Basile's passed," Selma said.

She meant dead. My father was dead and people talked about it. Society people. Art dealers. Other designers. Everyone I'd spent my adult life avoiding.

"To Basile." Mandy lifted her glass.

"Are you all right?" Logan whispered in my ear.

"Yeah. Sure." I lifted my glass with the last of the wine Logan had ordered with dinner.

"He may be gone from this world," Selma said, "but he left us Ella."

I clicked. I drank. I told myself it was all out of respect, because it was. I knew they didn't mean to turn a toast into a reminder of how much I'd squandered or what a disappointment I'd become.

"So," Selma said cheerfully, "let's talk about your work. This 'tinkering' you say you do. Who are your influences?"

David Hammons. Gordon Matta Clark. Doris Salcedo.

I could have mentioned any of those artists or a dozen more, getting into a perfectly enjoyable conversation about anything but me and my nonexistent work.

Logan's hand pressed flat against the base of my neck as if he was trying to steady me, and I was filled with the confidence to do something more with the question.

"Remember when LACMA installed *Levitated Mass*?" I said.

"Heizer, then?" Selma added.

"What's that?" Mike asked.

"It's a three-hundred-forty-ton rock," I said. "Just a big ugly rock. But it's so rare because it's flawless inside. No cracks hiding. They brought it from Riverside on a flatbed, right onto Wilshire Boulevard in the middle of the night. They took down streetlights and signs to move it through. I went with my friends to see it. We stood there at three in the morning, watching this big, ugly rock cut through the city. Witnessing something." I faced Selma fully. "That's what influences me, really. Creating an experience. A relationship. I've been to the final installation, and it's fine. But if I hadn't been there that morning, it would just be a rock."

"Yes," Selma said. "I get that."

"Hey!" Mandy said, snapping her fingers and pointing at Selma as if she was trying to remember something. "What did they call that house in Westlake? The one with the sparkly shit in it?" She looked right at me. "Who was that?"

Mandy needed to shut the fuck up.

"The Guerilla Arts Collective," Selma said. "*Geode House.*"

"What did you think of that?" Mandy asked.

"Sounds like a waste of horseshit to me," Mike said.

The check came. Logan picked it up and everyone reached for their wallets.

"I've been looking for them for years." Selma gulped her wine as if the GAC drove her to drink. "I was there. It was absolutely stunning. A statement on the value of human experience."

She'd obviously read Tasha's statement on our Twitter feed.

"On the unexpectedness and speed of inspiration."

That—on the other hand—hadn't been on any of Tasha's Twitter threads.

Mandy dug around her bag. "The demo guys gave out the rhinestones."

"They did," Selma added, tossing her credit card on the tray.

"Put it away," Logan said. "I have this."

"Thank you," Selma said, unsnapping a little wallet pouch.

"I got a yellow one." Mandy held an amber jewel in her palm. It was a cheap, silver-backed glue-on gem that still sparkled in the candlelight.

Selma inspected it. "Interesting. Not a Swarovski."

"Is yours?"

Mandy gave me a wide-eyed look, demanding I say something I couldn't. She was trying to help me, God bless her, but also fuck her because the GAC was a secret, and if I was outed, we were all outed.

Selma found a blue stone in the pouch and held it out. A spike of epoxy stuck to one side. "I called the man at the Swarovski buying office."

Shit. Swarovski did not fuck around. They'd know where it came from.

"Les Montcharion," Mandy added, putting her stone away.

"Right," Selma said, fisting her rhinestone. "He said it was a custom run from 1998. Big order, but defective."

Shit.

Shit shit shit.

"Logan," I said softly as he signed the bill, "we have to go."

"For Basile actually." Selma turned to me.

Logan's hand froze. My heart stopped.

"Wasn't that your dad, Ella?" Mike asked as if he hadn't been paying attention to a damn thing we'd been saying. "Maybe someone working for him did the house project?"

"Maybe." I took my napkin from my lap and pushed out my chair.

"I called to ask," Selma said, "but Bianca stonewalled."

"Nicely, I'm sure," Mandy said in a thickly sarcastic tone.

"Excuse me," I muttered as I took my bag off the back of the chair. "I have to run to the ladies'."

Leaving them, I passed the hallway to the bathrooms and wound up at the elevators with a pounding heart. I hit the button down and ground my teeth when the doors didn't open right away.

"Ella," Logan said.

"Leave me be." The elevator came and I got in.

"No," Logan said, standing beside me.

"I just want to go home." The doors closed and we descended.

"I'll send for the car."

"No! I mean home. *Home.* Not your house."

"Then I'll take you there."

I couldn't bear being in an enclosed space with him longer than I had to be. He'd try to fix it all. He'd promise me the world, but the world wasn't in the contract. Being his wife was what I'd promised and it was the thing that had halted my career and stolen my vision.

The doors opened onto the lobby floor, and I stalked out, knowing with every step that he was beside me. When I got to the curb, I tapped my phone for a car.

"Ella." Logan got right in front of me. "What happened?"

"What happened?" I entered the address of the warehouse on Highland. "I told you no. I said 'no Selma Quintero' and you didn't listen."

"I thought you were being modest."

"You set up a dinner with a totally powerful art dealer I'm not ready to meet like you wanted to be as vicious as possible in the shortest amount of time. Then you have the audacity to ask me why I'm nervous. But"—I pointed in his face—"lucky ass you, I know you better. I know you're not cruel. You're just selfish, self-involved, self-centered. You're the little piggy at the end of the line going"—I poked his chest with each *me*—"me, me, me, me all the way home."

"This dinner was for *you*, because I never see *you*, and if I have to meet with Mike, I might as well give *you* someone to talk to. It's what a husband does."

"Wait, wait. You never see me? Why does that matter?"

Why did it matter? It shouldn't. It didn't. I knew it didn't because that was the deal.

I'd let the cat out of the bag to both me and him.

I wanted him.

"This has been a humiliating disaster." I looked at my phone. The car was close but needed to be closer before I said more stupid shit.

"Humiliating that she knew your group?"

He thought the fact that Mandy and Selma had souvenirs in their wallets was some kind of social proof.

He was right. It was social proof that I'd given up more than I could ever get back.

"She knew about nothing." I put down the device. "Nothing that's mine. You made me leave it. I was doing something important and I dumped it to be your wife. What the fuck was I thinking? I let you ruin everything. You know what? I might as well take your name. Walk the walk. Be a placeholder for the next Mrs. Logan Crowne."

The car came, and the doors unlocked with a *clack*.

"I'm going with you." He opened the back door.

"Logan." I got between him and the back seat. "Stop. Jesus Christ, you don't *listen*!"

"You're talking crazy. This isn't Ella."

"Yes, it is. Please. It is." I sat and grabbed the handle, but he held it open.

"I don't want this to be why we broke up," he said. "This isn't the story I want to tell."

"You'll come up with something."

I yanked the handle and he let me close the door. When the car pulled away, I was completely alone, watching the streets go by with a driver who was blissfully untalkative.

Except I wanted to talk. My friends had moved on. My family was dead. On the way to nowhere, I'd burned every bridge behind me.

Doreen would know what to do, and if she didn't, she'd listen to me talk until I found the solution myself. I could tell her anything, except the problem of her son.

My mother in-law would never be mine. I had a dead mother and a stepmother who hated me.

Bianca stonewalled.

Asked about missing stones among the ones I'd skimmed for years, she'd said nothing.

I'd put her in a position to answer for things I'd done. I'd carelessly passed my wrongdoing on to her. She's been put on the spot because of me.

That wasn't fair.

Nothing she'd done was fair, but that didn't excuse me.

"Hey," I said to the driver a second before I actually decided what to do.

"Yeah?" he looked at me in the rearview.

"Can you take me to West Hollywood instead?"

———

BIANCA WAS, as always, a cartoon of herself, answering the door in a purple muumuu and full makeup. A white poodle barked at her feet.

"Ella!" she cried, actually smiling as if she was glad to see me. She scooped up the dog and moved aside. "Come in!"

"I'm sorry to bother you."

"Nonsense!" She closed the door and held up the poodle. "You haven't met Mr. Tubbs." She addressed the dog. "Mr. Tubbs, this is Ella."

"Hi, you're cute." I patted his head.

"Mr. Tubbs keeps me company now that you're gone." She clapped down the hall as if she hadn't just said something absurd.

"I moved out when I was eighteen."

"Of course you did," she called from the kitchen. "Do you want tea? I was having a little wine. You're not driving, are you?"

"No."

When I got to the kitchen, the dog was on the floor and Bianca was pouring a glass of Chablis.

"Whoa," I said. "Stop. That's—"

"Let's just finish it." She poured until the bottle gave out and handed me the overfull glass.

Why had I come? Was I looking for a mother? Bianca was the only one available of the three, but she didn't seem capable of comfort or wise words.

"Thanks." I took the wine and sipped it.

"So what brings you?" She sat at the nook and I sat across. "You can't need money."

"No."

Mr. Tubbs scrambled up next to me.

"Oh, he likes you!" Her delight seemed genuine. "What then? Tell me. You need something. Wait! I have it." She leaned in to look right at me, and even in a tipsy haze, she managed to look right through me. "You're bored."

"Oh, my God."

"What?"

"Is it that obvious?"

With a satisfied smile, she leaned back and crossed her legs. "I know you is what I know. You get this look like you're about to do something reckless. Whenever I saw that look, I'd have to run and find you something to do or you'd get 'fuck fashion' printed on all the hanger tape."

"It was 'fashion is for losers' and it gave Papillion a little edge."

"Which we were sorely lacking that season, I'll give you that." She raised her glass and drank. "After Basile died, we never really had the same... I don't know..."

"Authority?"

"No, not that. More..."

"Conviction?"

"Yes!"

"Like we were playing the old hits but didn't have the balls to stand by a new song."

"Cowards. We were cowards. No, well... I am." She nodded with a faraway stare then snapped out of it. "Drink up. Then tell me the truth. You have all the money you need, but you couldn't last six months without a job. You want to come back."

I nearly spit my wine.

"I guessed right again?"

"Why would I come here asking for that? You spent how many years trying to get me out?"

"My God, Ella." She seemed deeply offended, or at least I assumed she was offended. "You hated it. You hated it even before I got there. You just didn't know it. Of course I was trying to get you out. If I hadn't fired you, do you know where you'd be? You'd be there right now, at this hour, working your tail off and hating every minute of it until you exploded in some mischief or other."

I hid behind my wine, taking two big gulps and not even emptying half the glass.

"I don't want my job back," I said, holding down a burp.

"You need some water." She sailed to the fridge like a purple flag on a windy day.

With perfect instincts, Mr. Tubbs got up and went after her. As she filled a water glass in the refrigerator door, she took a treat from a canister and tossed it right into his mouth.

"I wanted to apologize for something," I said.

"Oh, let me sit for this event." She put the glass in front of me and got another bottle from the fridge. It was already half-empty. "What are we apologizing for?"

God, she was intolerable.

"I... stole some things from work. Some rhinestones."

"Some?"

"Some. A lot. Over the course of a few years. Overages. Defects."

"The Swarovskis."

"Yes."

"I knew, dear. But thank you for bringing it up. More wine?" She poured before I could refuse.

"You knew? Why didn't you say anything?"

"Out of respect for your father. And I admit..." She shrugged, cupping her glass. "I wanted to see what you were going to do with them. I have to say I was a little disappointed with that house thing."

"Wait. You knew?"

"Suspected. But *que sera*. You were always a mystery to me."

"You fired me for stealing the dress but not the rhinestones?"

"I fired you because you were ready to be fired. And by the way, I do love what you did with it." She flicked her hand at Daddy's dress.

I'd forgotten I was wearing something I'd have to explain.

But I really didn't have to explain anything to her. She seemed to know it all already.

"I want to be good," I said as the wine rushed to my head. "I want to be a good person who does good things and makes good decisions but it's just..." I drained my wine.

"It's just?"

"It's so hard when all the good stuff is blah." Was I slurring already? Of course I was. I'd had three drinks over dinner. All I needed was a few mouthfuls of Chablis to put me over the edge. "Life is just... it's this blah blah blah then you die alone anyway because who wants to hang out with blah? Nobody! They all want Bad Ella. Bad Ella's so talented and real. Bad Ella does such interesting things and we can watch from over here, where it's safe and we get to stay good."

"Ella, dear?"

"And oh my poor husband is so bored with me being good. He just doesn't know it. But if I go back and do Bad Ella things, we're finished and I'll have all the money in the world..." I threw my arms up. "But not him." I let them fall heavily to the table. "So. I'm here because you're the only mother I have and you're the only one who can tell me what to do."

"And you'll do the exact opposite." She switched our wine glasses. Now the one in front of me was mostly empty, which was good and wise.

"So you're going to tell me to rob a bank?"

"No. It's irresponsible of me to not tell you to rob a bank though. Lord knows, the financial sector should be paying me to tell you what to do as an insurance policy against you actually doing it."

"I'm sorry. Too many negatives. I'm confused."

"Be good." She slapped her palm on the table. "Be good and stay good. You'll get used to it. You'll keep your husband, who you obviously love—"

"How do you know that?"

"Don't be an idiot, Estella. Just keep yourself together. Life is mostly boring most of the time. Sometimes you meet a man like your father, or Logan Crowne if you will, who just makes it all worthwhile."

"It should be worthwhile just because. Without them. Just me. I should make it worth—uh, I don't feel so good."

Like a shot, Bianca gripped my arm and pulled me to the hall bathroom, where I unleashed a fifty-seven dollar salad into the septic system before its time. She held my hair back while Mr. Tubbs yapped at the bizarre noises coming from my throat.

"Hush now," Bianca scolded the dog.

"I stand by my assertion," I prayed to the porcelain. "It should be me. I make me happy. No one else."

"Happiness is other people."

"I thought hell was other people." I let loose again. It seemed impossible that my stomach could hold that much.

"Who said that? Was he French?"

"You said it when I broke your windshield." I pushed back and Bianca let go of my hair. I rolled to a sitting position on the tile. "I feel so much better. Thank you."

Bianca snapped a hand towel off the bar and ran it under the faucet. "I never knew you were such a lightweight."

"Did you tell me hell was other people so I'd believe the opposite?"

"No. You were hell and you were a person. I was probably angry."

"I'm sorry."

She wrung out the towel and handed it to me. "You must be truly, truly ill or possessed by something you haven't expelled from your system yet."

"I made it hard for you," I said after I wiped my mouth, abruptly more sober than drunk.

"You were a miserable bitch from day one."

"I said I was sorry."

"Alert the media." She took the towel. "Are you staying tonight? Your room still has a bed in it. I think there are a few of your things still in the closet."

My old room. Logan's house. The warehouse.

Three places to sleep for three stages of my life.

Which one did I want to live in?

None. But at least Bianca was finally being honest with me.

"Can I stay here?"

"Of course. Let's clean this up and get you to bed."

Shockingly, Bianca knew how to both clean a toilet and not complain about it. We made quick work of it together with Mr. Tubbs on the other side of the door, yipping for his mother.

On the way to the stairs, we passed my father's old office, and my eye caught on two urns side by side on a high shelf. My father's was polished gold. My mother's was pewter.

Instead of heading up the stairs, I stopped to gaze at the urns.

Appreciating Bianca's honesty meant I had to do her the same favor. I owed her the complete deal, not just carefully chosen admissions.

"My mother's urn," I said.

"Yes?" She scooped up the dog and made a kiss-face at him.

"It's in the same place."

"My goodness, Ella, did you think I'd throw it away?"

"It's empty."

She laughed brightly, as if cued by the *ba-dum-bump* after a perfect joke.

"What?" I asked. "You knew?"

"I knew it the day after your father and I were married."

She'd never said anything of course, because she didn't give a shit about my mother or what she meant to Daddy.

"Of course you did."

"Your jeans, that morning, after you declined to show up for the wedding? Strewn on the floor. Of course. You were sleeping, and your father and I were getting ready to go on our honeymoon. I turned them right side out to fold them. At first, I didn't know what on earth you'd gotten on the knees. What could you have been crawling through? A volcano?"

Was my secret a secret? Had my father known what I'd done? Did he die hating me and never telling me? Or did he understand?

"Did you tell Daddy?"

Instead of answering, she took two steps to the second floor and stopped with one arm under the white poodle and the other draped over the banister. "Are you coming up?

More steps, until her ankles were level with my eyes and I had to look up at her.

"Did you? Bianca! Did. You. Tell. Him?"

"Why does it matter now?"

"Because I never got to explain. If he died thinking I missed his wedding to throw mom's ashes in the garbage disposal or whatever… he'd think I did it out of spite."

"And you didn't." The statement was both a question and encouragement for more.

"No, I didn't. Mom up there, looking down at Dad and his new wife… I'm not saying I didn't hate you, because I did. But I wanted Dad to be happy and I wanted Mom at peace. So I spread the ashes over the front pavement at the Observatory, because she named me star and that's dumb, but it was all I could think of. Then I put the urn back. Without her inside, it was just a container."

"That's a lovely story," she said dryly.

"Did you tell him?"

"Did I?" She looked into space for a moment, head tilted. I assumed she was coming up with an extra biting retort. In the end, I kind of wished she had. "Basile found out a couple of years later. He moved it, and it was too light. He was… shall we say, distraught."

I swallowed hard. He'd never said anything to me. Bianca must have told him about my jeans and the mysterious ash. Why did he not come to me? "What did he say when you told him?"

"When I told him what?"

"About the ash on my jeans, Bianca. Stop fucking around."

She came down the steps, stopping in front of me with the banister between us. "I told him I'd been dusting up there and it fell. I told him the ashes came out and I cleaned them up before he could see. He was livid. He called me a liar. He said I was covering

231

for the cleaning lady. Then when she denied it, he said I was trying to purge your mother. He couldn't believe what a sneak I was. He said I'd done it out of spite. I didn't tell him that his daughter was the spiteful one."

Bianca, the stepmonster, had covered for me? Lied for me? Risked her marriage to an unforgiving man to protect me? Who was she?

Who was I?

Was I the kind of person who let that happen? Was I someone who did bad things and covered them up, thinking as long as I didn't get caught, no one was hurt?

"I'm—"

"Sorry, yes. I know, Ella."

"Daddy was wrong. He should have known you better."

"Well, he's dead now. So it doesn't matter."

Did nothing matter? Could a person do anything they wanted because we were all going to die one day anyway? Did all the scoreboards reset to zero? Was the plan to outlive everyone else's grudges and resentments and drop dead with your own, alone but clean?

"I have to go," I said, taking out my phone to call a car, which I did before seeing Logan's texts.

—*Are you all right?*—

—*Where are you?*—

He'd texted a few minutes after I'd left, then again.

—*You're not here*—

—*I'm fine. Go to bed*—

—*I need to know where you are*—

—*I'm going home*—

"You're perfectly welcome to stay," Bianca said, coming up next to me.

"No. I need to be... hell is other people, right?" I pocketed the phone, unable to look at her.

"You look upset. Will Logan be there when you get home?"

Yes, and that was a problem.

"Of course I'm…" I took a deep breath. "I'll be fine. Thank you for telling me. I know it looks like I'm running off mad, but I'm grateful for what you did and… I don't know. I have to figure out what it means."

"Maybe it doesn't mean anything."

"It has to mean something." I rubbed my temples to erase the impending headache. "It can't all be empty."

"It's not all empty." She rubbed my arm. "But you have to fill the *right* things."

My phone chimed. The car was pulling up the block. Bianca went outside and waited with me on the sidewalk.

"Did Daddy forgive you?" I asked as the Prius stopped at the curb. "For the thing you didn't do?"

"Who can say?"

No one could say whether or not he could hold a grudge against a woman he'd professed to love, letting it eat at him for years, or if he'd let it go. He didn't talk about what was in his heart.

"I get it." I hugged her. "Still sorry."

"Get home safe, and come by some time. Bring your husband." She winked.

I waved and got into the car. The driver turned down his radio.

"Good evening, miss," he said. "Still going to Hancock Park?"

"Actually, I need to go to Highland."

Cradling her poodle, my stepmother went into the house I grew up in and closed the door.

28

LOGAN

—I'm going home—

NOT "COMING" home. Coming home was with me, in the present —now. Coming home was "I'll see you there."

Going home was something completely different. It was the home of past and future, where she wouldn't see me.

I parked in front of the warehouse on Highland, where the mural commanded me to BREAK SHIT without saying what shit was or how badly it needed to be broken. I drove around the corner. Her car was parked in back, and the lights were off there too. I got out and listened for any sound from inside. Nothing.

I didn't like being cut off, and I didn't like having to figure out where she was. She was still my wife. If something happened to her, I needed to know where it was happening.

She had to be coming here. I'd just have to wait.

When I told myself I'd wait at Ella's back door all night if I had to, I didn't take myself literally because I didn't think I had to.

After the first half hour, I unfolded an old aluminum chair I found under the steps and waited on the landing. After the second half hour, I called Colton to see if Ella had gotten back yet. He

234

said "nah" and asked if he should wait for her. I told him to go to bed or whatever he did.

In the silence that followed a circling helicopter, I drank two-fisted from a well of worry.

My right fist clutched the fear that something terrible had happened to her.

In my left, I held onto the idea that she'd gone to a man's bed for comfort. There, they counted down the days until she was free of me.

What my right hand held was heavier, but my left got all the attention.

We were playacting at love. We were nothing. Nonexistent. Happiness didn't make a damn bit of difference. Fulfillment was for after the divorce.

For now we had roles, and every day we walked on stage and said our lines. In the morning, she cradled her cup and blew on her coffee, smiling at the first taste, tapping her ring on a mug with Van Gogh's *Starry Night* printed on the side when she was thinking about whatever we were talking about. My coming day. My hopes for it. My fears.

Me me me me all the way home.

Half our marriage was gone, and it hadn't occurred to me to make her happy until it was too late. She was doing everything I wanted and being exactly who I thought I needed.

She thought I didn't give a shit, but I did. I gave a lot of shits, and I didn't realize how much trouble that was until I was sitting in an aluminum folding chair behind a run-down warehouse, waiting for her.

Close to midnight, a car pulled down the alley and Ella got out. She looked disheveled and drawn, head down so she didn't see me until the car pulled away.

"Hi," I said.

She came up the steps and stood right in front of me, keys jangling off a finger. "Why are you here?"

CD REISS

I could have asked her the same question. She didn't live here. She lived with me.

Semantics.

"I want to talk to you."

"You're blocking the door."

I got up, folded the chair, and leaned it against the railing. Ella unlocked the steel security door, then the interior, and went inside, turning the lights on as she went.

"What did you want to talk about?" She dropped her bag and peeled off her jacket on her way across the length of the space, leaving it in a pile on the floor next to the huge white canvas. It had a red blob in the middle now.

"You decided what to do with this?"

"Not really." She stopped to kick off her shoes.

I hoped she'd tell me more so I could show an interest in her life. Take action to improve it or something... whatever she needed. All I had to do was listen.

"Can you undo me?" Her hair had grown, and she had to pull it over one shoulder so I could get at the back zipper of the dress she'd worn to dinner a few hours and a million realizations ago.

"You smell like throw up," I said.

Admittedly, of all the things I noticed, that was the wrong one to voice. She also smelled like wine and sounded hoarse, but those tangible, sensory changes were nothing compared to how far away she seemed.

I drew the zipper down, letting my finger course down the length of her back, over her bra, to the curve above her ass. I pushed the dress off her shoulders and let it drop to the floor. She stepped out of it, only in her underwear.

"Thanks." She didn't even look at me, walking away with her arms behind her to unhook her bra, bare feet on the concrete floor as she slid the straps down and tossed it onto the couch.

She wasn't being intentionally seductive. She wasn't asking me to follow her into the bathroom for a quick fuck. No, she was

236

tired and deep in thought, cavalier about my presence because I'd been cavalier about hers.

The shower sputtered twice before it hissed.

I caught sight of her phone. It was unlocked.

"You told Mandy and Selma I was sick, right?" she called.

"Yeah," I replied, setting up location tracking between our devices.

"Good. Want to keep the story straight."

I stood outside the doorway. She was down to her underpants, leaning into the stall with her hand under the water, waiting for it to get hot. Trying to avoid the peaks of her breasts, I looked down. The plain cotton fabric rode up the front of her cleft on the bottom, and hung at the line of her hips at the top. My eyes did laps around the shape of her underwear until the weight of her stare brought me back to her face.

"Are you trying to get me to ask for a fuck?" I asked. "Because it's working."

"If I wanted to fuck, you wouldn't have to ask." The room filled with steam. She bent down to get her underwear off and stopped with her fingers hooked in the sides. "You can come in, but if you can't stand the sight of me in my own bathroom, you can wait outside."

I sat on the toilet, averting my eyes before I did something stupid.

She went behind the curtain. "What did you want to talk about?"

"What you said to me before you left."

"I wouldn't lose any sleep over it."

"You were right. I've taken you for granted."

"Yeah, well, in a few months I'll realize that and get a lawyer."

If she had a twinge of doubt about the end of our deal, her voice didn't betray it.

Was that supposed to hurt as much as it did?

"I set up location tracking on your phone."

CD REISS

"Why?"

"I didn't like not knowing where you were. I'm a controlling asshole. You can divorce me for that too."

She didn't answer.

"Selma thought you were interesting," I said.

"Selma suspects I was part of the GAC. She's not interested. She's curious."

"Is that so bad?"

Water splashed behind the curtain. Plastic clicked as if a shampoo bottle snapped closed.

"What happens when she finds out that I'm not anymore? And I've got nothing but a rich husband and talent under the hood? Fucking pathetic."

It wasn't pathetic, but what was it? She rarely talked about herself or her career. My job was to buy out her father's company and sign divorce papers.

That was going to change starting immediately.

"Maybe art's not your thing," I suggested.

"What's that supposed to mean?"

"Hear me out," I insisted as if she had a choice. "Maybe you're at your best doing fashion. Maybe you got a whole other skill set and talent from your father. So when we get control of Papillion—"

"I don't want Papillion."

She shut off the water.

"I'm sorry?" In the damp air, under the sizzle of the shower, I couldn't have heard her right.

"It's not mine." Her hand stuck out from behind the curtain. "Can you grab the towel?"

"That was the reason you got into this with me." I handed her the thin white cloth.

"Yeah. I know." The curtain vibrated when she dried her hair, then stilled as it ran along her skin.

I had to be misunderstanding her.

238

"So am I buying it up or no?"

"You're not." She slapped open the curtain. The towel was tied under her arms and her wet hair hung to her shoulders in waves. Leaning on the sink, she plucked her toothbrush out of her glass.

"Can I ask why? Since I started already?"

"It's not who I am anymore. It's Bianca's mess. Let her clean it up."

"You are charmingly unstable."

"I was wrong about everything," she continued as she squeezed out toothpaste. "Nothing I wanted was ever actually mine." She brushed her teeth, stopping with a mouthful of foam to speak. "I'm entitled to nothing." Brush. Stop. "Doesn't matter what my name is." Brush. Stop. "Papillion. Crowne." Brush. Spit. "Lady McFuckstick."

My laughter was inappropriate. I wasn't matching her seriousness with my own.

But she smiled and wiped her mouth. "See, I knew you had a sense of humor."

Uptight Logan didn't know how to have a good time. Never went outside the lines. Kept his head so far down on his work, he couldn't see anyone around him and was never seen. I'd cultivated that image as if it was part of my job, and now she was surprised when I laughed at a corny joke.

She'd been everything to me, and I'd made sure I was no more than a husband to her.

"I want to know you," I said. "Really know you."

"No, you don't." With that, she went to her bedroom.

I followed like a puppy hungry for attention, helplessly watching my owner yank pajamas out of a drawer when I wanted to be taken out for a walk.

"Turn around," she said, about to drop her towel, and like a dog trained to sit, I did it.

This wasn't the story I told myself about who I was. I was in charge. I ran the show. But here I was, staring at a painting of a nude woman sitting on the toilet, clipping her toenails. I got close enough to see each brushstroke. I couldn't tell if it was garbage or a masterwork, but it was Ella's, and her presence was in the gestures.

"I want you to give me a chance," I said. "You think I don't listen, but I do. I've listened to the tone of your voice change from excited to bored. I've listened to the way you agree to do things you don't care about. You're like a woman waiting in line at the DMV, just trying to get through it. It's going to change, Ella. All of it. I want to know who you are."

I turned around as she was pulling on a T-shirt. The neck stretched and her head popped through.

She smoothed down her hair. "I didn't say you could turn around."

"You put the bottoms on first. I want to know that. Your warm socks are on the bed, so they go on after the shirt. I want to know that. I want to know the noise you make when you're sleeping. I want to know what soap you like, how you sit when you clip your toenails, how you brush your hair in the morning. I want to know how to take care of you so I can be there when you need me."

Her neck undulated when she swallowed. I'd said a lot. Too much. Way too much. I was out on a limb, and it was bending under my weight.

"What happens when you don't like what you learn?" she asked with her arms crossed. "Because you won't."

"Let me be the judge of that."

Her jaw set and her mouth tightened for a moment before she uncrossed her arms and threw open the armoire to pull out a black leather jacket. She shrugged it on over her pajamas and yanked an empty bag out of the bottom of the closet. "Let's go, Logan."

"Where—"

Before I could finish, she crossed to the working side of the space. Still leashed like a puppy dog, I followed. She threw open a cabinet and filled the duffel bag with spray paint cans.

"For a guy running a gabillion dollar company," she said, shaking a can with a click-click-click and discarding it, "you can't see the big picture." Red. Blue. Black. "How I put my pants on has nothing to do with who I am or the shit I've done." Zipping the bag with a single, loud screech, she threw it over one shoulder. "So let's start with that and see how you like it."

I held out my hand. "Let's start with me carrying the bag."

With a knowing smile, she swung the bag around and let go. It landed at my feet with a clatter.

I picked it up. "Lead the way."

At the back door, she jammed her bare feet in a pair of black boots. Her pajama legs bunched unevenly at the calves. The carelessness of it, the in-betweenness, was intimate in a way that made me want to slide the pajamas down and fuck her with her boots on.

Ready for anything, and satisfied in my role as both puppy dog and pack horse, I followed her out into the night.

29

ELLA

HE WANTED TO KNOW ME. Sure. Logan Crowne with tons of money and the perfect family wanted to know Ella Papillion the orphan who'd lost everything because she couldn't keep her shit together. Mr. Straitlaced who'd never broken a promise wanted to meet the woman who was breaking her promise to her father. The guy who'd lied one time and felt like shit about it every day until he lied about his marriage to me wanted to know a professional liar.

This guy.

I had to admire his willingness to go where I explicitly told him he didn't want to go. It took a strange kind of courage to trust me when I was so untrustworthy.

Once he was in the back alley, I pulled the telescoping ladder from under the stairs.

"We're going to the roof of the building." I snapped the ladder open a few rungs.

He looked up. The corner of the billboard was visible from where we were standing. "And then?"

"Then we do stupid shit we'll be sorry for."

He blinked. Considered. Shrugged. "Sounds good."

I opened the ladder fully and hooked the top to the roof edge. I went up it as if I'd done it a million times before—which I had— and Logan came after me without a moment's hesitation.

"Here we are," I said, showing him my little rooftop lounge. "It's not a mansion in Bel-Air, but you can see all the way to the Hollywood Bowl."

"I like it."

"You're in luck." I craned my neck to check out the towering, brightly-lit billboard. Obviously, no one had ponied up the money to buy an ad. The plywood was visible between three huge stripes of shredded white paper. It looked like a jar with the label half peeled off. "We're between last month's deodorant and next month's action movie. Reduced guilt vandalism."

Brightly-colored spray paint had a single, basic use as far as I was concerned. But Logan wasn't me, and I could tell he only made the connection when I said the word vandalism.

"You in or out?" I asked, putting my foot on the bottom rung of the billboard's ladder.

He picked up the duffel bag. "In."

He was still and always would be handsome. He was commanding and confident, assertive and poised. I remembered his dick with more fondness than any other. But on my rooftop with a bag of cans in a hard fist, the hottest thing about him was his readiness to follow me. I almost stopped myself from leading him further so I could protect him from the very intimacy he sought.

"Well?" he asked. "You want me to go first?"

No. I didn't.

He wanted to know me, but that was half the story.

I wanted to show him who I was, even if opening the gate and guiding him down the path to my heart ended up breaking it.

So I climbed.

Past the NO TRESPASSING sign. The DANGER warning.

The AUTHORIZED PERSONNEL ONLY badge. I went over the locked gate and dropped onto the catwalk behind the sign.

Logan slung the bag over the gate before he mounted it and launched down to the narrow walkway.

The lights were in the front of the billboard, but we were behind it, where the plywood didn't need to be seen or covered. Dwarfed by the scale of it and protected in the shadows, we were both very exposed and very alone.

"You're good at this," I said.

He cupped my face and kissed me before I could finish, pushing me against the raw wood as if he wanted to merge our bodies. His intensity had its own force, a gravitational pull I couldn't—and didn't want to—resist. If only I could fall into that depth of passion forever, with my unmet desires expanding to the surface of my skin and my fear sinking endlessly into darkness.

I pulled away, gasping for breath. "We're not done."

"I know," he said, picking up the bag. "I wanted to kiss you first."

This time, he led the way around the catwalk to the front of the billboard, where the lights were blinding and the faces were the size of a house.

"What now?" he asked, squinting in the light.

I took out a can of blue and shook it. *Click, click, click.*

"Whatever." I wanted to make a point, not art, so I scrawled a curly moustache over the newscaster's mouth because it was as high as I could reach.

"You live here." He popped a can of red. "Won't they know it's you?"

"Maybe they'll ask." I finished with a little flavor-saver under the lower lip because I was a child. "But they have to catch us red-handed, so hurry up."

He reached up and scripted *I want...*

"What are you writing?"

"Patience, my star."

...to fuck...

"Language, Mr. Crowne." I jabbed him in the ribs under his outstretched arm.

...my wife.

He tossed the can with the rest. "Now it's in writing."

His voice was liquid and solid at the same time. Forceful, impenetrable, and mutable enough to fit into the shape of my desire. His kiss was fullness, heat, the taste of what we could have had without the deals and contracts. He grabbed my ass and lifted me until my legs were wrapped around his hips and his erection was pressed against my heat.

"Inside you," he growled, grinding into me. "Now."

"Yes," I groaned.

Holding me up, he navigated around the billboard to the back where it was dark. He pushed me against the plywood, hands digging under my stretchy pants, past my ass, driving the elastic down my thighs. Reaching around, he ran his fingertips along my seam.

"I'm going to ruin this." He teased my clit. "Drive so deep you can't see where I end and you begin." He flicked the nub and I arched into him. "You want that?"

"Do it. Take me."

I held myself up on his shoulders as he undid his jeans, releasing his cock and positioning it to enter me.

"Don't." He jammed inside me, stretching me open. "Don't ever dare me to own you." He pushed again. "Once this cunt is mine"—with one last thrust, he was in to the core, so deep I existed only where we were joined—"it's mine to wreck."

I meant to make words, but I only found the vowels, and with every thrust, I found more. My world was his dick. The night was his voice. My life was the growing sensation between my legs as he stretched me, pushing his body against my nub as I clawed at his shirt.

"You want to come," he growled, driving hard.

"Yes."

"I want to know you."

"Okay. Please. Go."

Rolling his hips, pushing to the base with thrusts so deep and hard, he touched places I didn't know I had. He grunted right before I exploded into a cone of light and dark, blindness and vision, where the silence was as loud as a siren.

The world came back in stages. The sound of cars whooshing by on Highland. The smell of his cologne. The feel of his lips on my neck. The ache in my thighs.

He eased me down to a standing position and kissed my lips. "Let's get out of here before the neighbors call the cops."

We scrambled back into the warehouse as if the cops were chasing us.

He dropped the bag and came for me again as if fucking against the back of the billboard hadn't satisfied his hunger. As soon as he touched me, I knew it hadn't satisfied mine either. We groped each other's clothes, attached at the mouth, unbuttoning, unzipping, grasping for bare skin, finally naked when we fell onto the bed and rolled around like wrestlers on my little mattress.

We hadn't defaced much. Hadn't gotten caught or faced consequences, and yet it was enough. He didn't just accept me or tolerate who I was. He embraced how different we were and had dared to experience a little of my life.

Straddling him, I put my hands on either side of his head and shifted so his shaft ran along my seam. "You ready for me to run this show?"

"Ready for you to try."

I straightened, moving back and forth without letting him enter me. He took my breasts, kneading them as he jerked his hips with mine, trying to take control of how his shaft ran along my clit.

"I want you to fuck me," I said, putting my hand on his chest. "From there."

"Yes," he growled.

"Let me do it. Watch me." I took his hands off my body. "Just watch."

Crouching, I lined his dick up with me and impaled myself on him. He reached for me, but I pinned his wrists over his head.

"No hands," I said, letting go and kneeling straight.

"This is how you want it?" He seemed concerned he'd been doing it wrong the whole time.

"This time." Getting on my feet, I lifted myself and slid down.

When I rose again, he looked between us, at the place we were connected, and watched his cock enter me. "Fuck, that's so hot."

"Tell me what you want."

He glanced up at me, and I smiled. The shoe was on the other foot. I had the power to deliver his satisfaction. All he had to do was say it.

"Faster."

I gave him what he asked for, increasing the speed of my crouches by the look on his face and how hard he worked to not touch me.

"What do you want, Logan?"

"See you come," he snarled, demanding it from under me.

I put my middle and index fingers in his mouth. "Make them wet."

He did it, growling against my hand, sucking and licking. I pulled out and put my wet fingers on my clit, pushing him in and out of me, stretching the pleasure of his dick to a tingling fire.

"That's it," he said, jerking upward to push himself deep. "Show me how you make yourself come."

The command in his voice and the sharp jolt of his dick brought me closer, demanding a surrender to pleasure even as I tried to dominate him.

"Give it to me," he said. "Let me see it."

We moved together, each stroke pushing me just enough, but I needed more. Not more stimulation... more him.

"Say something!" I cried.

"Come on my cock."

Like magic, I exploded into an orgasm, pulsing around him as he'd told me to, bending backward until he slipped out of me.

When I opened my eyes, he was on all fours over me.

"Thank you," I said. "For letting me be in charge."

"You're good at it." His erection pressed against my thigh.

"You didn't come," I said, putting my hands on his face.

He took them away and put my wrists over my head as I'd done to him. "I'm saving it."

"For what?"

"I want to make a suggestion first." He rolled away.

"What?"

"I want to renegotiate the contract."

My lungs squeezed all the blood out of my heart. "Okay."

"Let's say this." He traced the line of my breast, over the last line of inked butterflies. "Let's say we don't have to get divorced."

"What?"

"I'm not saying we won't. But we treat this like a normal relationship. Just... married."

No. Everything in me said no. I'd clung to the security of knowing I'd be hurt and that I had control over how much and when. His change meant the sky was the limit.

"I don't know." I got off the bed.

"Why not?"

"Nothing's really changed. I'm not a good wife for you. And you..."

I couldn't finish with him reclined on my bed like a god, with his hammer of a cock waiting. I couldn't kid myself into thinking it was just his beauty or our sex. He was loyal and stable and sincere even when he was lying.

"Me, what?"

"I was going to say you're not my type. But..." I stopped myself again before I said a stupid thing. "I have to go to the bathroom."

Not waiting for him to answer, I did my business, sore from the violence of the first fuck and the pace of the second. He'd made me raw and I loved it. The way he'd given me control but taken it back exactly when I needed him to.

Naked in front of the mirror, I washed my hands with an unwilling smile because he'd listened. He'd heard me and adjusted.

Logan Crowne had changed just a little for me.

That was cool.

When I opened the door, he was standing there, dick still at attention.

"I want you," he said, coming toward me. "We're married. That is what it is. Whether or not you're the wife I need in six months or ten years doesn't matter. You're the woman I need right now. I'm not giving you up. You're mine."

I put my hands on the counter behind me. "I can't let you break me."

"Listen to me." He laid his hands on my shoulders, moving them to the sides of my neck. "No man is strong enough to break you."

"You're so sure?"

"I know they tried. But look at me. Compared to you, I'm empty. Hollow. The slightest tap from you and I'll crack in a hundred places. I belong to you. If anyone's walking out of this broken, it's going to be me. I want to risk it, and if I bleed when you leave me, it'll still all be worth it."

He wasn't lying, but he was misinformed. He'd misjudged my resilience and miscalculated my strength.

But as wrong as he was about me, and for me, I wanted him.

I wanted him for more than six months, more than a lifetime.

"Let's give it a shot then."

The light of his smile was so real I nearly had to squint. "Good." He kissed me. "Good girl."

His kisses went from loving pecks to deep passion.

As sore as I was, I was wet again. Then he pulled back.

"New rule," he said.

"There are rules?"

"No more playing wife. You have to do what makes you happy."

"Did the nineteen-fifties kick you out?" I ran my nails down his chest and stomach.

He laughed and kissed me again.

"What if you make me happy?" I asked.

He hitched me up and I wrapped my legs around his waist. "Then I'll be the happiest man alive."

That night, my husband slept in my bed for the first time, as if that was what I needed to do to let myself love him. The fact was, I already did.

ELLA

TED AND DOREEN had never claimed there was anything special about this wedding anniversary. Thirty-six wasn't a nice round number people usually celebrated. It didn't roll off the tongue, and my mother-in-law swore up and down there was no personal significance to the numbers. But the party was important to them. So important, Doreen wanted to wear her butterfly-wing dress.

But her body had changed, and it didn't look right anymore.

I'd offered to alter it. I didn't know if I could figure out how the thing even worked without taking it apart completely, but Doreen deserved every happiness, so I'd agreed to try.

I waited for her in my studio. My altered silver dress hung on the mannequin. I'd made some adjustments in the month since I'd worn it to our disastrous dinner. It had a leather corset belt and uneven hemline. I kept playing with it. Some nights, my mind was so alive with ideas, I couldn't sleep.

I'd recreated it in new fabrics, trying to emulate the pattern, eating at the cutting table Logan had surprised me with, staying on Highland later than I should. The shelves were soon stacked with boxes of false starts and bad ideas.

Logan had asked me if there was an end goal for all this time I was spending in the studio. He knew I didn't want to mass-produce clothing any more than I wanted to do custom couture. I told him I was amusing myself and he'd better not get in the way of it with dumb questions.

He laughed and kissed me, then laughed again when I jabbed him in the ribs. Then he pushed my wrists over my head and pinned them against the refrigerator. Then Colton had come in like a dog looking for a belly rub, and that was that until later.

Doreen knocked on the alley door exactly at two, and I opened it.

"Thank you!" she said, instead of hello.

Her driver was behind her, holding a huge garment bag.

"My pleasure, come in!" I held my hand out to the driver. "Here, I have it. Are you coming in?"

"I'll come back when she's ready. You have it? It's heavy." He let the weight of the hanger fall on my fingers.

"Wow, it is."

He said his goodbyes and I closed the door.

"Do you want to sit?" I said to Doreen as I hung the garment bag on a rack. "It's not as clean as you're used to, but I vacuumed the couch."

Doreen stood in front of the mannequin, shaking hand pointing at the silver dress. "This is what you wore to the Crowne Jewels?"

"Yeah." In my fervor, I'd done things to that beautiful dress a sensible person wouldn't, and in front of my mother-in-law, I was suddenly ashamed of reimagining my father's legacy.

"It's really something."

Unzipping the bag, I smiled at the nice-person code for "terrible." I couldn't disagree with her, but I was undaunted. The process made me happy.

"God," I said as the butterfly wings bled out of the open zipper. "This is more amazing the second time I'm seeing it."

Doreen wrung her hands together, which made them tremor together. "What do you think? Can you fix it?"

"Let's get it on you."

She undressed down to her leggings and tank. I helped her get the gown on, tucking in the NORA WARREN tag, and stood behind her in front of the mirror. She looked pretty good, but I made a list of things I'd change if I could. Which I couldn't. Forget it.

"See?" she said.

"Tell me what it feels like."

"Tight here." She put her hands on her waist. "And here." Top edge, under her arms. "And when I do this"—she twisted her hips —"it moves too much."

"All right, get it off and we'll see what we've got."

When she got it off, I laid it out on the cutting table.

"God damn, Daddy," I mumbled.

"What?"

"Well, it's so clean inside... I'm going to have to rip some seams. Do you mind?"

"Have at it."

I took out my seam ripper, and for the second time in my life, I laid it in the seam of one of Basile Papillion's gowns.

"How are you and Logan doing?" she asked, walking around the silver dress to see my work.

Riiiip. Didn't hurt at all.

"Great." Truthful, if still part lie. I inspected the construction at the top edge. Wait. This couldn't be right. I ripped deeper.

"I have to admit, I didn't think you'd last a minute with that boy."

"We haven't been together that long."

"I was worried. I mean, he's so tightly wound and you're such a free spirit."

The edge was easy, but the way the butterfly wings were

attached from the inside? It looked like glue. Brushed-on clear glue.

"And I thought," Doreen continued, "he was either going to crush you or you were going to get bored and run like hell."

I sniffed the inside of the lining and almost got a contact high. "I don't believe it…"

"I'm starting to."

"Moth-er-fucker. I cannot even with this." I stood away from the table. "He used rubber cement on a ten-thousand-dollar ball gown."

"Is that bad?" Doreen peered over the gown to see the glue.

Basile Papillion wasn't such a genius after all. Or at least he wasn't a perfect genius.

"If finding out your father took shortcuts is bad, yeah."

"Can you make it fit again?"

"Well, I don't know what's going to happen if I start cutting. The glue's old, so the wings could drop and you'll have bald spots." I gathered the garment and draped it onto a second form I'd bought. "And if I take it in here, it's not going to drape unless I…" I stepped back, dismissing the idea.

"What?"

"It's too much. It'll change the entire thing."

"You mean, a little different? Or like this?" She pointed at the silver dress.

"Somewhere between." I waved, wrinkling my nose to describe mitigated damage.

Doreen clapped as if I'd delivered fantastic news. "Perfect! Make it like this." She took my face in her cold, spindly hands. "Make it as special as you are."

I pressed her palms to my cheek, overwhelmed with gratitude for her, the most loving and supportive of the three mothers I'd had in my life.

31

LOGAN

ESTELLA PAPILLION. My wife. Soon after I slept in her bed, I stopped thinking of our marriage as fake. In the month since, we'd woken up together every morning, and every night I came home as soon as I could because that was where she was.

I'd been wrong about marriage. It wasn't a role. Nor was it a proper division of duties. Marriage was knowing that no matter what happened, she existed in the world. Our world.

"What are you looking at?" Ella asked as Loranda opened the back of the car for her.

"My wife." I put my hand on the door, and my driver—our driver—retreated to get behind the wheel.

"Not the dress?" She swung her hips, and the pleats in the skirt rose above her knees, opening to reveal bright pink fabric that glittered.

"The...?" It was one of her father's that she'd pulled from a closet in Bianca's office. "No. It's nice, but it's not the dress. It's you."

"Careful," she said. "Or you might get laid tonight."

I traced the length of her collarbone. "If there's a Ferrari parked in the garage, it's a guarantee."

Her mouth curled in a knowing smile, and she got in the car. I sat next to her and closed the door, arm around her as we pulled into the street to Bel-Air. I kissed the diamond in her nose.

Estella Papillion was my wife. My partner.

If she left me, she'd rip half my world off with her.

———

THE ANNIVERSARY PARTY wasn't a tenth the size of the housewarming where Ella and I had announced our marriage. No paparazzi. No faces I knew but didn't quite know.

"Darling!" Bianca cried when she saw us. "It's magnificent!"

She was talking about Ella's dress.

"So is the woman wearing it," I said after greeting my mother-in-law with a kiss.

Ella nudged me in modesty, and I kissed her humility away.

All the Crowne sibs were there, except Dante, who was known to go off the grid every once in a while. Colton wore one of his better suits and a backward cap. Liam's son, Matt, was old enough to run around with second cousins and leave his dad to mingle. Lyric was in a corner with her friends, faces lit by their phones. Byron had Garrett on his shoulders, looking over the patio at the sunset, naming all the colors.

We went to the bar as the band played gentle versions of songs popular the year my parents were married.

"Mr. and Mrs. Crowne," the bartender said, placing square napkins with the number thirty-six printed in gold foil in front of us.

I left it up to Ella to decide whether or not to correct her name, but she didn't.

"I don't know." She scanned the bottles lined up behind the server.

"Gin?" I asked her. "Or a Shirley Temple, for old time's sake?"

"How about..." She bit her lip, clearly thinking. I admired how

—down to the smallest things—she didn't get caught in a rut. "Something old school."

"How about a gin rickey?" the bartender suggested.

"Great! I'm in."

"Sounds fun," I said. "I'll have one too."

"Who are you?" Ella said when the bartender turned away. "And what have you done with my husband?"

"Keeping you on your toes."

"I'm not sure I like it. There's something nice about a man who knows what he likes."

"I can also be a man who finds new things to like."

"True." She put her back to the bar. "Look at them. They're so perfect."

I followed her gaze to my parents. My father wore a suit, as always, and Mom was in the dress that she'd worn on her tenth anniversary. Ella had added sleeves, and the butterflies crammed together on the skirt thinned on the bodice as if they were taking off, like the tattoo on my wife's chest.

"You did a good job on the dress," I said.

"It was fun."

"How about more?" I waved to my parents, and they made their way to the bar, greeting guests on the way. "A gallery full of them."

"It's not quite art."

Our drinks came.

"Then make it art. Call it sculpture. Start from scratch, like you said. Or buy another designer and destroy them. Could be a good business."

She looked away from my parents to me and fixed my tie. "Not everything is business, Mr. Crowne."

"But not everything isn't, Ms. Papillion."

She laid her hand on my chest, about to say something, and stopped. "What's in here?" She tapped the place where the contents of my breast pocket made the jacket stiff.

"My first anniversary gift," I whispered. "I'm taking you on a honeymoon."

"Where are we going? Did you get tickets already?"

I laughed when she peeked into my jacket, but I pressed down the lapel and pulled her into me. "It's just a card with a list of ideas. But I hear dinner on an oil rig in the South China Sea is nice."

"Sounds romantic." She wrapped her arms around my neck and kissed me.

"That's enough of that," my father's voice came from my left.

Ella and I separated.

My mother was flushed, mouth agape, eyes shifting from me to my wife and back. She quivered as if a chill ran up her spine, a very different shake than the one caused by her Parkinson's.

"Mom?" I asked.

"Oh my! It's just even when I expect it, it's unexpected."

Ted laughed. "Finally!"

"I knew it was coming, Theodore," she said.

"What was coming?" Colton said, breaking into our circle. Always late to the conversation.

"I have no idea," Ella said.

"The tingle," Ted said. "It came late."

Arm around Ella, I pulled her closer.

We had the final approval. I picked up my drink and lifted it. "To the tingle!"

We all toasted, and I kissed my wife.

"About damn time," Colton said. "I live with you guys and I'm always thinking you're half broken up." He took a swig of beer, and Ella's hand tightened around my waist.

I needed to change the subject. Whatever he thought he'd observed, I didn't want him revealing it in front of my parents.

"So, Dad—" I said, trying to change the subject without knowing what I was changing it to.

"Fighting's healthy," Mom said.

"Nah, nah, they don't fight. This guy—" Colton punched me affectionately. "He's so old-timey he had them like... what's that show? *I Love Lucy*? With the separate beds." He pointed between Ella and me. "They were in separate rooms until, like, what? A month ago?"

"No," Ella said, but didn't elaborate.

Mom seemed unmoved—as happy as ever—but Dad looked deeply into his drink.

"It's cool, El, you wore him down." He tipped his beer toward my wife in respect.

"What were you doing upstairs?" I growled, missing the point.

"Checking it out. I was bored. Then I went to look for my buddy's ball—up on my roof? I told you?"

"I knew it," Ted said, looking at me. "It was too easy."

"Dad—" I started, but he held up his hand.

"This is disappointing." He put his drink on the bar. "But not surprising."

"What?" Colton asked.

I could explain. Maybe Ella had had a cold when he went up there, or maybe I snored. I had to say something, anything, but no excuse looked strong enough to get through my father's newfound disbelief. For the first time since Colton started running his mouth, I looked at Ella.

The color had drained from her face and her expression was frozen.

"You're right," Ella said, and with a hitch of breath as if she had to stop herself from saying more, she clamped her mouth shut and looked at me. She wasn't asking what to do, but if she should do anything at all.

"Teddy," Mom crooned, "I told you this would happen."

"I didn't expect to be lied to."

Dad walked away. Damnit.

"I'm so sorry," Ella said to my mother.

"Let me talk to him," Mom said, following her husband without accepting Ella's apology.

"I have no idea what the fuck just happened," Colton said.

My wife had been hurt by two mothers, and she was about to be hurt again. Without even realizing it, I'd let that happen. I had to fix it, and I didn't know how. I just wanted her out of the line of fire.

"Ella," I said. "You should go."

If I thought getting her out of the way would reduce the pain she was about to suffer, I was proven wrong by her expression. She looked as if I'd slapped her, and I couldn't explain myself. Not right there. Not right then. I needed to be in that room with my family, and huddled in a dark corner with her at the same time.

"Just go," I said urgently, trying to sound encouraging at the same time.

She had to know I would take care of it, that I wasn't abandoning her, but I'd clearly just slapped her again, reddening both cheeks and filling her eyes with tears. "Okay."

She left. She just did what I'd asked her to do and walked out, and suddenly I was in a room I didn't want to be in, getting pulled away with every step that echoed against the high ceilings.

My family stared at me with wide eyes as if I was a man they'd never known.

I had a moment to choose between them and Ella. We were partners. She was my bulwark against the unexpected. The mitigation of all risk, and yet, I'd told her she didn't belong.

My family could wait.

I chased her into the house. "Ella. Wait."

"You're right," she said, descending the stairs. "And I'm not family. I never was. But I hoped…" She blinked, and lines of water dropped down her cheeks. "I hoped you saw it differently, and you don't." She laid her hand on my chest, where the honeymoon card stiffened the fabric. "It was wrong of me to work so hard to not love you and then fall in love with them."

"Just go home. Wait for me." I pulled a hankie out of my pocket and tried to dry her eyes for her, but she snapped it from my fingers and did it herself. "I'll talk to them, and if it means you stay away from my parents until they come around, then that's what we'll do. Okay? I still run Crowne, so they can't get rid of me."

"It's always about you." She shook her head, refolding the hankie. "That's never going to change. I should have seen it, I mean…" Her short laugh was aimed directly at herself. "God, you wanted me to sign off on naming our fictional children, for fuck's sake. I'm so stupid."

"If you're so stupid, maybe I should make the plan." I crossed my arms. "Because mine was pretty good."

"A plan? I love you, you stupid shit."

She loved me. I could barely hear that from behind the soundproof wall of my frustration at the collapse of our plan. I was turned around, facing the wrong direction, pulled by the tide of needs that I had assumed conflicted. Maybe they didn't. Maybe it was all going in the same direction, and that direction was out to sea.

I'd had it all in my hands. Everything I'd worked for my adult life had been mine, and now it was all at risk because she loved me and I was a stupid shit.

Emotional inertia kept me full speed on the path she'd abandoned, grasping for what I thought I'd attained.

"That's not relevant," I barked.

My head must have sprouted a second face, because that was how she looked at me. As if I was insane. What was so hard about this? We had a fire to put out and she was adding gasoline.

"Of course *you* decide what's relevant."

I reached for her, but she turned and ran down the stairs, holding the handrail so her diamond ring scraped the wood. At the landing, she turned to look at me.

"We'll talk when I home," I said.

"Just stay away from me."

She went down the next flight, and I was about to chase her when I heard my name.

"Logan!" Byron called, running.

"Later," I said.

"It's Dad." He grabbed my wrist.

When I saw my brother's face, I stopped cold.

————

MY FATHER WAS NOT a young man, but he wasn't old enough to have a heart attack.

Maybe having his first son at twenty did it. Or the hours he worked could have weakened him. Or the travel.

Or me.

Maybe—probably—it was me. When I broke his trust, I broke him. He'd given me everything, and I'd stopped his heart with lies and deceit.

"Nice going, asshole," Lyric said, taking her phone away from her face long enough to glare at me across the hospital's VIP waiting room.

"Stop it," Mom scolded.

"She's right," I said. "It's my fault."

"You're not that important," Byron muttered as he paced. Olivia and Garrett had gone home, and he looked naked without them.

"Wow," Colton said, flipping channels on the flat screen TV. "It's Take Shots at Logan day."

"He deserves it," Lyric said.

"We oughta call Liam in case he wants in on the gang-up," Colton added. Liam had gone to put Matt to bed. "If we could find D-Tay, he'd have something to say too."

D-Tay was baby Lyric's pronunciation of Dante.

"Sorry you're made of Teflon, jerk-off," my sister spat back.

"Enough!" Mom cried. "Logan, you did what you thought you had to. We pushed you."

I scoffed. I was a fully-grown man who'd taken a risk without considering any of the personal impacts. I'd hurt my father, my mother, disappointed my brothers and sister, shamed myself, and worst of all, I'd lost the one thing of value I'd gained in the deal.

Ella.

Overwhelmed with remorse and grief, I bent over in my seat, putting my face in my hands to block it all out. If I had my wife there, I'd be able to look my family in the face. Nothing would erase the guilt of what I'd done to my father, but with her at my side, I'd feel redeemable.

The cushions next to me sank, and a shaky hand was laid on my back.

"He just has to take it easy," Mom said, rubbing my back. "You're just like your father. You both work so hard you forget why you're working in the first place."

I folded my palms together and put the edge to my forehead, looking at my feet spread on the beige carpet. "He never lied."

She laughed. "Of course he's lied. Like a rug, that man's lied."

"Ma," Lyric said, dropping her phone next to the fruit bowl. "Not cool."

"Shush, you. Byron, sweetheart, sit down before you wear out your shoes. And you"—she tapped my back—"Stop hiding your face. You're not the only sinner in this family."

"Yo!" Colton raised his hand, still flipping channels. "I'm right over here."

"Don't call Daddy a liar just to make him feel better," Lyric said.

"I agree," I said. "I don't want to feel better. And Lyric? That time you fell into the Wilkins's empty pool? I lied. We didn't follow you over there. You followed us." I looked at Byron. "Sorry."

My brother laughed. "I forgot about that."

"I'm devastated." She rolled her eyes.

"Get it out, brah," Colton said.

"I'll tell Dad when we can see him," I said. "And I'll resign from Crowne."

"No, you won't," Byron snapped. "You're not dropping that in my lap."

"I thought you wanted it."

"It's a time-suck. I have a wife who needs me."

And I didn't.

I had a wife who loved me and who I'd hurt—not with lies but indifference. We'd had a short time together, and I'd spent it taking her for granted. And when I stopped for a moment to appreciate her needs, I'd torn her open like a Christmas gift, shredded her defenses, only to take her for granted as soon as she said she loved me.

My family couldn't leave me, no matter what I did to them. They'd never stop loving me.

But Ella? My star? The light source I revolved around?

"Ella," I said, the name bittersweet on my tongue. "We got married based on a lie. I'm sorry for that. I can't make it up to you guys, or her."

"You love her?" Mom asked.

"Is it love if I tricked myself into it? Because I don't know what to believe anymore."

Mom sighed and folded her hands in her lap, which made her shoulders shake more. "Byron," Mom said with a definitive air, "you aren't my oldest child."

We all shot up straight, asking "what?" at the same time.

"I had you two years after I married your father, but I was six weeks pregnant for our wedding."

"Mom, what the—" Lyric started.

"We rushed a wedding to save face," Mom interrupted. "I cried for a month. I wasn't ready to be a mother or a wife, but I couldn't tell my parents because if I did, they'd push to annul it. We were both still children, but I wanted to make my own decisions. Your grandparents were so controlling, and I couldn't wait to get out of that house. If they knew, they'd try to convince me to raise the baby. I didn't want to."

"Byron's still oldest if you terminated," Lyric said.

"But I didn't. Your father's uncle died, and he had to figure out how to run Crowne. We made a deal. I trusted him to keep his promises. I left school for one year. He got trained in the London office, and I went with him. Holed up in that drafty old house in St. Luke's." She shuddered. "I had the baby there, and the agency whisked it away."

"We have a brother?" Colton asked.

"Or sister," Lyric shot back.

"Apparently," Byron said, as if this seventh child was both threat and curiosity.

They were all focused on the existence of a sibling and not the marriage of Ted and Doreen Crowne.

Our parents were perfect. They'd done everything right. They loved each other fully and had built a life on mutual trust and affection.

"When I cried," Mom continued, "Ted held me. When I lashed out at him, he didn't even blink. I didn't love him when I married him, and that's the truth." She waited for us to digest that fucking tidbit. "But by the time we came back to the States, I did. With all my heart I loved him, and still do." She put her hand on mine. "So what I want you to know? Love grows where the soil is rich. And sometimes... well, you know what fertilizer is made of."

"Love grows in shit?" Colton asked. "What a fucking story to make that point in."

My parents couldn't have been built on a lie. Or circumstance. Or convenience.

That couldn't be true, and yet... it was. Everything I believed, everything I wanted, everything I'd modeled my future on was a lie.

"Where's the kid, Mom?" Byron's even tone demanded an answer.

"I don't know," Mom said. "It was a closed adoption. All I know is, they're set financially for life."

"So," I said. "This is what it feels like to be lied to."

"Sucks, don't it?" Lyric said.

"It's not as bad as lying to yourself," Mom said directly to me, as if she knew something I didn't about what I told myself.

She did. She knew everything.

3 2

ELLA

I PEELED off the black dress and stood in the middle of my living space in my underwear.

The studio was huge and empty. A hollow repository for meaningless work created as I fell in love with a man incapable of loving me back.

Another wasted effort.

I wasn't pushing for unattainable goals anymore. From now on, I was staying in my lane.

Once I found my lane, of course.

Logan wasn't in it. He wasn't even on the same freeway. My heart had done something stupid and reckless. Something I should have seen coming a mile away. I'd surrendered more than my body or my bed. I'd surrendered my soul to him, and he did exactly what I should have expected. He threw it away because he knew his lane. He knew how wide it was, how fast he could go, and who had to get off at the next exit.

I was tired. So tired. My limbs weighed half a ton and my brain had broken under the constant hammer of self-recrimination.

He didn't call. Didn't text.

Not that it mattered. What was he going to say that would change who he was or how he saw me?

Nothing. He'd said from the outset he didn't want a woman who'd nag or push him to love her more than he was capable of loving. He wanted to be what he was without pressure. I wasn't that.

Sadness crushed me into a tight ball too small for the bed, too tiny for the space, too rigid for change.

I didn't want to be this way, and I wasn't. Ella Papillion didn't hold pain until it ate her alive. She acted out. Stole the ashes. Changed the hanger tape.

I was an alchemist who turned hurt tangible.

Non. Again.

Fine, Daddy. An alchemist who turned pain into art.

Non. Again.

Still in my underwear, I approached the Big Blank. The red enamel was dry, but the gloss made it look wet and fresh, like a new wound in unblemished skin.

After fishing a razor out of my toolbox, I cut the canvas away from the stretch frame along the edges I could reach. The bottom corners curled away. I flipped it horizontal and finished the job, slashing the last inch of the rectangle so hard, I gouged the wood behind it. The canvas folded in on itself, hiding the primed side and leaving the raw linen side up.

I dragged the fabric across the studio and laid it over the cutting table.

The first thing I thought when I spread my hands on the red blotch was how much I wanted to share my plans for the Big Blank with Logan Crowne.

That was when I started crying.

MORNING.

Our time, every day.

Me in fuzzy socks and pajamas and him in his suit.

He'd ask me how I wanted my coffee because it constantly changed. He found that charming and him being charmed meant nothing. Charming women were a dime a dozen when he sat at the head of the table at Crowne.

As a woman, I meant nothing. I was a hammer in his toolbox.

Non. Again.

I was a nail.

Company to keep. A body to use. A valve to release the pressure of his dream job.

Guilt-free, because I'd told him I didn't have feelings.

My fault? My lie? Sure. I'd take that on. Just add it to the luggage. I had plenty of room inside the hole in my heart.

Round and round, my thoughts found new ways to hurt me. When I stopped crying, my father's voice would say, *Non. Again,* and the loop would start until I found just the right length blade to stab myself with.

With a straight razor, I sliced the stiff, primed canvas of the Big Blank into a shape I didn't need a pattern to reproduce. I knew the curve of the armhole and the length of the shoulder without checking. The Papillion sloper was a part of me, crafted into my myelin, burned into my cells with the blowtorch of Daddy's approval.

I sewed the shoulders and the sides together. The bodice stood up on its own, a legless, headless form in the middle of my floor with a red splotch over the heart.

Ah! Oui, little peanut.

It was too corny to be compelling, but it married my craft to my creativity, and despite what the artist class would think of it as a piece, it was the statement I needed to make to myself.

My past was my own.

My skills had value.

I was enough. Good enough. Talented enough. Free enough.

Loved enough? I was too hurt to know.

Early in the morning, in the middle of this litany of self-recrimination made worse by lack of sleep, my phone buzzed.

In socks and pajamas, I went to the kitchen counter. The phone was glass side down.

Who else could it be at this hour?

Was he in his kitchen, making coffee?

Did he want to know how I wanted mine?

Non. Again.

I wasn't charmingly unpredictable any more. I was useless, or worse, a liability.

My eyes ached as if they'd been punched, but they were dry. Tapped. Outta juice.

It buzzed again, rattling against the linoleum surface so hard it tugged at the cord. I caught it before it fell off.

—Ella. We should talk—

—I'm sorry I didn't text sooner. Dad had a heart attack. He's fine—

Shit.

I had the desire to reach out to him—not to update him on my life but to comfort him through his.

If I prioritized self-preservation, he'd be shut out until I was ready to talk to him.

But I loved him, the fucker.

How much was I willing to take?

I loved him. Like a fucking idiot, I loved him. I wished I knew how much that mattered. Was it as important as sticking to a decision I knew was right? My whole life, I'd acted out when I felt like it, taken dumb risks out of rage or boredom. I hadn't made a single, important deliberate choice about my path until I decided to walk away from this man.

I wouldn't impulsively undo this one thing. Not for love. Not now. Not ever.

But I cared about him and the family he'd shut me out of, so I called, and he picked right up.

"Ella?"

"How's Doreen?" I asked.

He didn't answer right away, as if I'd caught him off guard by starting the conversation in the middle.

"Fine. She's sleeping. Dad's going to be okay. It was mild, as these things go, but scary."

He sounded tired and flat, and a new kind of pain jabbed me. I wasn't allowed to soothe him the same way.

"You sound like shit," I said.

"I'm okay. It's been a long night."

"Well, get yourself some rest."

"Ella."

I sighed and sat on a kitchen chair. I didn't want to get roped into this, but as soon as he said my name, I knew I'd be lassoed and hogtied. "What, Logan?"

"I'm sorry about last night."

"It's fine. You were just being you. I'm the one making it messy."

Messy was an understatement. This was supposed to be business and I was four seconds to tears all over again.

"So what do you want to do?" he asked.

I wanted to love him, but when I'd told him that the night before, his silence had been clear.

What I wanted wasn't an option.

"We can get divorced now. Since everyone knows. If you want."

The last sentence was an exit ramp. A lifeline. A softball pitch to a home-run hitter.

"What if I don't want?"

"What would you want then?"

He was supposed to say he wanted me. All of me. Married.

Together. Just the way I was. All the messiness and recklessness I had to offer.

"I don't know."

"We're a mess," I said, dropping onto the bed.

"Yeah. You should get some sleep. You sound tired."

"That's the pot calling the kettle silver."

He gave me one laugh, then a breath. "You modernized a cliché."

"I did."

"Well done, star."

My body relaxed, and my eyes stopped throbbing enough to close. "Yay, me."

"Yay, you."

"You can call me if you need me."

"So can you."

"Okay." I was already breathing more slowly. The dull thickness of sleep pushed against the corners of my consciousness.

"I miss you," he said. "Already."

Like the tide coming in, oblivion rose and rose, scrambling my words and thoughts into a kind of truth.

"I miss me too."

33

ELLA

LOGAN and I were on opposite sides of a dinghy in the middle of the ocean with no land in sight. The boat was sinking and we were looking for holes, but there were none on either side. It was sealed tight and sinking anyway. Just as I thought to look away from my end to check for a hole under the center bench, a chime rang so loudly, I thought God was calling.

The phone was on the pillow, right by my ear. I fumbled for it, clearing my eyes to see who was calling.

Amilcar. I answered to the sound of people laughing, shouting, and music.

"Hello?"

"You sleeping?"

"Was." Out the window, the western sky was the deep dark blue of sunset. "What's going on?"

You and Logan are having an amicable breakup.

I covered my eyes. Crying in front of Amilcar wasn't going to go over well.

"She's sleeping!" he called to the room.

"Damn!" Liddy said. I heard him take the phone. "Lady of leisure."

Not for much longer.

"You know how it is."

"I do, Fance."

My old name. Before star. Before everything.

"She coming or not?" A woman's voice from the room. Maybe Irma.

"Where?" I asked, getting my elbows under me. My brain was awake, but my legs hadn't gotten the memo.

"My place on Echo. The GAC is on, baby. We're ready-set."

"When?"

Amilcar grabbed the phone. "Bring your ass over here before this knucklehead opens his mouth on cellular."

He was always the paranoid one, and rightly so.

"Okay," I said, finally awake enough to put my feet on the floor. "Coming."

———

I'D HAD the cab stop at the liquor store on the way. I picked up a bottle of vodka and a bag of lemons, then ran back in for ice.

They always needed more ice.

The little house hummed with music and the laughter and chatter of a few dozen people.

Did I know everyone? Or were there new people?

I walked up to the porch with my loot, and through the door, hoping for no more than a celebration. But I got more than that. I was greeted with exultation and embraces from friends who had known me when I didn't even know myself.

I was home.

———

"THIS *PENDEJO*"—LIDDY filled the wet shot glasses from the pitcher with one hand and flicked the other in Amilcar's direction—"had a bug so deep in his ass like, 'We have to show Fance, man. She always has these ideas.' And I was like, 'Nah-nah, leave her alone.'"

We snapped up the glasses of lemon drop.

"And I did so, what are you complaining about?" Amilcar said.

"To complaining!" I cried.

Seven—maybe six—maybe a dozen and a half glasses clicked mine. The drink slid down my throat as I swayed. There was a puddle on the table, and the room shifted back and forth like a dinghy on the ocean.

"Fuck, I missed you guys." I side-hugged Irma, who was sitting next to me. "And I'm so happy you're still wrecking shit. We need to toast." I grabbed a glass Liddy had filled. "To fucking the system."

"Slow down." Amilcar took my glass and downed it, slapping it back on the table. "Your husband can pick you up or no?"

Irma thought she was getting one over on me by filling my glass with water.

Whatever, I was thirsty.

"Fuck him!" The water felt good, but only made me want more. "That stick up his ass? It's, like, all the way in." My glass was full, so I drank. "That's why he stands so straight. True story."

"*Mija*," Irma said, "you tied it up too fast. You got to give him time. Five years at least."

"Fance is a five-day kinda girl," Amilcar said. "Then he's out. Now, me? Five minutes, and I know it's off or on."

"You guys! I have to say something! You don't know, and it's like... big big big and suuuuper secret. Guerilla secret. Like, I'll have to kill you and be mad forever, okay?"

Not waiting for a response, I pushed the glasses away and leaned my arms on the table without giving a single shit that I was getting the sleeves wet.

I made eye contact with each of my old friends, trusting them the way I did in high school. "There's a contract. A trade. It's not a marriage. Logan Crowne and I are... fake."

As if I was a TV on Super Bowl Sunday, they all reacted to a touchdown. Raising arms. High-fives. Shouts of "shit," and "yes," with Amilcar crying, "I told you," with his hand out.

"Pay up," Amilcar said.

Liddy reached into his wallet, head shaking.

"You took *bets*?"

They didn't seem to care that I'd lied or held back a secret, and I didn't know whether to be hurt or happy.

"Girl." Amilcar folded the twenty. "Who are you? You're not the type to run off with some dude. Not no-risk Fance. No way."

"Why would you say that?" I was offended. Maybe they didn't know me, and that was why they didn't mind that I'd lied.

"You stayed at that dumb job you hated for how long? Because you were afraid of not inheriting it or something? Meanwhile you coulda worked anywhere?"

"Had me though," Irma said.

"I figured for love you'd loosen up." Liddy poured the last of the lemon drop.

"That cost you twenty." Amilcar grabbed a glass.

The doorbell rang, and Liddy went to get it.

"Logan thinks I'm wild and crazy," I whined for reasons my addled brain couldn't add up. I felt as if I was getting drunker even though I'd been cut off. "Cossa my nose and I guess art or I dunno."

"Please," Amilcar said, pouring water into my glass again. "Save it. You're an old lady inside."

"Was it a good deal?" Irma asked. "You got the fuck you money?"

"I got the fuck you money, and the fuck me man."

They laughed, and I toasted with my water. I didn't think I could explain about the divorce coming sooner than we'd agreed. I didn't feel articulate enough and I couldn't find a starting point. Was it high school? Or his father's ultimatum? Should I even mention that part? It wasn't my story to tell; it was Logan's.

"This guy yours?" Liddy asked.

He was talking about the guy he'd brought in. Tall, strong Logan standing by the refrigerator with his arms crossed. Or maybe I was tipsy enough to mistake some random guy with cheeks and jaw as overgrown as an abandoned lot for my husband, who I'd never seen unshaven for a minute the whole time we were living together.

"Nope," I said. "That guy right there? No. Uh-uh."

"Sit." Amilcar kicked a chair toward the man with the beard, who opened his jacket before spinning around and straddling it with his arms on the back.

The wrists. The hands. Could still be my fake husband.

"Thank you," he said.

Sure sounded like him. And the way he looked at me across the table? Only Logan Crowne could sober me up with his eyes.

"I slowed down enough." I flicked a glass toward the man with the scruffy chin and wide hands. "I got something to say and I wanna drink to it."

"Oh, shit," Liddy said, snapping up the vodka bottle and pouring.

"You're driving her home, right?" Amilcar asked.

"I'll get her home."

I lifted my glass and picked up a lemon wedge. "To Logan Crowne. Who tried to get me to change my name, but wouldn't change."

We clicked. I downed the vodka and sucked the lemon. Everyone did the same, except Logan, who waited, watching me before he followed suit, cringing at the bite of cheap vodka. No lemon for him. Just the stare, holding me in place.

Silence, except for the music and shot glasses hitting the table.

"This song sucks," Irma said, getting up.

"Don't put on that merengue shit," Liddy objected, following her to the living room. Somehow, it was just Logan, Amilcar, and me left.

"Fance." Amilcar snapped his fingers between Logan and me, breaking the tether between us. "You cool?"

"I'm cool."

"All right." He put his hand on Logan's shoulder as he passed, patting it hard twice.

We were alone in a crowded house.

"You cool?" I asked. "Logan? Are you cool or no?"

"No. I am not cool."

True. He was hot. Very hot.

"You want another shot?" I picked up the bottle, but it was empty.

"I want to talk," he said.

"It's all still about what you want."

"It is. And I want my wife back."

"You gotta find her first. The real one. She's out there somewhere."

He got up and turned Irma's seat to straddle it, facing me while I looked forward. "Her name's Ella Papillion. Have you seen her?"

"Don't know her. Thought I did, but no."

"I miss her." His hand drifted along my arm. "We met up every morning, in the kitchen. She wore fuzzy socks and had her hair up. She called me at lunch to see how my day was. When I got home, she put slippers out for me. I never wore slippers until I lived with her."

"It was an act."

"When I made her come, her whole body twisted like she was possessed, and one time, she came so hard she cried in my arms. Tell me that was fake and I'll walk out right now."

Lying would have been easy, but I was done with lies.

"She's mine," he said, pressing his finger under my chin and turning me to face him. "And I'm hers."

He meant it. Everything in his posture and voice screamed a truth he believed. But it wasn't a truth I shared. He'd fallen for someone I wasn't, and I loved who he really was. The imbalance would break us.

"That's not who I am. Logan, I was fake with you. You gave me yourself and I gave you a lie. I'm not that way. I was so bored. I fell in love with you, but at the same time, I wanted us to change. It's all wrong. We're wrong." I turned my body in his direction. "I don't want us back. I love you, but that doesn't mean I'll be happy with you. There's no point to love if you have to pretend to be someone else to feel it."

"I love you when you're not pretending." He leaned forward to kiss me, and the anise and musk of him cut through the vodka, setting my skin alight with desire.

"No." I pulled back. "Don't. I just... we're not ready. Neither of us. We're a mess."

"What do I have to do to prove it?"

"Drop everything that's important to you. And I don't want you to. You're Logan Crowne. You run it all. You can't be fully present. The world has to revolve around you or nothing works. Are you willing to give that up?"

"I can't." His hand fell away from me, cutting the connection so abruptly, my body moved forward to get it back. "Byron's out. And my father..."

"Is Doreen okay?"

"She is. Everyone's okay but us."

"You work your ass off and you have crumbs left over," I said. "That's who you are. I need more. This is the right decision, and for once in my life, I'm not going to just smash something because I'm mad or run to the wrong man for me because it feels good. I'm going to think about the future and plan and know I can look back and say, 'Good fucking job, Ella.'"

He believed me, but I didn't want him to. As much as I knew I spoke the truth, I also wanted him to speak a different truth. If he'd only say he loved me and that love could conquer our identities, that he could give me everything right now, right then, with his whole heart open.

But he didn't.

"This is what you want?" he asked.

"No, but it's what we both need."

"All right."

He stood and kissed my cheek with a tenderness more real than his name, his dreams, or his acceptance.

It took him seconds to walk out the door, but it seemed to take the years with him that would never happen.

34

LOGAN

Driving away from that house in Echo Park was the hardest thing I ever did, but if I ran back in for her, I'd be showing her that what she wanted didn't matter to me.

It took two weeks to wake up from a nightmare. Fourteen days without her. Half a month of making too much coffee in the morning, an empty bed, a live-in brother who constantly asked me if I was all right—if Ella was around or nah.

Two weeks at a massive headquarters I'd lost the desire to run, skipping meetings to go home to nothing, delegating fires for someone else to put out so I could get home to a house as empty as my heart.

What was she doing? Was she happy? Was she laughing with the friends I'd taken her away from? Was she working on the Big Blank? The silver dress? If I went to her, would she let me see it?

Dad was out of bed in that time. His doctor told him to do something with himself. Jogging. Parasailing. Horseback riding. After a week of recreation, he admitted he only wanted to do one thing.

Check in at Crowne.

I didn't become a workaholic on my own.

He came in to fight his own boredom, made an effort not to get in my way, and failed. Except that I didn't care. He could charm the lobbyists over the conference room table where I couldn't anymore. I was world-weary, living a life with Ella in an imaginary universe filled with laughter and surprise.

"I'm going," Dad said, peeking his head into my office. "Don't stay too late."

"I'm leaving too."

He looked at his watch. "Really?"

"Mel has the quarterlies." I pulled my jacket off the back of the chair. "She'll brief me in the morning."

Instead of walking out, he closed the door behind him. "Son. It's six o'clock. Are you sick?"

"I'm fine, Dad." I put my jacket on, in no mood for a discussion about my feelings or anything else.

"You haven't been yourself." He sat down on the other side of the desk.

"You're right. Maybe I'm sick."

"Where's Ella?"

"That's over. I told you."

"You did."

"I'll be back to normal soon. I can't put in the hours right now. It's covered. Don't worry."

He crossed one leg over the other. "You get it now."

"Get what?"

"What's important. You finally got it."

"Okay." I sat down across from him. "I'm sitting. You got me where you want me. Again."

He nodded, accepting the jab he didn't deserve but not retreating either. "Has anything exploded this week?"

"No."

"Has your team done anything you wouldn't have done yourself?"

"No."

"Major fuckups? Bankruptcies? Anybody dead?"

"What's the point, Dad?"

"You can run the show and still have a life. That's the point. That was always the point."

"What if I don't want to run it anymore?" The words left my lips before my brain could put the brakes on, and with that failure, more spilled out. "What if I leave it? But not to go be happy or get married. What if I was a bum like Colton? Or just did my own thing?"

"What thing?"

"Whatever. Like Byron. What if I asked for my One Big Thing and went off and built shit? Or made sculptures out of tin cans? What's the difference? I wouldn't be here. There wouldn't be a Crowne at the helm and then what?"

"I guess we'd all survive." He shrugged. "Would you?"

I'd live. My blood would flow and my lungs would fill with air. But that wasn't what he was asking me. Obviously, I'd survive, but without Ella, I wouldn't be alive.

"Logan," Dad said, leaning forward. "Son. You're a Crowne, but you aren't Crowne Industries. Do you understand me? Piping oil to customers isn't the whole of who you are. It's not enough."

Was that how he saw what we did? Just getting fuel to people who needed it?

No. That wasn't what he was saying. He'd made this point before, but for the first time in my life, I heard it. He wasn't talking about the company or the Crowne legacy.

He was talking about me, and the family, and what held us all together.

Love. History. The stories we told and the mountains we climbed together. Ella was a part of that, and when I'd chased her out of the room, she'd been shut out of more than my life.

"I'm ready," I said. "For my One Big Thing."

"What's that?" he asked with a raised eyebrow.

"It's not money, or an object." I cleared my throat. "I want you and Mom to forgive Ella. I don't care if you ever forgive me, but she loves you guys, and I want you to bring her back into the family, no questions asked."

"That's it?"

"I know a big check would be easier, but the OBT is guaranteed, and it's what I want."

"I'll have to talk to your mother."

Mom didn't need any convincing, but he wouldn't agree on her behalf any more than admit he was the one holding a grudge.

"You do that."

He stood and stopped before turning to leave. "You're sure?"

"I've never been so sure about anything."

———

MY FATHER HADN'T CLEARED the miasma that hung over my mood. I didn't go home with a spring in my step or cheerfully concoct a life plan from his encouragement. But after we spoke, I rubbed some of the fog from the mirror.

My cleaning lady left my mail on the table by the front door. A manila envelope had been sent by courier. I opened it and slid out the document.

Divorce papers.

Ella Papillion wanted to divorce Logan Crowne, and suddenly—with those two names in front of me—I knew what I had to do.

3 5

ELLA

"Isn't this what you wanted?" Bianca asked, exasperated.

In the showroom, with Papillion's most expensive pieces displayed before me and Bianca offering me everything, I was at a loss to explain why it wasn't enough.

"You'll have full creative control," she reiterated. "If it's money you're after, just say it."

The brand had completely lost its reputation for innovation. Profits flowed from discounters and licensing, but it had plateaued before taking a nosedive last quarter. I had to give my stepmother credit for not only seeing the writing on the wall, but for swallowing her pride and coming to me for help.

"It's not money."

"What is it then?" She sat across from me. "Shares? If you want me gone, you can put that out of your mind."

I didn't want her out. She knew the business, and despite everything—or because of everything—I trusted her. If Logan and I had gone through with the buyout, I would have been stuck without a partner who knew the company like she did.

She wanted to make me president of design. Creative direction put back in the hands of a Papillion, with no responsibility for the cheaper side of the business. She wasn't just willing to give it all to me, she was eager, and I could have gotten her to agree to anything.

"I'm not in a place to negotiate this right now," I said.

"When will you be?" The impatience in her voice was lined with control, and the seams were ripping.

I looked at my watch. My meeting with Logan and his lawyers was in an hour. Would I be ready after that? I couldn't promise I'd be able to function, much less weave a path through her offer. "Look, Bianca, here's the deal. Straight up. Daughter to mother."

She brightened a little. Softened a little more. She'd never be warm and fuzzy, but she wasn't ice and steel all the way through. "Go on then."

"You know about Logan. That the marriage was fake, right?"

The news hadn't made it to the press, but in circles where people whispered over cocktails, people knew.

"I suspected as much," she said. "It's been talked about. Not by me, of course."

"We're signing divorce papers in a few hours." I cleared my throat when the word "divorce" created a lump right where my voice was. "And it's complicated. More complicated than I thought it would be."

"Is he trying to screw you?" She pushed her index finger into the table. "Because when Janet Bolivar's husband left her, she got a lawyer who ate him for breakfast. I can get you the number."

"No. That's not it."

"Well, what is it then?"

"I love him." My face scrunched, tightening to hold back tears.

"Oh, darling." She rushed around the table to sit next to me. "Don't you dare cry."

"I don't know what to do."

She put her arms around me and I leaned into her, letting the sobs come.

"It's okay, sweetheart." She stroked my hair. "If he can't love you back, then… well, all his money's worthless. I mean, what the point of it if he can't see what a gift you are? How smart, principled, loyal… your spirit is so strong. Any man would be lucky to be loved by you."

"He thinks he loves me."

"Then what… wait." She shrugged me off to look in my eyes. "He does or he doesn't?"

"He wants, like, this helpmate wife, and I've been that just to keep up appearances. But he doesn't know me and if he did? I'm not the person he always wanted. We'll only break up for real and then I'll be alone again."

Again? What did I mean by again?

Mom left me, then Daddy. Left behind like a dinghy on the ocean with nothing to navigate by but memories. How could I wake up from that pain again?

"Estella," Bianca said, shaking her head.

"What?"

She shifted straight in her seat. "I hate this business." She waved at the roomful of samples. "Just despise it. It's taken all the fun out of clothing for me."

"Really? Why are you here?"

"Because I met your father halfway. He needed me, and I was there. Now, I admit when he passed, I could have sold it. I kept it up because money, you know. And when I needed him… did you know he went quite literally broke paying off my father's gambling debts?"

I didn't know a damn thing, except that this business meeting had taken an off-ramp to deeply personal and set the road behind it on fire. "I didn't know that."

"I thought I could take care of it, so I didn't tell him until after we were married. He was an absolute saint about it. Took you out of that school to save money."

"I thought you pulled me." I was down to sniffling over Logan.

"We both knew it had to be done. There were men—bad men

287

—who were going to use my kneecaps to make a point." She rubbed a wet trail from my cheek with her thumb. "Can you imagine?"

"I can't actually."

"When people tell you marriage is about sacrifice and compromise... well, you should believe them. I mean, you have to draw lines, of course. Cheating's right out. And I'm assuming he hasn't raised a hand to you?"

I remembered his spankings and decided that wasn't what she meant. "He'd pull back a bloody stump."

"Indeed. Does he make you feel good?"

I raised an eyebrow.

"Not like that. My God, Estella. Get your mind out of the gutter. This is all quite simple. Do you like who you are around him? Are you happy with yourself?"

I looked at my hands. I did, and I was. When I thought of living without him, the way I felt around him was what I was going to miss the most.

"Does he say nice things or hurtful things?" Bianca added, brushing my hair away from my face the way my real mother used to.

"He's good to me."

"Can you meet him in the middle?"

"I don't know if he'll take the middle."

"Can you ask him?"

I nodded, intending to ask but not knowing if I'd have the courage to hear the answer.

———

LOGAN CROWNE LOOKED magnificent in his navy suit, strong hands folded in front of him, standing next to his lawyer, a red-haired woman in her fifties wearing a lavender pantsuit under an armor of confident impatience. They stood when I entered the conference room with the lawyer Mandy had found for me. He had warm brown eyes and a nose textured like cauliflower, and he'd promised he'd get it over quickly.

Logan checked his watch. I hadn't thought about that leather strap on his wrist in a long time. When I first saw it, I thought it hinted at a little darkness. A touch of the wild in him. In the daily grind of marriage, I'd let myself forget about that first impression.

I'd missed an opportunity. I should have arrived earlier, without the lawyer. I should have texted him before and asked if he could meet me halfway. I should have called the whole thing off to give myself a moment to think about what Bianca had told me.

But there we were, sitting on opposite sides of a shiny table, flanked by lawyers looking out for our best interests without knowing what our best interests were.

Not that I knew either, but did he know?

I couldn't look at Logan's face, so I kept my gaze on his hands and their reflection on the glossy tabletop, his gold wedding ring bouncing as his fingertips tapped one after the other. Nerves? Impatience?

"My client agrees to all the terms set out in the consent decree," his lawyer said, taking out a folder.

I meant to look at my lawyer to gauge his reaction, but I looked at Logan instead.

Blue eyes fixed on me, lush mouth twitching as if he held back a smile. Shoulders relaxed. Not uneasy or anxious. He was happy to be there. Enthusiastic even. That was what the drumming fingers were about. He wasn't nervous or impatient. He was excited.

There would be no halfway.

He was already gone.

"Just one correction to initial." The lawyer in the lavender suit slid the pages across to my counsel. "Then we're good to go."

"Logan," I said.

"Ella?"

"I just want you to know—"

"This isn't the divorce agreement," my lawyer sniped.

"I want him to know..." I snarled at him before turning back to my husband. "That it was never you. I think, under different circumstances, with different expectations... we could have been happy."

He nodded. No words. No change in his expression. Not even a whiff of agreement.

Just a nod to recognize that he heard me loud and clear.

I willed myself not to cry, because fuck him and his control. If he could shut off his emotions like a faucet, I wouldn't let my tears flow like one.

"What is this?" my lawyer said, flipping through.

"My client wants this revised first," she replied.

"This?" He held up the pages. "It's the initial contract."

"Yes." She slid a pen across to me. "Just initial."

I leaned over to look at the document. It was our initial deal, with redlines we scratched over terms in Bianca's office a million years ago. I took the contract from my lawyer, looking for something significantly different.

I found it.

Children resulting from this union will be named Crowne.

Next to the red *to be decided* he'd written on our wedding day was a new line, in black and initialed, which amended the line to:

CHILDREN RESULTING *from this union will be named Crowne-Papillion*

"I DON'T UNDERSTAND," I said.

"Me neither," his lawyer grumbled.

"Logan?" His name was confusion and sadness, a cry to his back as he walked away.

And still, though his fingers stopped tapping, his expression didn't change.

"I'm not initialing this until you explain it." I spun the papers to him. They opened like feathers and flattened,

A smile played at the edge of his mouth, breaking the stoic control for a moment. He rotated the papers and pushed them back. "It's pretty self-explanatory."

"That you're mocking me?" I turned the contract over, word-side down, and crossed my arms to protect myself against a final hurt I couldn't bear to imagine.

He folded his hands in front of him, leaning forward as if he was ready to launch himself in my direction. "I'll say it plainly with counsel present."

The intensity of his gaze ran right through me like a shot of heat through a frozen system, turning ice into steam.

"Give me another chance," he said. "I'll write your name into every part of my life."

"Why?"

"Because you being in my life isn't enough. I want more. I want to be part of yours."

Did he just offer to meet me halfway?

"I can't…" I stood so fast, the chair shot back and hit the wall behind me.

I wanted him to meet me in the middle, but something about this was wrong, and I couldn't put into words neither the shock that he'd read my mind nor the disappointment that he'd pulled a stunt that got it all so wrong.

"Why not?" He stood.

We were on opposite sides, hands on the table like opposing parties in a heated negotiation, eyes locked in heated combat. Looking away was impossible.

"Because I don't want you to change. I want you to be happy. I want you to have everything you want."

"I. Want. You." He pounded the table between each word.

Out of the corner of my eye, his lawyer closed her folder. "This is now outside my legal purview."

"Go," Logan commanded, eyes still on mine.

"Yes," I said to my counsel. "You can go."

My lawyer sighed, picked up his bag, and left right behind Logan's. The door clicked, leaving me alone with my husband.

We didn't move.

"You want me?" My question came out as a challenge.

"Yes."

"You sure?"

"You think I won't change? That's the least I'll do. I'll get rid of everything. Every dollar I earned and the billions I inherit. I'd give it all to you if that's what you want. But you want my name? Take it. You're the only asset worth a damn."

"I don't want you to change. I don't want to take who you are."

"Then take my time. Take my career. Take it all and throw it away. I don't care. Just take me. With nothing else. After all the changing is done—all the work, all the decisions—take the part of me that's always the same. The part that loves you."

Unable to stand another second of his intensity, I looked down. My fingers were splayed on the table, pressed so hard the knuckles were white.

"This is real," I said.

"You bet your ass it's real." He wasn't across the table. In the seconds since I'd broken our gaze, he'd come around to my side. "I know you didn't like being my wife. So don't be. Be my One Big Thing."

My spine straightened, hands off the table, head up in surprise at the contradiction. "You want me and a divorce?"

"No." He put his hands inches from my biceps, pausing before he touched them as if waiting for a signal that it was all right. I took half a step closer to him, and he let himself touch me. "I don't want a wife." His thumbs drifted upward, caressing my jaw where the skin was sensitive. "I want to be married… to you."

I didn't know how badly I'd needed to hear those words until he said them.

Not a husband and a wife—two motionless objects on top of a wedding cake—but two people tied to one another, engaged in the living, growing act of being married.

Like my parents. Like Ted and Doreen. Like every other marriage that seemed perfect from the outside because the inside constantly evolved.

"I'm trouble, you know." I gripped his lapels and shook him.

"You are so much damn trouble." He kissed my forehead.

"And you're no fun."

"I'm too boring for you." His breath caressed my ear as he ran his lips along my neck. I ran my fingers through his hair with a sigh and a groan. "We're a perfect mess, my star. Say yes anyway. I love you. I love you more than this life can contain. Finish the year with me. Then the next and the next. Let's break shit and glue it back together for the rest of our lives."

We were perfect, and we were a mess, and that was all it was.

I pushed him away to hold his face still, up against mine so I could feel our separateness and intimacy. Both existed at the same time, in the same space.

It was him. I wanted his mess. Our mess.

"Logan Crowne," I said, "I take you to be my husband. To love and to honor. To break shit and put it back together 'til death do us part."

"Do I kiss the bride now?"

"You'd better."

He kissed me, and of all the times our lips had met, that kiss buckled my knees the most. When he held me up, his arms were stronger because his promises were real, and so were we.

Happiness didn't come neatly packaged. It found you in the moments between tears and laughter, in the fights and brokenness, in the support and in the bond with someone who loved you as broken as you were and as whole as you'd become.

EPILOGUE ONE

LOGAN

"Do I look okay?" Ella asked as I put the car into park.

The valet opened her door first, the dome light making her eyes glint like stars twinkling with jitters.

"You look gorgeous."

"I'm supposed to look approachable."

I took her chin and kissed her, getting out without another word. I met her on the passenger side and helped her out of the car and into the Crownehome garage, where I'd first taken her on the hood of a Ferrari.

She wiped her palms on her jeans.

"It's just dinner." I offered her my arm and we entered the elevator.

It had been a few weeks since I'd asked my father for my One Big Thing, and though he'd laid the burden of forgiveness at my mother's feet, he was the one who needed to be reassured that the marriage that had started out as a game had turned very real. Colton, who was allergic to getting the hell out of my house, had intervened with eyewitness accounts of how we'd become so disgustingly in love, he made his own coffee in the morning rather than interrupt us.

"I don't know why I'm so nervous," she said, tilting her chin up and closing her eyes to calm herself.

I took her hand. "I'm here."

"If they still hate me, I'll know."

"They don't, and you will." I pulled her into my arms. "My parents fell in love with you before I did. And now that you're mine, you're one of us."

The elevator car stopped, and the doors opened. I barely had a moment to register that my parents were standing there before my mother rushed into the elevator with her arms wide.

"Ella!" Mom hugged my wife so hard, Ella got pushed into the elevator's back wall. They rocked back and forth, laughing as if they shared the funniest, most delightful joke ever told.

Dad stood in the entrance, hands in his pockets, watching them.

"Doreen, thank—"

"No, no," Mom interrupted Ella, pulling away just a little. "You call me Mom."

Dad held the doors open to let them out, and I followed into the house.

"Thank you, and..." She looked at my father, making eye contact, which I knew was hard for her. The possibility that Dad was delivering on his One Big Thing to me, but without really forgiving us for all the lies, was her biggest fear, and she took it head-on, first thing, like a boss. "I'm so sorry about everything. I understand if you aren't ready to say it's all okay. But I'm going to earn your forgiveness."

"Before you take another step into my house, know this," Dad said sternly enough to make my body react.

The only thing that kept me from getting physically between him and my wife was Ella's hand, gently keeping me still.

My father saw the split-second interaction and smirked. "Know this," he said more softly. "My son should be mad at me. I tried to enforce happiness, and he did what was necessary to protect himself. I brought the lies on myself, on the one hand. On the other hand, if I hadn't? He wouldn't have found you, and he wouldn't be as happy as he is, so…" He shrugged. "It worked."

"It did," I said, putting my arm around Ella.

"That's not a cue to do it again," my mother said to Dad, her voice heavy with consequences. She turned to Ella. "Just tell me you're happy too."

"So, so happy." Ella pulled me closer.

I believed her, at least. Three weeks into the real beginning of our real marriage, after an unplanned honeymoon in Palm Springs where we did nothing but fuck and laugh, I believed she was happy. We had years to go, and some of them would be harder than others, but I couldn't imagine any of them without her by my side.

"Dinner's on the east patio," Dad said, leading us.

"Which one's that?" Mom asked, taking his hand to slow him down.

"The one on the east side of the house."

"There are two to the east. The one over the pool or the one over the cliff?"

"Well, now I'm not sure."

The four of us strode at an easy pace, joking about the size of the house, the number of pools and patios, until we found dinner for four. I held the chair out for my wife and kissed her cheek. When I sat and put my hand on hers, I knew I had what my parents had and no less. Ella and I were perfect partners and perfectly in love.

Marriage was a deep and abiding partnership where two people took on separate roles to build a more complete life together.

My wife would pull when I pushed, go left when I went right. I wasn't looking for control, just a unique life with her and for us. That was my choice.

My first goal was making her happy, and with that in the bag, Crowne Industries would take care of itself.

EPILOGUE TWO

ELLA

FROGTOWN WAS a sliver of land on the west side of the Los Angeles River—a dry rift in the city three out of four seasons, with trees and wildlife in the center, and an unruly, fast-moving waterway in winter. Every year—well, into the 1970s—thousands of red-legged toads would leap into the streets, hopping on lawns and shitting on windshields. Toads were miscategorized as frogs, and the name Frogtown stuck even after the riverbed was paved in concrete and the toads stopped coming.

Things changed. People changed. Sometimes the idea of yourself that you'd nurtured your whole life was shattered, and the pieces glittered in the moonlight.

"They're late," Logan said.

The GAC's LA River piece had been slated for sunset, but the sky had been dark for half an hour already. Twitter didn't have an update for the hundreds of people crowded along the River's path.

"That's what happens when you get the city involved."

The GAC was more than half an hour late. They were actually months late. The frogs would have been out and gone already, but the delay was unavoidable. Irma and Amilcar had been caught setting up, and Tasha—who was too savvy by a mile—got the principal of her school to contact the mayor's office. He pitched it as a free speech project. The city issued permits but demanded changes, and a deposit for cleanup.

Amilcar wouldn't come to me for money, but Tasha did, and I demanded to pay for it. I was folded back into the GAC with my friends—one of the many places I belonged.

Logan pulled me close and kissed my temple.

I belonged with him too.

"They better hurry up," he whispered. "I have a hard-on with your name on it."

I turned to him, rubbing the scruff on his chin. "The whole thing, Mr. Crowne-Papillion?"

"Every letter's going to be inside you, Mrs. Papillion-Crowne."

Things had changed. I still set out his slippers, and he still wore them. I saw him in the morning, but also next to me, in our bed. He came home most nights, and when he had a late-night overseas call, he still kept the camera covered.

Things changed all the time. Sometimes I was the one who didn't make it home for dinner. Getting Papillion back on its feet wasn't a small job. But when I worked late, Logan brought takeout to the office for us, and we ate together in the same room where my father had made me set in a sleeve again and again until it was perfect.

We were separate people, but one and the same, locking our lives together over and over until we were perfect too.

"New tweet!" Mandy said from beside Logan. "It's going now!"

In the darkness of the ravine, a line of green dots lit up.

"I see it!" I cried.

The crowd bustled and hummed. Fathers put children on their shoulders, and the green lanterns lifted over the treeline all at once, like little frogs floating into the air, tightly at first, then drifting apart into the sky. Then the paper lanterns fell downward onto the street and the children lifted their arms to catch them.

A little boy next to us grasped for one, but it bounced off his fingers, over the railing and out of reach. He screamed in disappointment, and his mother had to grab him to keep him from falling over the rail.

"I have it," Logan said, catching it in one swift motion. He handed it to the boy.

"Thank you," his mother said, then whispered in her son's ear. "What do you say?"

"Thank you!" The boy hugged the lantern, crinkling it.

It was over in five minutes, but like all great art, it lived as an experience to be remembered and shared.

"That was a good one," Mandy said, scrolling through her phone. "You guys in for dinner or—" She stared at the screen. "No."

"Yes," Logan said, taking my hand. "Amelia's."

"No, no, no, no."

"Olivia's meeting us there," Logan replied as if Mandy's denial was directed at the restaurant.

"What?" I asked, peering at her screen.

Instagram.

I recognized Renaldo immediately, then the woman he was kissing as the actress Gertrude Evans. America's Next Sweetheart. There was no mistaking that picture for a friendly peck on the lips.

"Mandy..." I laid my hand on her arm to push the phone down, but she pulled away to study the picture like an X-ray as we were jostled by the crowd of people leaving the river path.

"Well—" Logan started, but I kicked him before he could say he told her so.

"How could he?" She moved to the DMZ app, where Renaldo and Evans were top of the news, picture after picture. "We just went public last week. Everyone knows. He said he loved me. He promised..." She let her arm drop. Her face contorted into a flinch against an oncoming blow. "This is humiliating."

Her chest heaved and she spit out a sob, dropping her phone before emitting a wail.

I picked up the phone. The glass was cracked.

Logan put his arm around her, practically holding her up.

"Oh, look," one in a cluster of half a dozen girls said, holding up her cell phone, "the homewrecker herself! Say cheese, cunt." She took a picture.

Her friends looked up from their phones.

"Bitch can steal a man," one of them said, displaying the Instagram photo, a frog lantern looped over her thumb. "But bitch can't keep him."

"Better watch yours, lady," a tall girl said, pointing at me, then my husband.

"Watch yourself, you dumb twat, before I—"

Logan grabbed my arm with the one that wasn't holding up Mandy. "Let's get out of here."

———

LOGAN and I had framed our divorce papers and hung them in the kitchen, where we'd met every morning in those first months. I'd started taking them for granted, until Mandy sat at the center island in her yellow T-shirt, pouring white wine as if it was soda.

"He divorced her for *me*," she said through sobs. "Not so he could fuck around with—"

"Easy there." Logan plucked the wine from her hand. "Eat something."

I dropped a few bundles of half-wrapped cheese in front of her, next to the box of crackers. Logan gave me a worried look. I shrugged helplessly. We didn't know what to do for her.

"I told everybody. It was public. There are pictures. And it was okay they called me a homewrecker, because I had him. At work? They whisper. And these people work for me. They're still like, 'what she did to Tatiana blah blah...' behind my back, but I could handle it because I had him." She took two gulps of wine and snapped up a plastic-wrapped, quarter-pound wedge of brie. "My personal shopper... my favorite one—I told you about her. Lannie? She wouldn't even look at me the other day. And I had to run a gauntlet in sunglasses and a hood to get there. I made a joke about Unabomber chic and the look on her face... like at least she respected the Unabomber. But you know, with a huge pink smile of course." She wrestled the cheese free. "Like someone glued a big wet pussy to the bottom half of her face."

"Like a cat?" Colton said, walking in without the joke-cowbell we'd bought him for his birthday. "Because the other kind... not so much."

"Shut. Up." Mandy bit off the corner of the brie wedge. "You don't know what you're talking about."

Colton stuck his head in our fridge because his didn't have jack shit inside it and came out with a bottle of beer. "Renaldo slipping Gertrude his meat or nah?" He cracked open the top.

"Colton," I snapped. "Really?"

"I want to die." Mandy rested her forehead on the stone counter. I rubbed her back.

"What?" he said. "I figured everyone knew."

"Can we talk about something else?" Logan suggested. "Papillion stock's up."

I shook my head at him sharply. He threw up his hands, at a loss for what to say.

"Let's talk about Dante," Colton said, getting onto a stool. "He called Mom today."

"What?" Logan's hands balled into fists.

Dante hadn't been seen or heard from in weeks. He was never forthcoming, according to Logan, but he'd gone darker than usual this time. No phone calls. No forwarding number at the private clubs he owned and Logan wouldn't tell me more about. Nothing.

When Doreen started worrying herself to distraction, Logan

hired a private detective to find him, but he'd come up empty so far.

"Right out," Colton said, slashing his hand definitively. "He's all 'I'm disappearing.' Not to worry, but basically, tough shit."

Logan tapped his fingertips on the counter, staring at—and through—his brother as if debating whether or not to interrogate him further.

"I wish I could disappear." Mandy drained her glass. "Just until this dies down."

Logan's attention went from Colton, to Mandy, to me, and I knew that look. It was the same one he'd had when he got the idea for us to separate for a while. It was a plan hatching.

"We can arrange that," Logan said, getting onto a stool. "Ever been to Cambria?"

———

BY THE TIME we got to bed, it was after midnight. Logan had gone to his parents' to get the keys to the Cambria house, and Mandy and I had gone back to her place to pack her up.

She'd kissed us and thanked us with tears in her eyes before driving west and out of reach.

"She looked more relaxed just getting the hell out of here," Logan said as he slid under the covers.

"Honestly?" I scooted back so he could spoon me. "She wants the idea of Renaldo more than she ever wanted the actual Renaldo."

"I'd never work that hard for an idea." He reached around me and under my shirt.

"Of course not." I guided his hand downward. "That would be so not Papillion-Crowne."

"Nope." He wrestled his way under my waistband and right between my legs.

"Totally Crowne-Papillion though." I twisted to kiss him.

"I love the idea of how wet you are." He pushed down deeper, reaching for proof of the idea.

"It's too late." I got onto my back so I could spread my legs wider.

"We'll sleep late." He put two fingers inside me. No resistance, just swollen wetness waiting for him.

I kissed him and was running my hand down his chest when his phone rang. I groaned with annoyance into his mouth, and he smiled, reaching behind him while two fingers of his other hand were still inside me.

"Shh," he whispered, then answered the phone. "Hey, Cooper."

He circled my clit so gently my body screamed for more.

"You found him?" His hand stopped for a moment. "Is he all right?"

Logan and I made eye contact. His brow was knotted. I sat up, and his hand fell away as he got himself next to me.

"So"—he held the phone between his shoulder and his ear and got a pen from the night table—"where then?" He put the pen down. "All right. No... forget it. That's good enough. Thanks."

He hung up and tossed the phone next to the pen.

"Dante?" I asked.

"Yup."

"Where is he?"

"On his way to Cambria."

———

WHAT'S GOING to happen when Dante finds Mandy in the Cambria house?

PREORDER NOW

ACKNOWLEDGMENTS

Before you send me a strongly-worded email, let me get this out of the way.

If you chose to change your name to your spouse's, I'm not judging you.

It's your name, do whatever you want with it. Seriously. Marriage is a series of compromises, realignments, and changes directed toward the greater good of two individuals. If that includes having the same name for whatever reason, go for it. It's not my decision and honestly, I don't care.

However, these characters had things to learn and using name changes to shape their commitment really jazzed me. It's my book, so it is what it is.

Also, in case you're wondering, I didn't change my name when I got married. One, I'm lazy. Two, my (real) name is rich with a cultural heritage that my loving husband doesn't share. I didn't want to lose it. My call.

All the same things go for being a stay-at-home spouse, with or without children. Ella was bored with that arrangement. If you're not, that's awesome.

Your life, baby. Make yourself happy.
Please thank a feminist for making the choice possible.

THE END

Margie Drazen has a story and it's going to blow your mind.

THE SIN DUET

———

CONTEMPORARY ROMANCES

Hollywood and sports romances for the sweet and sexy romantic.
Shuttergirl | Hardball | Bombshell | Bodyguard | Only Ever You

CPSIA information can be obtained
at www.ICGtesting.com
Printed in the USA
LVHW110014120621
689977LV00001B/23